Olivia

OTHER BOOKS AND AUDIO BOOKS
BY JULIE WRIGHT:

Eyes Like Mine

Cross My Heart

Hazzardous Universe

the Newport Ladies Book Club

a novel

JULIE WRIGHT

Covenant Communications, Inc.

Cover images: *Sitting on Deck Chair Enjoying Vacation*, © Jacob Wackerhausen, iStockphotography.com; and *Umbrella Icon* © o-che, iStockphotography.com

Published by Covenant Communications, Inc.
American Fork, Utah

Printed in the United States of America
First Printing: February 2012

18 17 16 15 14 13 12 10 9 8 7 6 5 4 3 2 1

ISBN13: 978-1-60861-843-9

To women—
So often we are unaware of how much
one smile,
one kind word
might mean in someone else's life.
Thank you for all the smiles and kindness
that have saved my life
on a daily basis.

Acknowledgments

In November of 2009, Josi Kilpack and I went on a Western United States book tour together. Not only did we have a blast (and I learned that Josi is an amazing person to put up with me the way she did), but we also had a pivotal conversation about how much we wished Heather Moore and Annette Lyon were with us. Josi came up with the idea of all four of us writing a series together, which created the opportunity for us to spend time all together.

We met with Heather and Annette for breakfast when we returned home and pitched the idea to them. They were as excited about the idea as we were. That was the birthplace of the Newport Ladies Book Club.

We decided to write from the viewpoint of different characters. In each of the books, you'll get some of each character's story, but only by reading all four books will you get the full picture and discover the ending to all four lives.

Writing this series was an incredible process. Each story is unique and beautiful in its own way. During the creative process, something struck me: friendships are so important, and we as women have so much to bring to the table and offer each other. There are many who have been there for me through the years, who likely have no idea how their kindnesses saved me from despair, and I want to thank them. Thank you:

To the grandmother who stayed on the phone with me when I was home alone late at night and afraid.

To the mother who drove me on my paper route when it was cold.

To the woman who called me one day and invited me to church, even though she didn't know me and I was only a name on a roll sheet. In that one moment, you changed my future.

To the girls who got me through the teenage years and, now in our adulthood, are helping me get through the old lady years.

To the countless strangers who've complimented me and made me feel comfortable when I've felt dowdy, ugly, and out of place.

To the lady in the hospital who was unlucky enough to get into an elevator with me when it seemed my life was falling apart and who took the time to cry with me.

To the online friends I've never met yet who uplift and encourage me with their words.

To the women in my town who have their own Heaven Reminders and are always there for me.

To my sisters, of both the natural and in-law variety, who love me when I'm absurd, who make me laugh, let me cry, and care so very much.

To my daughter, who reminds me of all the beautiful potential in the world.

To the incredible strength and dedication of the women at Covenant Communications and all the authors who inspire me, encourage me, and stand by me as a writer.

To the three women who were willing to let me write a series with them.

It amazes me how much we need each other—to build, to bear up, to simply be kind. It amazes me how often I witness women stepping up to the plate to do what is needed—to hug when needed, to kiss better when needed, and to love always.

Thank you to all the women in the world. You're beautiful. You shine. Be happy.

Other books in this series:

DAISY—by Josi Kilpack
PAIGE—by Annette Lyon
ATHENA—by Heather B. Moore

For ideas on hosting your own book club, suggestions for books, and recipes, or information on how you can guest-write about your book club on our blog, please visit us at http://thenewportladiesbookclub.blogspot.com.

Chapter 1

He wasn't coming home.

The grandfather clock I'd inherited when my mom died chimed eleven times, each marking the late hour and seeming to mock me for waiting as long as I had. The candles on the dining room table had burned to stubs, white wax dripping off the collars of the candlesticks and onto the table.

I stared at the wax, pooled and dried to the shiny oak surface, and couldn't even muster the ability to care that it was likely leaving a waxy ring that would never come out of the wood without stripping, sanding, and restaining. It was all work I'd do on my own. He'd be mad, and he'd comment on how it showed my lack of . . . whatever it was I should have. And then he'd fume silently for a while longer before moving on to something else that actually interested him, something that wasn't *me*, something that wasn't our anniversary dinner sitting cold around the two flames bobbing above their almost-spent candles.

Nick hadn't even called.

Hours had gone into preparing the dinner. Hours of my life I'd never get back. Creamed peas, asparagus with that maple-mustard sauce he loved, grilled lemon garlic halibut, and fresh homemade rolls. I scraped my chair back and blew out the flames, my breath sweeping more wax down onto the table.

I flipped on the light switch and pressed my palms into my temples as I paced around the table. *When did we come to this? How did we get to uneaten anniversary dinners?* We used to be a fun couple. We used to be the couple everyone envied—the one everyone wanted to be like. He used to be the one surprising me with flowers and kissing me loudly in front of our small children just to hear them say, "Ew! Gross!"

The pendulum of the clock ticked off every moment he wasn't home as though it were personally keeping track. *What should I do?*

With a sigh, it occurred to me that the only thing to do at the moment was clear the table and throw out the food since it had been sitting out for more than four hours. I'd picked at it after the first hour, taking nibbles from the sides where it wouldn't disrupt the visual effect—as if it had mattered. At least the only dishes I'd have to wash were the serving dishes and the cooking pans. *There. That's better. Find something positive. Breathe deeply, and look for something to be glad about.*

It sounded Pollyanna but was a habit I'd picked up as a child when my mom had snuggled under a lap blanket with me and watched old classics, *Pollyanna* among them, while thunder pounded the sky and wind howled through the rafters of my childhood home. Those had been good days in years filled with good days; I'd been held in the safety of my mother's arms, warm and loved and needed. The glad things in my life seemed endless at the time, and counting them all had sounded like fun.

Mom had encouraged me to be like Pollyanna. And later she told me my personality quirk had gotten her through some rough times in her own life. She'd once called me her life preserver. What would she say if she could see me now, clearing an uneaten meal from my dining table in a home too large to feel cozy and too cold to feel homey? A forty-one-year-old woman with four kids and a husband who didn't remember the plans of a special anniversary dinner? A woman who hid the gray sneaking into her brown hair with bottles of blonde dye? A woman who could find precious little in her cold, silent house to feel glad about?

The china plate I'd been holding slammed into the wall and shattered into an explosion of porcelain, startling me enough that I jumped.

But what startled me more than the fact that I'd thrown a grossly expensive plate into my decorator wall, leaving a dent of chipped blue paint and white drywall, was the fact that the action offered real relief.

I felt better having thrown the plate.

So I threw the other one.

And smiled.

Then frowned.

"You're an idiot, Livvy," I told myself. "Who do you think is going to clean that up?"

Talking to myself was a habit I'd picked up after my mom died four years ago. My dad had died before her. I had no siblings. Mom's passing left me vacant. She'd had a blood clot that had found its way to her brain when she'd been out watering her red hibiscus. The hose was still running, pointed up at a crazy angle, caught between her arm and body, when I'd found her. The mulch had floated on top of the little pond of water, and the drenched flowers had drooped with the water weight as though they were bowing their heads in respect for the woman who would no longer care for them.

I bowed my own head now. She was no longer caring for me either.

Even at forty-one, I needed my mommy. I blinked back the sting in my eyes for the want of her arms around my shoulders.

I went to the kitchen and came back with the dust pan and a little sweeper. "The same person who made the mess is the one who's going to be cleaning it, that's who." It's one thing to talk to yourself, but I'd started answering myself two years ago when I'd realized no one else ever did.

I stayed on my tiptoes to keep from crunching the glass into the hardwood floor as I swept around and under me, running the hand broom along the edge of the open cardboard boxes and into the dust pan before I dared to actually look *inside* the two boxes—donations to the library book drive in one box and my son's fourth grade volcano project in the other. Books and volcano both had a new coating of porcelain chunks and splinters.

Perfect.

"Just perfect!"

I stood up and dumped the contents of the dust pan into the trash then pulled out the vacuum and the hose attachments so I could suck the little shards out of the boxes without cutting myself. A lot of the sand used to make Tyler's volcano look more realistic and a couple of the plastic palm trees I'd picked up at the Newport Birthday Party Supply House went the way of vacuum bags. By the time I was done, I'd scratched up a couple of the books with the end of the hose and made the volcano scene look like the remnants of a long-dead planet. I hoped the books weren't first editions.

"What's all the noise in here?" Amanda stood in the doorway of the dining room, her arms folded across the pink tank top she slept in, which completely clashed with the green flannel bottoms covered in smiling skulls. She'd been studying at her friend's house and had planned on spending the night. Her brown hair strayed from the sloppy ponytail.

"Why are you home? I thought you were staying at Cassi's." It was just as well she'd come home. It wasn't like the big anniversary plans had panned out anyway. When Amanda said she'd be at her friend's and my oldest child, Chad, had said he'd be doing a game night at a buddy's house, I'd called the in-laws to see if they'd take Tyler and Marie. I didn't ask for those kinds of favors very often from my in-laws—even if they did live only a half hour away. The in-laws were complicated in ways that made me tired.

"Cassi's brother is a creep. He and his friends ate all the good food and then wouldn't turn off their stupid games. I finished the project and just want sleep now. What are you doing?" She stepped farther into the dining room.

"I dropped a plate. I needed to clean it up."

"You could do that in the morning. You're going to wake up Dad. It's like . . . midnight."

"Dad's not home yet." I didn't bother correcting her about the time. It was only just past eleven.

Her eyes swept quickly over the table, the candles, the dinner, and the dent in the wall. In less than a glance, understanding dawned on her face. "*Dropped* the plate, huh?"

I swallowed and looked down, feeling stupid for having been caught throwing the kind of tantrum she was famous for in our family.

She laughed. "Looks like you dropped it real hard against the wall." She wandered over to me and traced her fingers over the new dents. "Looks like you dropped it real hard against the wall *twice.*"

Nothing could be said to dignify my actions. Not denial or admission. So I stayed quiet, feeling the heat crawl up my neck and into my face.

"Did he at least call?" she asked, the humor gone from her voice.

I shook my head and coiled the vacuum hose.

She took a sharp intake of breath, as if she'd been about to shout something but then had changed her mind. She nodded and gave me a gentle hug. "I'm going to bed. You should too." Her whisper was barely audible. She turned and left, her feet treading softly on the stairs like she still worried she might wake up her father who wasn't home.

By the time I'd cleaned up the dinner and the tantrum, my soul felt scoured. I checked the boxes again to make certain there weren't any stray bits of plate still hanging around and inspected the top book in the library box—Barbara Kingsolver's *The Poisonwood Bible.*

The dust jacket had been scratched pretty badly from my raking the hose nozzle over it. Donating something so damaged seemed uncharitable in every way. And they'd already asked us not to use the donations as a chance to discard worn and unwanted items but instead to try our best to donate quality merchandise. It had been quality merchandise when it had been donated by one of the neighbors.

I ran a finger along the new scars of the book. Reading had once been a favorite pastime. What had happened to time that actually belonged to me?

I hefted the book out of the box, liking the weight of it in my hands. It felt like something of substance, something more than the emptiness the evening had brought me. I opened the book and began to read.

Imagine a ruin so strange it must have never happened.

I read a few pages in, right up to the sentence:

I had washed up there on the riptide of my husband's confidence and the undertow of my children's needs.

I snapped the book closed, looking at my surroundings anew with those words echoing through me. I wasn't in Africa, wasn't in any jungle more ferocious than the 405 freeway, and yet, sitting there on the floor between boxes of charity and childhood, my hands dried out from antibacterial dish soap, I felt I *had* been washed up on the riptide of my husband's confidence and the undertow of my children's needs.

The house was in perfect shape, no dust—not even on the blades of the ceiling fans—nothing out of place or amiss in the Robbins household. Nicholas didn't yell or throw tantrums. He certainly never threw dishes at a wall. But over the years, he'd become silent. The silence felt like disapproval in so many ways. I kept thinking if I did things better, worked harder, he would start talking to me again.

He'd been married before, but it had ended badly . . . with him catching her and his best friend together having breakfast in bed—*his* bed. We had dated for almost two months before he'd confessed to having an ex-wife. Along with that information came the confession that he also had two small children.

He'd expected me to walk away. Looking back, sometimes it felt that he'd told me about his past and his two children with the *intention* of me walking away. But when I was excited to meet his kids and take on this new challenge, he finally opened up.

I felt like I'd passed a test. He knew my devotion was total. If an ex and two kids didn't make me waver, nothing would.

It had worked out well enough . . . in the beginning. His kids became my kids. And then we started having *our* kids—four of our own to add to his two. We should have been a happy family of eight. But somewhere along the way, Nick had compartmentalized his life from before and his life with me, no matter how hard I tried to mesh us all into one family unit. He distanced himself from things that weren't perfect. His previous marriage had been imperfect, and he distanced himself from that life—even the kids from that life.

But I was also imperfect. Is that why he distanced himself from me? My body had filled out over the years, going from a toned size six to a softened size twelve. And I *did* throw dishes at the wall—not that he'd ever know about that because I'd never admit to it and Mandy would never rat me out. I'd pull out the spackle and paint tomorrow and fix it myself. Calling someone to fix it would require paying a bill I'd have to explain later. I stared at the newly bruised wall and hoped a repair job was possible.

But so what if it wasn't?

What if my patch-up job looked worse? Who was around to care? My undertow children were all nestled away in beds somewhere, and my riptide husband had yet to make an appearance. I scrambled to my feet—my body not reacting to my brain's commands as swiftly or as easily as it once had—dropped *The Poisonwood Bible* on the table—I'd been right about the wax leaving its mark on the table—and headed to the front door.

I needed some air.

Walking at night was not a habit of mine. I lived in an upscale area, but it was still California, and smart women didn't go walking around on their own at midnight without at least a bottle of pepper spray and a cell phone. But anger fueled the walk. Any punk kid who might try messing with me would find himself turned upside down in a dumpster.

My anger flowed from one source.

Nick.

He would excuse himself tomorrow with, "I had to work late." And that would be the last of it.

But it wouldn't be the last of it. He'd do it again. And again. And again.

What killed me was the wondering. Was it work? He was a CFO at Soft Tekk. Could that work be exciting enough to keep him hours away from his home? Was it a woman—a secretary, a coworker, a barmaid he'd met in some dark, smoke-filled place where he could watch a Lakers game without the kids running through the house making noise? Or was it worse? Was it simply the fact that he'd rather do *anything* than be with me?

He escaped our marriage every day through the convenient excuse called work. And yet his life spun a web around me that held me cocooned in place while he came back on occasion to feed on my energy.

His house. His children. His community. *My* responsibility.

Riptide.

I turned toward the shops. Too bad it was the middle of the night. No comfort shopping for me. I passed a nail spa in a strip mall. No comfort manicures either—not that I ever really indulged in things like that. It was an expensive habit, and the kids were always needing something that competed for the financial attention. A few doors down from the nail spa, a blue flyer taped to the door flitted in the night breeze. In a brief moment of need, I imagined it was waving to me—asking me to stop and read whatever message it had for me and me alone.

Looking for serious readers to join the Newport Ladies Book Club.
Women only! Eating and good conversation!
Space limited. Call Ruby Crenshaw asap.

I looked up to see the sign above the shop. *Grey's Used & Rare Books.* A book club. How long had it been since I'd held a novel in my hands for the sheer pleasure of losing myself in its pages? How long had it been since I'd held any book without needing to stuff it in a box for charity or a backpack for a child or a shelf to put it away for when the riptide wanted it?

No. That wasn't fair. Calling Nick a riptide every four seconds would get me nowhere. Find something glad.

But there wasn't anything glad I could associate with Nick at that moment. Even the fact that I lived in a beautiful home and had beautiful children just made me tired—not glad at all. It reminded me of schedules and soccer games and visits to the dry cleaners and grocery shopping and school functions and Junior League meetings and volunteer work and cleaning a house that never felt like home anymore. Tired.

The breeze picked up, and the little flyer waved at me again. I pulled the blue paper from the door, feeling guilty for removing it and hoping the bookstore owner had a spare to put up. Even if I didn't have to face my minister every Sunday, I hated taking anything that wasn't mine.

Depression replaced anger for the walk home. I blinked away the sting in my eyes again, imagining him cuddling up with some flirty female who wasn't me.

But the accusation in that image wasn't fair either. Nick had once been the victim of infidelity. Cheating was something he abhorred, something that made him physically ill. Nick was the last man on the planet who would be the cheater. He didn't even cheat at Monopoly back when he'd stayed home long enough to play a game with us. And there had been no evidence of infidelity—aside from his absence.

But what did absence prove, if not infidelity? It proved he didn't care enough to be with me. Another woman or not, I'd been rejected. He didn't need or want me.

I looked down at the paper in my hand and considered it. The woman's name was Ruby. I needed something with the ability to shine in my life. A ruby was as good as anything. And for the first time since setting the table for dinner, I found something to be truly glad about. Because I was going to, for once, do the selfish thing. I was going to join a book group, read, eat, and have good conversation.

Chapter 2

He came home after I'd already changed into a nightgown and curled up under the blankets on my side of the bed. He didn't turn on a light but bumbled around in the dark, undressing himself, tugging off shoes and dropping them to the floor. All the noise he made overrode any show of politeness in keeping the light off.

He whispered my name once, his voice soft like a caress in the darkness. I didn't respond, not wanting to hear the excuse now, not with the stinging back in my eyes and my pillow already damp. For as sweet as the whisper might have been, the excuse without apology would be a slap. I couldn't handle the slap, not when I clung so desperately to the little bit of glad the idea of a book group gave me.

When his bulk settled into the space next to me, he stretched a little, his toe touching my leg. Surely the touch was an accident. Surely he hadn't meant to make contact with me, like he'd done at the beginning of our marriage when he'd felt he needed to touch me every moment we were together. It almost burned where his skin connected with mine, but I couldn't move away, not without him realizing I was still awake. The few tears that had trickled out before became a steady stream of quiet mourning for the love I'd once felt in such a touch.

His foot stayed against my leg.

When I awoke, my eyes felt scratchy; my head ached from crying. Nick still slept the sleep of an oblivious, stupid, dumb, uncaring ox of a husband. I took a deep breath.

No, Livvy. That doesn't help you. Stop casting insults at the man who can't defend himself in his sleep. But no self-admonishment replaced my desire to fill his shoes with oatmeal. Grateful he still slept, I slid out of bed and went to the bathroom to quickly get ready. I had a lot to do, and not dealing with him would help the morning run more smoothly.

I frowned at the mirror, noting the dark roots against the blonde dye job. I'd have to go back to the hairdresser. I hated getting my hair dyed all the time. But Nick had come home one day talking about how he thought blonde hair would highlight my blue eyes.

At the time, everything in my life had swirled around Nick's opinion. The next day I'd walked into the hairdresser a brunette and walked out a blonde.

He'd been wrong. The blue in my eyes faded with the blonde, becoming typical and uninteresting, whereas the brown hair had offset my eyes and made them more vibrant. Nick loved the change though, and I loved what Nick loved.

Until today.

Today I wanted to shave my head just to teach him a lesson, except, like the dishes, I'd be the one dealing with the mess that would follow. I finished getting ready, pulling my hair back into a ponytail to keep it out of my face.

He rolled over as I tied my shoes in front of the closet. *Stay asleep*, I thought. *Stay asleep until I leave.*

It wasn't until I was downstairs and starting breakfast that my body relaxed into the routine of the day. I put some eggs on to boil, remembering to set the timer so I didn't let them get too hard, lest Nick turn his nose and mumble something about catching breakfast on his way to work.

Amanda followed the smell of bacon to the kitchen, her hair now in messy clumps around her shoulders and her eyes squinting in that way she did when she really hadn't slept enough. "Morning, Mandy." I handed her a plate so she could serve herself. The rest I would pop in the warmer oven for whenever Nick pulled himself out of bed, which hopefully wouldn't be until I was long gone.

"Is Dad home?" she asked, accepting the plate and piling on most of the already cooked bacon. Someone once told me that having a teen boy would cost me a fortune in food, and they were right. Chad ate a ton. But no one had warned me about the teen girl. Mandy ate twice the amount of food her older brother ate.

I nodded. "Still sleeping."

She snorted. "If I came home that late, I'd still be sleeping too. You *do* know you would totally ground me and *not* let me sleep in if I came home that late."

"I'm not his mother," I said.

She moved to sit on the barstool at the island while I finished cooking. "Then you should call his mother, because if he's going to act like an immature brat, he ought to be punished like one."

I shot a warning look over my shoulder and went back to the fry pan. "Don't disrespect your father, Manda-Bear. You know that's never okay with me."

I felt her tensing behind me, wanting to say more, but she didn't. Mandy had always clashed with her father. They'd been butting heads since she was two and wanted to have her own puppy. She'd finally gotten her way, but when that dog died, he'd refused to get another one. Not much had changed. They still clashed, and I still came between them and smoothed out the wrinkles of the impact. If I ever divorced Nick, Mandy would choose to live with me like his other kids had lived with their mother.

I blinked and exhaled sharply. *Divorce?* Where had that thought come from?

The phone rang, cutting into the tension of Mandy's mood and my worry over the appearance of a word I'd never really allowed into my mind before.

"Hello, DeeAnn." I greeted my mother-in-law. "How were the kids?"

DeeAnn once asked me to call her Mom, but I already had a mother and wasn't looking for any replacements—and DeeAnn never felt motherly to me. She was still in love with the wife who hadn't worked out.

The voice on the other end of the line informed me that Marie had a fever and refused to eat breakfast because she didn't feel well, but Tyler was fine.

"I'll come get them as soon as I finish making breakfast," I said. "I'm so sorry Marie's sick!"

"Oh, don't worry about it. I know how to care for a sickly kid; she'll be better off here with some grandma spoiling. I really don't get to see them often enough. Get whatever you need to do done and then come by. I just wanted to let you know she wasn't feeling well so you aren't surprised when you pick her up."

DeeAnn was like that, helpful, willing, pleasant. And yet there always seemed to be a barb under the pleasantries. Marie would be *better* there? I knew how to take care of a sick kid as well as the next person. I'd raised four of them just fine, thank you very much! Nick accused me of looking for unintended criticism, so I stopped mentioning my feelings of inadequacy around his mother to him. The fights weren't worth it.

I considered throwing the phone against the wall after she'd hung up but remembered how the plate incident had turned out and instead placed the phone gently on the counter.

Mandy rolled her eyes at me. How was it that she could look so cute while doing something so infuriating? "You had his mother on the phone and failed to mention that he needs a timeout and a spanking."

"I am not about to confess to that woman that I have no control over my own household. She's already thinking she can handle things better than me anyway."

"You're being paranoid, Mom." Mandy finished her bacon and eggs and eyed the rest I'd cooked in the interim.

I pulled the plate of bacon away from her view so she didn't get any funny ideas about eating everyone else's breakfast. Chad would come home soon and be starved. Chad was always starved. And Nick would get up sometime and be unhappy if he had nothing waiting. I was too sick-to-my-stomach mad over the previous night to be hungry. Maybe anger would work where diets had failed me. "It isn't paranoia if they're really out to get you," I said, feeling sullen at having my daughter call me paranoid.

Mandy laughed, got up, and kissed my cheek. "But it *is* paranoia if they really *aren't* out to get you. But paranoia's kind of a cute look on you."

"I'm glad you're my daughter." I pulled her into a light hug.

"Any mother would be," she said, smiling. She shook her head and went back upstairs to get ready for the day.

I grimaced at the fact that her plate still sat on the counter, not in the sink or, heaven forbid, the dishwasher. I considered calling her back to put her own dishes away but decided getting her back downstairs would take more energy than my rinsing them and putting them away on my own.

All food went into the warming oven. All dishes went into the dishwasher. And the counters were cleared and ready for the next meal. I went to the dining room, where it joined with the front hall, so I could fetch the book box for the library. I glanced at *The Poisonwood Bible* sitting on my table and remembered my decision to join Ruby's book club. My schedule for the next month ran through my mind. I had Junior League, Marie's piano lessons and her recital, Mandy's dance academy stuff to deal with, Chad's play rehearsals and performances if he got the part, and Tyler's speech therapy. Where would a book club fit?

Nowhere. I'd have to forget about adding one more thing to my life.

I scooted the book off the table and into the box to go to the library. Maybe they wouldn't care about the dust jacket. It would be best to let the library decide. They could donate the stuff they didn't want to Goodwill. I glanced into Tyler's volcano box. I'd have to stop at the party supply place and pick him up some new trees. He certainly couldn't take the project in like that.

As much as I wanted to get Marie and Tyler home, I couldn't ignore the fact that the library and the store would be faster errands without them. So with the book box balanced on my hip, I grabbed my keys from the key dish on the counter and opened the door leading to the garage.

"Where are you going?" Nick's voice called from behind me.

My eyes squeezed closed, and a few words that were less than admirable raced through my mind. "To pick up the kids from your mother's."

"What are they doing at Mom's?"

There would be no quick escape, so I steeled myself against tears and turned to face him. He looked good for a man who'd been out all night and had barely pulled himself out of bed. His messy hair had fine highlights of silvering, nothing major, not enough to call him gray. I hated that I loved the way that looked on him. His bathrobe hung open, revealing his bare chest, which was still toned and solid, and flannel pajama bottoms. He looked like he was doing an advertisement for men's sleepwear. "They had a sleepover last night. Your mom thought that since it was September twenty-first we'd want to have some time alone together." I kept the words factual, removing the icy bitterness and the icier accusations. A confrontation wouldn't help anything.

He considered my words before his expression widened with comprehension. So he at least remembered what September twenty-first was *supposed* to mean, even if he hadn't remembered that I told him to plan on a special dinner for the occasion. "I had to work—"

"I know." I cut him off before he could tack on the word *late*, though his tongue was caught between his teeth in the *L* position. "Breakfast is in the warmer. I have errands to run before I pick up the kids, so I'd better get going."

"What errands?" he asked, though his voice carried a hint of contrition, which wasn't typical.

"The library and then to the party supply store." I wanted to tell him to mind his own business. I hadn't asked him where he'd been until two thirty in the morning.

"Who's having a party?"

Not me. "No one. It's for Tyler's volcano project. I need some trees."

The contrition was gone. He pursed his lips in that way he did when he was about to be critical, cynical, or outright rude. He looked like his mother when he did that. "I'm surprised you call it Tyler's project. I'll bet you did all the work on it while Tyler played with his friends."

I really should have filled his shoes with oatmeal when I'd had the chance. His words embarrassed me enough to cause the heat to climb through the collar of my shirt and onto my face. I knew that meant my neck had red splotches and my cheeks were stained as though I'd used too much makeup. He'd know his words hit their mark.

I didn't respond, just nodded to acknowledge he'd spoken and turned to get out of the house.

His voice from behind me ripped out any shred of dignity left in me. "Really, Liv. The kids need to take responsibility for their own work. You can't follow them around once they're in college, doing their homework and mopping up their dorms."

I shut the door hard enough that the noise made me jump.

Riptide of my husband.

My heart pounded, and my throat burned with the need to cry some more. After waking up with a headache, the last thing I wanted was to cry again. I shoved the box into the back seat of my Pacifica. It was outdated and the manufacturer didn't make them anymore, but I loved that car and had decided to run it into the ground before allowing anyone to make me part with it.

I pulled the blue flyer out of my purse, where I'd stuffed it the night before, and dialed the number on my cell.

Ruby answered, sounding cheerful enough in her hello, but when I mentioned the book club, she moved from cheerful to ecstatic. "You saw my flyer then? Wonderful. Wonderful! And I suppose you're a great reader?"

Did it count if I *had been* a great reader once? "Of course I am."

"What's your favorite recent read?" she asked.

I looked down into the backseat of my car at the book with the scratched cover. "*The Poisonwood Bible.*"

My answer delighted her. She hadn't read it yet but had heard wonderful things about it and certainly wanted to give it a try. I hadn't read it either. But I *did* have it in my possession, which sort of counted. Ruby grilled me on my schedule, making sure I would actually make it to the monthly Saturday night meeting.

I walked around the car to the driver's side, agreeing with everything Ruby said, promising I'd be there, promising I was serious.

She ended the call with the statement, "And I'm not a serial killer, so you can feel safe when you come to my house." She laughed and hung up.

I stared down at my phone. "And somehow that's supposed to make me feel better?" I asked myself.

"No. No, it really doesn't," I answered myself as I turned the key in the ignition and backed out of the driveway, wondering how crazy it made me to have full conversations without the addition of any other person. But I took a liberating breath. Hang that stupid man! I was going to do something for me for a change.

At the party supply store, I picked up some little plastic dinosaurs in addition to the palm trees, knowing I was only buying them to spite Nick. I was grateful the store carried little cake decorations that could be used for anything.

The woman in line in front of me had her cell phone wedged between her shoulder and ear as she paid for her purchases. "Oh, honey, leave him." She paused while the person on the other end said something. "I know you don't want to live alone, but living alone is better than living lonely." She nodded her thanks to the cashier then took her crepe paper and phone call with her.

And that word that had never crossed my mind before this morning came back to me. *I could get a divorce.* Because, really, the woman with the cell phone was right. Living alone had to be better than living lonely. And I'd been living lonely for a lot longer than I wanted to admit.

* * *

"Hi, DeeAnn. I'm here for the kids." So many of my smiles around this woman felt painted on—as pretend as a china doll's smile on her cold, glass face.

A smile like that could break if not handled carefully.

I knew that from past experience.

"Oh, they're on the back patio. We were having a picnic. They'll be so sorry to have to leave early."

I flinched.

Paranoid, Livvy. You're being paranoid. She couldn't be criticizing me for coming at this exact moment. She couldn't be hinting that I'd ruined my children's day by showing up.

She wasn't a dragon.

Seemed like a dragon, certainly . . . but wasn't.

Though she *had* been the one to call me and say Marie was sick—which hinted at her wanting me to get them earlier rather than later. She *had* been the one to hem and haw until she couldn't think up one valid excuse to not take the kids for the night in the first place. She *had* been the one to cry on my wedding day and say, when she thought she was alone, when she thought no one else could possibly hear her, that if Nick would have just *tried* harder the first time around, she wouldn't have to be attending this current disaster.

I wouldn't have believed that anyone, certainly not my new mother-in-law, would be calling my wedding day a *disaster*. I wouldn't have believed it except I had been the one to overhear.

I was the one witness to DeeAnn's confession. No one else knew. Not even Nick. Why tell him? It would put a wedge between us that would end up damaging us. I couldn't allow that. DeeAnn warranted proof that she'd been wrong to cry alone in the gardens of my reception hall. I would make Nick so happy that someday she would have to approve of me.

That had always been my plan: to be glad, to be grateful, and to give everything my very best.

I didn't wait for DeeAnn to lead me to the back patio. I didn't need an escort and hurried off toward the French doors before we were forced into conversation that would make me drive too fast after it was all over. It scared Tyler when I got like that.

It scared me too.

"Hey, my babes!" I said, thrusting as much cheer into my voice as possible as I planted a kiss on Tyler's head and pulled Marie out of her chair and into my arms. She was way too big to actually pick up anymore since she was seven now, but I didn't have her full weight on me since I was bent down and she was still half on the chair. She was a little flushed, and her forehead was warm but nothing dramatic—nothing that popsicles and Tylenol couldn't fix. I pressed my lips to her forehead then pulled away as if she'd burned me. She giggled.

"I heard you weren't feeling well, lady love."

She nodded emphatically. "I'm *sick*," she declared.

"Have you eaten anything?"

She shook her head but stopped herself as if the action had caused her pain. "No," she answered instead. "And my head hurts too."

I tucked her in closer and started to croon soothing words when, from around the table, I noticed a pair of blue eyes peeking out from a bob of light brown curls. She'd been hidden by the large bouquet sitting on the middle of the table. But now that I was down at her level, I could see that my own kids hadn't been sitting alone.

Grace—my step-granddaughter—was with them. She sat on a box so her two-year-old body could eat comfortably at a table made for big people.

Before I could process the information or greet the little girl, Jessica, my stepdaughter, arrived on the patio, holding a chubby and smiling baby Kohl in her arms. She came at the same time DeeAnn finally showed up.

"Jess!" And this time my smile was real. I wanted so much for Jessica to feel my love for her—wanted so much for us to have a relationship in some capacity beyond the typical, evil stepmother stereotype. I'd never wanted to be that stereotype for Nick's kids, and yet I had failed.

Jessica barely knew me beyond the cards on holidays and passing phone calls where I was usually only taking messages for Nick. The kids had come over all the time in the beginning. I couldn't pinpoint when it had all changed, but one day Nick had just stopped caring that they existed. He couldn't look at them without his face twisting into one of irritation. He hardly spoke to them except in grunts and shrugs. I tried to help—to make things better. It was as if I'd pushed them on him—pushed him to really see his children—and that had caused him to retreat into himself.

He'd paid the child support without question and without requiring anything in return. He hadn't expected them to come for holidays. He hadn't asked for them to come on weekends or during the summer when they were out of school.

And then one day . . . they'd just stopped coming.

Who could blame them?

He hadn't been the one to walk Jess down the aisle at her wedding. It also hadn't been her stepfather, Andrew—the man who'd once been Nick's friend and the same man who'd been caught cheating with The Ex before she'd become The Ex. The man who had walked Nick's daughter down the aisle had been her new father-in-law.

Nick had been slighted by the whole situation. It had never occurred to him that he wouldn't be walking Jessica down the aisle. He'd left the wedding early, but I'd stayed—stayed and watched Jess glow and smile in this new family who adored her as much as she adored them. I liked her in-laws and made a point of being friendly with them. These would be the people who would share Nick's grandchildren. I didn't want to see those new babies pushed away the same way Jess and her brother, Kohl, had been pushed.

Yet, I hardly ever saw those babies—hardly knew little Gracie or little Kohl—named after his uncle.

I gently nudged Marie back on her chair and gave a hug to Grace and made a big show of loudly kissing her cheeks and neck so she'd giggle. It had been a long time since I'd had little ones like this.

Jess grinned while I kissed on my grandbaby. And I *did* consider them my grandchildren. They were Nick's grandchildren, and I was Nick's wife. That meant they belonged to me too.

"Hey, Livvy!" Jess said, the smile in her greeting as real and as warm as my own. She didn't hold me responsible for Nick's bad parenting anymore. She knew I'd tried to make things work for all of us. But she hadn't really understood until she had married and started having children of her own. The realization that I wasn't the evil stepmother had come about very slowly for her.

I didn't blame her for that. How else would she have been able to view me? The Ex had told her a lot of untrue stories about Nick and about me specifically. Nick's "hands off" approach to everything made the stories seem true. Who could blame a child for believing her mother?

"Hey, Gracie, love. How are you doing?" I asked.

"I good!" Grace said in that high-pitched, sing-song voice that only a two-year-old girl could ever manage to create. I looked over the table of food and tried not to roll my eyes.

"You've got finger sandwiches. How elegant!" I said, trying not to feel hypercritical of the fact that DeeAnn was feeding dry, old, boring, grown-up food to little kids.

"Wanted hotdog," Grace muttered.

I leaned close and whispered in her ear. "When you come to my house next, we'll have hotdogs and cake and cookies, and we'll eat it all up under a blanket."

Her eyes lit up, and she almost burst out loud with whatever kind of excitement she now had, but I hurried and put my finger to my lips so DeeAnn wouldn't hear things that could make this moment awkward.

It was wrong to try to outdo DeeAnn, but it was a fault I spent a lot of time *not* worrying about.

I stood up, hating that it hurt my knees a little to make that effort. “So how are things, Jess? The kids both look perfect. How’s Mike?”

“Mike’s great. He’s being promoted—that’s why I needed a babysitter at the last minute. He’s been in training down in San Diego, and they put him up in this insane hotel suite with a hot tub in the room. He asked me to come spend the night last night so we could have a little time together. I hadn’t seen him for a week.”

“You could have called me to babysit,” I declared before thinking about it.

DeeAnn narrowed her eyes. “You needed a babysitter last night as well.”

Jess either didn’t notice or outright ignored the cool tone in DeeAnn’s voice and said, “Exactly. I know when your anniversary is. I wouldn’t have dreamed of infringing on anniversary time. So how was it? Did you two do anything fun?”

How to respond? The truth was unpardonable, but lying would be bad too. “I possibly made the best meal of my life last night.” There. Those words were true. The meal had been beautiful. But I couldn’t let Jess or DeeAnn dig for more information, so I changed the subject. “How is . . . Natalie?” I asked, having to pause to keep myself from calling her The Ex, like I always did in my mind.

“Oh, you know . . . same as always.” Jessica seemed to have taken an extra breath as she looked down at the baby as a distraction. I’d suspected her relationship with her mom wasn’t great, but I couldn’t have imagined the look on Jess’s face just now. That was a look worse than *not that great.*

“I’m sure she’s doing wonderfully,” DeeAnn said with a smile. “Natalie always manages to sparkle everywhere she goes.”

The only thing that kept me from falling into immense amounts of self-pity at having my mother-in-law compliment The Ex like that was noticing the way it made Jessica shift her weight and look away.

“Well, our baby Kohl is sure losing some of that chub I love so much.” I switched the subject again, for Jessica’s benefit this time, and kissed his feet, which made him smile and coo while he drooled down his shirt.

“He’s walking all over the place—no . . . running is more like it. Baby fat doesn’t stand a chance against that kind of exercise.”

“And how is Uncle Kohl?” I asked, still cooing at his namesake.

Her head jerked up, and she glanced at DeeAnn as if somehow deciding what could be said in such company. “You know my brother.

He's doing great. You know . . . school, getting good grades, being smarter than everyone else."

"Well, that's wonderful." I glanced around the table at the biscotti and dry sandwiches. The possibility that Marie's sickness might have something to do with the lameness of the menu didn't escape me. "Are you staying for their tea party?" I asked Jessica.

"Oh no. There's a whole list of things I need to do today. I'm afraid I have to be the bad mom and rush the kids on out. I just needed to change Kohl's diaper before we left."

Her mouth twisted slightly, and I wondered if it was because DeeAnn hadn't changed the diaper soon enough—which was totally believable—or if it was because she thought dry sandwiches and biscotti were nasty excuses for a lunch too. I would have stayed and endured DeeAnn if it meant getting to spend time with Jess and the kids. But since Jess wasn't staying . . .

"I get to be the bad mom too." I tsked and put my hand on Tyler's shoulder as he was about to say something to the effect of not minding leaving early. "It was good to see you, Jess. Tell Mike hello for me, and make sure to call me if you ever need a sitter. I'm happy to take my grandbabes for a bit. They're just so kissable!" And I attacked Grace with more kisses. She giggled some more—a sound I loved like I loved sunshine.

"C'mon Ty-buddy, help me gather yours and your sister's stuff and take it to the car." He shot out of the lawn chair without needing to be asked twice. "Say good-bye and thank you," I reminded him.

"Bye, Nan. Thanks for letting us stay."

"You're welcome, Tyler," DeeAnn said. She never let the kids call her anything besides *Nan*. She felt that *Grandma* or *Nana* made her sound old, in spite of the fact that she *was* old. So she shortened it to *Nan*.

Tyler gave Grace a quick hug and tickled Kohl's belly until the baby made the sort of chuckle that brought a smile to everyone. Tyler really did like his little niece and nephew.

He turned to go when DeeAnn said, "Are you forgetting something, Tyler?"

It appeared as though he'd hoped she'd forgotten too, but he pecked a quick obligatory kiss on her cheek then disappeared through the French doors before he could be instructed to do anything else.

"Well, I'll be off too. Everything's already loaded in the car and ready to go." Jess managed to pick up Grace one-handed and settle the toddler on her other hip. The girl really was a very good mom. "Thanks, Nan. I'd offer to stay and help clean up, but I know today is your maid day, so I won't worry about it."

I almost laughed at that as I moved through the house to the front door. I never worried about trying to help clean up anymore because the woman threw fits about everything being done wrong. I always ended up feeling like I'd inconvenienced her—rather than actually helped. I'd have hated to be her maid. DeeAnn's expectations were borderline criminal. It wouldn't have surprised me to find out she went through a new maid service every week simply because no one would work for her longer than a few days.

I took a deep breath. *Stop it, Livvy. You're being unkind.* I muttered out loud, "I always feel like I need chocolate when I leave this house."

I hadn't realized how close behind me Jess was until she caught up the few steps and said, "Could you give me a hand buckling these two in?" She didn't mention the chocolate comment, either because she really hadn't heard or because she was too polite. My face warmed because she likely *had* heard, and it was not a nice thing to say.

"Of course." I sent Marie, who seemed to be feeling better already, and Tyler off to buckle themselves in while I followed Jessica to her car.

"So . . . I thought I should tell you because he refuses to say anything to Dad, but you know how Kohl signed up for the marines so he didn't have to have Dad help pay for his college?"

I nodded.

"He's being deployed. He'll be gone for a whole year. I'm gonna miss him like crazy."

"Deployed where?" I asked, feeling sick about Kohl being all on his own for a whole year. Idiot Nick! Giving his son no other options.

"Djibouti, Africa. I don't even know if I pronounced that right. He leaves in January. Anyway, I wanted to have a good-bye party for him—a way for everyone in the family and all of his friends to wish him well and show their support and all that, but he totally shot me down. He says no one in the family wants to see him off, and he doesn't want to see any of them either." She blew at her bangs and grunted as she battled against Kohl's waving arms to try to get them inside his seatbelt restraints. "I'm not sure what to do. This is huge. I want to make a big deal out of it exactly because it *is* a big deal. And he keeps shutting me down. What do you think? Should I just let it go?"

"Tanks, ma-maw!" Grace called out in her toddler language as I finished buckling her into her car seat and straightened to face Jessica directly. Jess had the warmest brown eyes I'd ever seen—like wet sand when the setting sun hit it just right—kind of golden brown and filled with light. They were the same color as her father's eyes.

"You're welcome, baby," I said absently to Grace. I pondered Jessica's question. It was a dilemma I always found myself caught in. How much pushing toward family togetherness was too much pushing?

"I don't know," I said finally, leaning against the car. "You're right. It is a big deal. It totally matters and should be given the attention it deserves." I almost picked at the paint on the side of the car door where it had peeled away under the humidity of Southern California but stopped myself. Jess would be mortified if I did something like that. Since Mike was being promoted, they'd likely be upgrading the car. This car represented another thing I admired about Jessica. She lived within her means, rather than overspending on play like her mother or overspending on appearances like her father. Jess was so much like me that it seemed wrong that she actually belonged to The Ex.

Kohl? I didn't understand him nearly as well, if I understood him at all. Kohl may have had his mother's looks, but he had his father's stubbornness. He seemed to push people away just like Nick did.

Jessica waited for me to continue.

"Why doesn't he want a party? Is it because *he* doesn't want it? Is he happier as a hermit? Or is it because he's afraid no one will really care and you'll be the only one to show up?"

Jessica shrugged. "He doesn't say anything, but probably both. He says Dad won't come, and Mom's never civil."

The Ex really never was civil. She brewed poison as a hobby—no one could convince me otherwise. Who could blame Kohl for not wanting that to be his farewell before he left for Africa? Add DeeAnn to the mix, and you had the perfect storm. Jessica's wedding had been proof enough that the family was a sticky entanglement.

"I don't blame him for worrying, but I don't blame you for wanting a get-together either. One would hope we could all be in the same room and play nice for the sake of Kohl getting one night where it's about him and not about the past."

Jessica nodded.

"The past!" Grace shouted like it was the punch line to the best joke ever.

Grace had it right. The past certainly felt like a joke—only not the funny kind.

That pushed away the indecision. "I think we should do it. I'll help you set everything up, but maybe let's pick a neutral location to hold it at. Somewhere where none of the major players get to claim being in charge."

Jessica smiled. "You don't think forcing him to do this will make him mad at me?"

I snorted. "It might, but at least he'll know you love him enough to make the effort to give him a special day."

"Will Dad come, do you think?"

"Of course he will," I said with far more confidence than I truly felt. I would have to approach it right. I had until January. That was three months to try to work it out. Hopefully that would be enough time to soften him.

"It's just that after what happened at the wedding . . ."

"That was almost four years ago." I almost added that Kohl had been a hotheaded teen at the time, but it hadn't been Kohl's fault. He'd just tried to keep Nick from walking out on the wedding, and they'd argued. Kohl hadn't been wrong to try to get Nick to stay at Jessica's wedding. Nick had been wrong to leave. They hadn't talked since—not even when Kohl had graduated from high school. Nick had planned a business trip that weekend on purpose so he had an excuse not to be there.

I patted Jessica's hand. "He'll come," I assured her again.

He'll come if I have to hit him over the head and drag him there unconscious. He owes it to me after ruining our anniversary.

Jessica smiled and nodded again, her face clear and relaxed with the relief she must have felt to have someone to help make a special day for her brother.

"Hey, Livvy," Jessica called as I turned to leave.

I turned back.

She broke a Kit Kat bar in half and held one of the halves out to me. "I always need chocolate when I leave Nan's house too."

Chapter 3

Almost two weeks had passed since our failed anniversary dinner.

Nick had actually come home early for the evening and found me in the kitchen baking cookies for the book club meeting. He took one for himself, which irritated me, but I'd made extra for the kids, so it shouldn't have bothered me—it just did. He lounged against the counter in his creased suit pants and pressed-perfect white shirt, his tie loosened at his collar. He never used to wear suits on Saturdays. He'd reserved the weekends to play with Chad and Tyler and to be with me—no matter what I was doing. He looked pleased for a change, a look I hadn't seen on him for a long time.

The timer chimed, letting me know the other batch was ready to come out.

"What's say we go out for dinner tonight—just you and me," he said.

I almost dropped the pan of cookies I'd just pulled from the oven. "What?"

"You heard me. Mom could watch the kids, or Chad could."

"Chad's going to a friend's house to run through lines for a play tryout."

"Then Mom could do it. It's been a while since . . ." He trailed off. It had been a while since a lot of things.

"I can't," I said, feeling bad for saying no. And yet, was he serious? Dinner? As if that made up for *anything*? And without any warning? He completely expected I'd just be home waiting for some whim? For years I had been waiting for that whim. He was two weeks too late.

"You can't?"

The timer was still beeping, but it had turned to little more than background static as I tried to make sense of the conversation. Tyler and Marie came tearing through the kitchen at just that moment.

"Cookies!" Marie shouted, filling up her tiny seven-year-old hands from the already-cooled pile and then running out again. Tyler didn't shout but did stop to fill up on the baked goods before leaving.

I met Nick's eyes, almost wavering, almost changing my mind and doing what he wanted, but then I stiffened, thinking of the dinner, the unmentioned anniversary. He still hadn't said anything. Not a "happy anniversary" or a card or a gift or a kiss or *anything*. Eighteen years was suddenly meaningless. Besides, I'd given my word to be at the book club. I lifted my chin. "I can't. I have a book club tonight." I turned my back on him and moved the cookies from the pan to the cooling rack.

"You can't? Just like that, you can't?"

"The plans were made a while ago. It wasn't *just like that*."

He wiped his hand down his face and said, not loudly enough to be shouting but close enough, "Would you shut off that timer? It's driving me insane!"

I hit the button, leaving us in silence.

"Whatever," he said, and he walked away, the casual, pleasant demeanor gone from his step.

I heard doors slam and listened to his car pull out of the garage before trudging up the stairs to ask Mandy to watch Marie and Tyler. Her eyes focused on my trembling lip while I asked, but she didn't mention it, which spared me from breaking down until I was in my own car and driving away.

* * *

It took a bit to clean myself up from the crying on the way to Ruby's house. How would it look if I showed up with red eyes and a runny nose?

The temptation to turn around and not go to the book group nearly overtook me on several occasions. But my hands never actually turned the wheel to make the car move back in the direction of my house.

I'd meant to be early but ended up on time, walking up to her doorstep, ringing the bell, clutching the plate of cookies like a weapon. The strange comment about her not being an axe murderer or whatever came to mind again. Wouldn't that be my just desserts? I deny my husband for the first time in our marriage and end up chopped to bits and stuffed in a cooler.

"Stop it, Livvy! Be glad your cookies turned out."

Yes. Be glad. Ruby had sounded sweet and sincere. Be glad.

The door swung open, and the older woman standing in front of me with way more jewelry than I even owned, let alone would wear all at once, stood in front of me, her smile wide and welcoming.

I relaxed. Or tried to.

She was like a sparkling jewel and not at all like a crazy fiend. Before I knew what was going on, she'd enveloped me in a hug, nearly knocking the cookies out of my hands, welcoming me to her home. She reminded me of my mom and all the things I missed about not having a mom anymore.

"I brought cookies," I said, feeling silly for it now. She'd told me not to bring anything, but it seemed so wrong to show up with nothing to give in return. That would be like showing up at a potluck with nothing but a fork.

"Oh, honey, you didn't have to do that, but they look lovely," she said as she ushered me into her home that was startlingly similar to Nick's mom's house—the same sort of show-house appeal with expensive rugs and paintings.

Yet Ruby's house felt warm and lived in—a direct contrast to the way my mother-in-law's house felt to me. Ruby's house was a place I was welcomed into without question or judgment. I realized immediately that it was Ruby, herself, who made the difference.

She showed me into a room where two others waited.

"Olivia," Ruby said, "meet Daisy and Athena."

I tried to smile as I handed off my cookies to Ruby.

Athena had dark hair that came just past her chin in one of those chic, trendy cuts I'd learned long ago I could never pull off. I loved that haircut. Loved the way her dark hair contrasted with her blue shirt, the way my dark hair used to contrast with my eyes.

Stupid Nick. Stupid Nick and his stupid, "But you'd look so nice with blonde hair . . ." I felt dumpy next to these women. But I took the hand Athena offered me and shook it. Her grip was firm and confident and, in a way I couldn't explain, made me smile briefly and like the girl.

"Call me Livvy," I said, blowing a stray hair out of my face. Why hadn't I put it up in a ponytail? I smoothed it all back, hoping it would stay that way, and vowed to put it up next time. I might not have been able to pull off the cute, short haircuts, but I definitely knew how to style it so it looked better than it did now. I turned to Ruby. "I know you didn't want us to bring anything, but this was a new recipe I just had to try. White chocolate chip cookies." They had cranberries in them too, but I couldn't remember the word *cranberry*, I was so nervous.

Ruby thanked me as the door chimed, and she went off to answer it.

I turned back to the others, feeling stupid and inadequate. Why had I brought those dumb cookies? I smiled again, hoping they wouldn't notice the splotchy flush that had already invaded my neck and cheeks.

"It's wonderful to meet both of you. I've been looking forward to this all day," I said, noting that Daisy's clothes were creased in all the right places. I smoothed my hand over my black shirt, which I'd thrown together with a pair of black slacks that hid a little of my fluffy midsection. I took great care to keep Nick tidy at all times but, in my fury over the fight I'd had with him, hadn't taken that same care for myself. What would a woman who looked so put together like this Daisy did think of someone as unkempt as me? Her pink cashmere sweater hung beautifully on her frame, which made me shift slightly. I'd worn black to hide my out-of-shape body but knew the pants bunched up in the wrong places. Daisy was probably the same size as me, but her clothes fit her in a way that flattered her and made her look elegant.

Athena also had a look of togetherness about her, with her dark hair and young, toned body. But I'd felt warmth behind Athena's firm handshake, and when she smiled, she looked to be encouraging me. Time to stop comparing myself to these others and to stop the paranoia. I seriously doubted anyone else would agree with my daughter that paranoia was a cute look on me.

"And this is Paige." Ruby showed up with the newcomer to our group.

I felt immense gratitude at the distraction Paige offered everyone. No longer was I the focus of scrutiny.

Paige was young and sweet looking. She had the look of "new mother" to her that made women her age shine—like Jessica. She smiled and gave us all a shy little wave. Definitely sweet. She also looked frazzled. I knew that look. It stared at me in the mirror most mornings. She probably had a husband like mine—the distant kind who never helped out with the kids. She sat on one of the folding chairs, and I kept my smile up.

Think of something glad, Livvy. Stop thinking about Nick and his tantrum earlier. Stop thinking about the anniversary dinner that never happened.

And yet, that failed dinner never strayed far from my thoughts anymore. In nearly two weeks, hardly a minute ticked by without the pain of that night burning through my nervous system.

I will not break down in the home of a stranger, I insisted to myself. There were millions of better places to break down. I could do that later, in the privacy of my own home or in my car or at the beach where the sound of the waves crashing into the sand would drown out my screams.

It shocked me how much I really did want to scream.

But I gritted my teeth and smiled while Ruby went to answer the door again.

She came back with another woman in tow. This one looked like she'd just come from work. She had a green shirt with the word *Walgreens* written on it. She looked exhausted—probably from having to stand on her feet all day long checking out ungrateful customers. I'd decided long ago to never work in customer service. I had a tendency to take it personally when people were mean to me. This was something I'd learned about myself during my teenage years when I'd worked my very first job in a fast food restaurant. I'd gone home in sobbing fits because people had been so outright unsympathetic while I'd struggled to get their orders right. Mom had held me and smoothed my hair and rocked me gently before informing me I had to go back the next day.

I'd already planned on quitting and started crying even harder when she insisted I go back because "you have to make sure you never quit until you know you did everything in your power to give it your best. If you still don't like it after that, fine. But never quit without trying first." I'd stayed on for another year and become pretty good at learning how to make people happy so they didn't yell at me very often.

But even though I'd learned how to handle the insults of people in foul moods, it didn't mean I liked it. They'd promoted me to assistant manager. That was the day I'd quit. I'd proven I'd given my best and felt free to leave.

I half admired and half pitied this girl for working in customer service and then having the strength to show up at a book club. If I had been her, I would've gone home and put in a movie.

"This is my niece, Shannon," Ruby said.

Ah. That explained it. Shannon had likely been pressured into the book club by her aunt—just in case only a couple of people showed up. Shannon gave a wry smile as Ruby explained. "She needs to make room for a book in her life now and again, so I'm thrilled she could come."

Shannon seemed to genuinely love her aunt. She must have because she'd shown up to the book meeting despite the fact that anyone looking at her could tell she wasn't exactly thrilled about being there. It was another way Ruby reminded me of my mom. She could do that to people—make them do things they didn't want to do simply because everyone hated to disappoint her. In just a few moments, I had decided I loved Ruby.

"Everyone have a seat, and we'll make the round of introductions." Ruby waved Shannon over to one of the white couches. Having young children and teenagers, the idea of white couches filled me with dread. As I looked Ruby over, in her bright blue tunic and her grandmotherly face, I doubted young children were a worry to her any longer—not unless they were visiting grandchildren. If she was anything like my mother-in-law, that wouldn't be an issue, since she rarely took the kids. But Ruby's warm eyes and quick, easy smile reminded me that she wasn't anything like the shrewish woman who'd raised my husband. She was definitely more like the woman who had raised me.

Shannon, looking resigned, sat next to Paige.

"Maybe next time we'll get more ladies coming," Ruby said, almost to herself. Then she brightened again and began the conversation, since it seemed none of the rest of us had any such intention. "As you all know, I'm Ruby Crenshaw. I just turned sixty-two last month. I've lived in this gorgeous home by myself since the passing of my husband. It's been nearly two years, but sometimes it seems as if Phil has just left for work." She paused for a moment and took a deep breath. "I have one son who lives in Illinois with his wife. My brother and his wife, Shannon's parents, recently moved to Phoenix—I can't imagine why they would want to live in the middle of the desert." She shook her head like her brother was insane, and I agreed with her. The mild humidity of Southern California kept me from feeling like I was drying out and shriveling up. "Shannon lives in Laguna Hills; it's wonderful to have her so close. No grandkids of my own just yet."

So she definitely wasn't worried about young kids on the white couches. But I was willing to bet she wouldn't scowl if a chubby-legged toddler who called her grandma accidentally spilled red punch on one of them. She might sigh and shake her head, but she'd love the child no matter the imperfections. She'd love the child and be grateful for the inconvenience children sometimes are.

Ruby smiled, and her eyes had the shine—as my mom would have said. It was her way of saying someone looked like they were about to cry, but I was probably just projecting my own desire to have another good cry. Nick always said I needed to stop assuming people felt the same way I did.

Ruby twisted the large diamond ring on her finger. I touched my own ring but pulled away when the desire to rip it off and throw it into

Ruby's fake fireplace nearly overwhelmed me. Imagine me showing up and making such a display like that—dumping all my anger onto these strangers. They'd think I was a lunatic for sure, and that would be before they discovered that I talked to myself.

Ruby smiled. "I've always read, especially when my husband traveled." She looked at her hands. "Since I've been widowed, I haven't socialized like I used to with our friends. They're always there with an open invitation, but I find it harder to enjoy myself around them since I'm always the third or fifth or seventh wheel. So I spend a lot of time cooking for myself and reading, of course." She brightened. "That's enough about me; let's go around the circle."

Daisy was first, giving a summary of her family and job, where she dealt with insurance. "And I'm looking forward to getting to know more people now that my kids are older and I have my own life again," she said. She laughed.

I didn't join her in her laughter. The words struck me with fear. *My own life.* What would that be like? A house with no bickering kids—but no laughing ones either. A house filled with the silence of my husband's absence, and on the rare occasion when he did come home, the house would be filled with the silence of his apathy. I shuddered, terrified for the future that inevitably awaited me.

Daisy didn't mention anything about books at all, and I felt instantly glad I hadn't brought in the copy of *The Poisonwood Bible* I'd pilfered from the library donations. It would have made me look overeager and needy. It was bad enough I'd brought cookies.

I was next, and I wished I'd sat to the other side of Athena and Paige so I could have been last. I babbled about my kids, carefully not mentioning much about Nick because I didn't trust myself not to burst into tears. Forgetting the anniversary was one thing, but then to go two weeks without mentioning it? Not one word? And the one time I'd mentioned Kohl's farewell party, he'd rolled his eyes and left the room. The man was pushing my limits. The scream that wanted to escape seemed caught in my throat. But I managed to swallow it for the time being.

"My daughter's babysitting for me tonight, which means the kids will likely be having frozen pizza for dinner, but at least they've got homemade cookies." I smiled, feeling stupidly like a commercial for home-baked goods and wishing I could make myself shut up. I should've stayed home with them. As Daisy had reminded me, soon the job of raising my children would all be over, and I would be left with nothing but the riptide. That reminded me of the book—the reason I was here. "I haven't read a novel in a long time, so I'm hoping to get a kick start with the group."

What was wrong with me? This wasn't a confessional. Ruby didn't need to know I'd overstated my recent reading habits when we'd talked on the phone. I half expected her to kick me out of her house. But instead she leaned over and patted my hand, reminding me once again of my mother.

The pain of missing my mother shoved its way to the surface like an angry, raw wound. I felt my eyes prick with the sensation of tears and ducked my head so no one else would see the shine before I could blink it away.

Paige came next. I'd been right about her. She was a young single mom from Utah—a Mormon, apparently—having recently come to California after a heartbreaking divorce. That haggard look in her eye wasn't because she had a nonhelpful husband but because she didn't have anyone at all. "I still can't believe I'm actually divorced—it wasn't supposed to happen to *me*, you know?" With every sentence she uttered, she hurried to follow it up with an explanation and then said something else to explain the words that came before the explanation. Poor girl. I wanted to hug her and tell her she would be okay—she'd make it through this horrible event that had obviously shredded her insides. I thought again about that girl in the party supply store on her cell phone.

I know you don't want to live alone, but living alone is better than living lonely.

I almost repeated those words out loud but caught myself.

Oh, how that girl needs a hug and a mother to bundle her up, make her a cup of cocoa, and whisper comfort to her.

"I came tonight because reading is one of my few escapes—or, well, it used to be, and I miss it. I also came in hopes of making some new friends."

While I'd nearly opened my mouth to repeat the words from the woman in the party supply store, Ruby had hurried to offer condolences, or whatever the kind words you said to someone who was divorced were called. Ruby's interruption gave me the moment I needed to filter my own words. Paige had made her choice already, so she knew better than I what the difference was between alone and lonely.

Shannon was next. "I'm a pharmacist," she announced right off the bat. That explained the Walgreens uniform. She wasn't a cashier after all. I had a cousin who wanted to be a pharmacist, and it was grueling work for him to get through his schooling. The fact that Shannon had made it through that same schooling spoke volumes about her. She was a professional woman. And she was smart. She wasn't that much younger than I was, yet she had a completed education under her belt. An education *and* a career. Where would I be if I had taken that same kind of time for myself?

"I live in Laguna Hills," she continued, "like Aunt Ruby said, and have one son. He's twelve. I've been married for fourteen years, and honestly, I can't remember the last book I read. I think Aunt Ruby's hoping I'll develop some hobbies."

"She works too much," Ruby said with a smile that looked conspiratorial. That smile meant Ruby fully planned on changing the *works-too-much* description. "I'm really glad you're here, Shannon."

Shannon shrugged, and I guessed that if she'd been here without an audience she'd have rolled her eyes like an insolent teenager at her aunt. The thought made me smile too.

Athena was last. She looked down at the plate of cookies on the mosaic coffee table, and I hoped with all my heart she'd take one. They really were good. And her handshake, so firm and full of friendship, made me want to offer something in return.

"I'm thirty-two and single," Athena said and paused as though she were waiting for us to kick her out for her lack of attachment. I found I envied her too—so full of possibilities, a whole life ahead. The pause went long enough that I thought she might actually not say anything more.

Finally, Ruby said, "Oh, come on. There's got to be more to you than that." Her smile looked encouraging and helpful rather than nosy.

Athena must have recognized the nudge of good will and finally continued. "I own the online magazine called *Newport Travel*. It keeps me pretty busy . . . so much so that my boyfriend broke up with me a few days ago."

When everyone started in on how sorry they were, she held up her hand. "It's not exactly what you think," she said. "I wasn't ready to move into anything deeper and . . . Karl was . . . so he ended it."

Paige and Athena shared a look. They were both just freed from a relationship. Did they feel lighter? Or were they still lonely? I wanted to know and wished I knew them well enough to ask. I thought of The Ex. She'd had Nick once and didn't care so much that she'd lost him. *She'd* been the one to walk away. What did she know about Nick that I didn't know? Did it make me a fool to have stayed with him for so long? I thought about Nick's relationship with his other kids—strained and near enough to nonexistent that it actually *could* be nonexistent. Did I want that for my children? Of course not. So was I dumb for staying with a man who didn't really care about me anymore?

Stop thinking about that, Livvy.

"He thinks I'm a workaholic." She took a deep breath, looking at me. I nodded for her to keep going.

"I am. I know it. But I want to do better. So here I am." No mention of happiness, just an admission of working too much.

Ruby clapped her hands together. "We'll straighten you out."

We all laughed. Well . . . everyone except Shannon, who seemed to instinctively know that the last comment was meant as much for her as for Athena.

"Well, now that we know one another, let's eat," Ruby said with a huge smile. "Then we'll talk books."

Athena finally took one of my cookies, and it made me feel glad to have given her something in return for her warmth and friendly handshake. As they all shifted into more comfortable postures, I couldn't help but think that Ruby was exactly that shining thing I needed in my life.

Food was one of those things that settled me. And with everyone eating and talking, I felt more comfortable. I could belong here. I could fit here. Paige looked pale and shifted in her seat several times. Poor thing. How hard it must be to find yourself on your own with little children.

But even as I pitied her, some small part of me envied her.

Free.

She'd never have to wonder if her husband would make it home for the anniversary dinner she'd spent the whole day preparing.

"I think we should read *The Poisonwood Bible* by Barbara Kingsolver."

Athena's voice calling out the title to the very book I'd thieved from the library donation box startled me out of my private thoughts. I glanced up, realizing the conversation had flowed past me without me even noticing.

Athena seemed confident in her choice for the first book our new group would tackle. "It came highly recommended to me by a bookstore owner."

"I actually own that already," I chimed in. "I haven't read it through all the way yet but was hoping to. I'd love the excuse to finish it now rather than wait 'til later." Ruby didn't look ruffled by my admission of *not* having read the book already, in spite of what I told her on the phone. Maybe she didn't remember.

Everyone agreed, and Ruby seemed pleased to have settled that task of book choosing so quickly. I smiled at Athena. Her choosing that particular book out of the blue felt like a sign. I belonged here, and I had the book to prove it.

The evening was done much too fast, in my opinion. I dreaded the idea of going home to face Nick after the afternoon's conversation. The guilty apprehension in my stomach told me I probably should have just given in and gone with him to do whatever he wanted to do for the night. But then . . . I'd have missed out on all of *this*.

The time spent in Ruby's home reminded me that other people had worries and problems too—well . . . everyone *except* Daisy, who seemed genuinely content with her life. For the first time in a long time, I felt emotionally fed rather than fed upon. These women reminded me that I wasn't alone.

I loitered a bit afterward, taking my time getting up, time clearing away a few scant dishes from the evening, time removing the extra cookies from my tray to a paper towel on Ruby's counter so she could have them for later.

Daisy held back too, seeming hesitant to let the evening end. She thanked Ruby several times for pulling off a group like this.

Daisy intimidated me a little. The way she held herself showed she felt secure in her own identity. She wasn't in the middle of a midlife crisis.

"You don't have to do my dishes," Ruby said, looking up from where she and Daisy talked quietly at the kitchen entrance.

"I know," I answered, not stopping. There were only a few things left to put in the dishwasher, so what sense was there in not finishing?

"Well, you're a jewel to help me out like that. I appreciate it," Ruby said when the work was done and the dishwasher hummed to life.

"It's pretty much what I do: clean, cook, clean some more . . . I actually don't mind. It makes me feel useful."

Daisy tilted her head, her brow furrowing slightly at my words, and I felt the warmth of the red flush on my neck and cheeks. I tried to think of something else—anything else—that might make me useful to the world or interesting enough for someone like Daisy to want to talk to me, but nothing else occurred to me.

I really had been reduced to housework and cooking.

Once upon a time, I'd been involved in all sorts of activities—things that could define me, things that were even interesting.

Somewhere in the midst of my own life story, I'd become lost. I should be my own main character. And yet . . . How had I been replaced? I wasn't even a strong secondary character in my own story. I was more like an errant housekeeper who clung to the background and blended in so well no one noticed her presence anymore.

The horror of that realization made me look away, down at my shoes—scuffed and worn and needing to be replaced. I had become such a background character, I failed to notice the details about myself. Not until this moment had I even noticed I needed new shoes.

"Are you okay, dear?" Ruby asked.

"Fine." I breathed, turning back to the sink and grabbing the dishrag as though it were a life preserver in a turbulent sea. "Fine," I repeated. "Just wanting to finish the job properly." I wiped down the counters, folded the little dishrag over, and placed it on the back of the sink.

When I turned back to the two women, they both stared at me as though I were an exotic insect inside a glass cage—a little creepy yet something strange enough they couldn't look away.

"Are you sure?" Daisy asked, her voice kind and compassionate.

The kindness startled me, and a nervous sort of laugh escaped me—the bubble of the scream threatening to follow closely behind. "It's just been a long week . . . no, year . . . no, *four* years." It really had been four years. Since Jessica's wedding. Everything went wrong after the wedding. I forced myself to meet Ruby's warm eyes. "You just remind me of my mother. I guess I'd forgotten how much I still miss and need her."

Ruby stepped forward and enclosed me in a hug that stifled the scream inside me . . . for a little while longer.

Chapter 4

I LET MY CAR ENGINE idle at the end of our street for several minutes before daring to face him again. What would I say? How would I excuse myself for ditching him like I had? The guy finally asks for some of my attention, and I blow him off?

All those worries vanished the minute I hit the button on the garage door opener and the light from the garage flooded out, revealing the empty space where his car should have been.

Should have been.

But wasn't.

New worries replaced the others. Where had he gone for such a long time? Was he angry? Regretful? Did he feel anything at all?

"Enough, Livvy!" I shoved my door open and stepped out of the car. I wasn't going to take this back. I would not regret a couple hours spent on myself. He could do or feel whatever he wanted, but I wasn't going to back down—not from this. I needed this. I needed one place in the world that belonged to me.

I pulled the empty plate from the passenger side of the car and made my way into the house. "Hey, Manda-bear. Anything exciting happen while I was gone?" I tried to keep my tone pleasant. This wasn't the kids' fault.

Mandy looked up from the computer in the study nook that took a corner of our kitchen. She had Facebook up and was on a page with a boy's picture in the corner. I tried to scoot closer to see who the face belonged to, but she clicked over to her own profile page.

"Marie's in bed. Tyler's watching TV, and Chad hasn't come home yet." She rattled off her report with a hint of boredom. Her foot tapped against the chair leg impatiently, and I knew she wanted me to scoot out of the kitchen so she could get back to the page of whatever boy she'd been staring at before I showed up. She reported on every nonpresent member of the family.

Except one.

I opened my mouth to ask the question that hovered at the edge of my tongue but closed it again. Amanda grew more bitter about her dad on a daily basis. My attitude surely rubbed off on her. How could she not notice my emotions when she caught me slamming plates against the wall?

I nodded instead and kissed her on top of the head. "Thanks for watching them for me."

Before I'd made it out into the hallway to check on everyone else, Amanda said, "I don't know where he went. But he slammed enough doors on his way out that we can only hope he stays gone awhile."

Any hope I had of reconciling this evening and smoothing things over deflated with her words. Amanda knew me so well—to know and to be able to answer the unasked question. It felt wrong that she had to be so aware of the dance her father and I waltzed around her. She shouldn't have such concerns dropped on her. No kid should.

I nodded and made my way toward the rec room where the TV blared. "You should be in bed," I said to Tyler as he looked up.

"Hi, Mom. How was your meeting?"

"Good. And you still should be in bed. Don't go changing subjects on me."

He smiled wide, showing off his missing canine teeth. He'd had them pulled because they wouldn't fall out of his mouth on their own. We were prepping him for braces and hoping his teeth would move into their proper place so his speech patterns would improve. He slushed his *S* sounds way too much. "Doesn't hurt to try."

"It'll hurt if you end up grounded."

His gaze conveyed anything but fear. "I got an A on my volcano. And a ribbon." He pulled a ribbon from his pocket, crumpled from having been stuffed there since . . . I closed my eyes. He was wearing the same jeans he'd worn to school yesterday in order for that ribbon to still be in his pocket.

I determined to focus on the glad part. He had a ribbon. Now was not the time to lecture on hygiene. But the wrinkled little ribbon looked so forlorn sitting in his hand that I couldn't help but say, "Hey! If I got a ribbon for a volcano, I'd take better care of it than to just shove it in my pocket with all my pocket lint. Aren't you proud of your accomplishment?" But even as I said the words, Nick's comment seared through me. *I'm surprised you call it Tyler's project. I'll bet you did all the work on it while Tyler played with his friends.*

Why would Tyler care about the ribbon? He hadn't earned it. It was exactly like Nick had said. Tyler took no responsibility for his work. Why would he care about the ribbon or even the grade for that matter? I hated admitting Nick was right—even if the only person who knew of my admittance was me.

"Ty . . ." What could I say? I wanted to explain that he needed to care about that ribbon—that it should mean something, but no words came.

"You need to do more of your own work," I said instead.

He looked confused.

I tried again. "Are you proud of your accomplishment?"

His shoulders jiggled in what might have been a shrug. "Yeah. It was cool having my name called out."

I ground my teeth together. "But wouldn't you have felt even better—prouder—if you had done more of the work yourself?"

"I probably wouldn't have gotten the ribbon if I'd done it all myself."

And there it was—the real reason of my shame. It wasn't just that he didn't do his own work, but he felt incapable of doing his own work. Nick's words continued to tumble through my mind. *Really, Liv, the kids need to take responsibility for their own work. You can't follow them around once they're in college, doing their homework and mopping up their dorms.*

I took a deep breath. *Dang you, Nick, for being right!*

"What's your next big project?" I asked, trying to keep myself from screaming at Tyler. It wasn't Tyler's fault I'd ended up doing his homework—not exactly. It was just late when he'd started working on it the night before it was due. If I'd asked him about it sooner, we would have had more time to plan and get things ready, and he wouldn't have been whining because he was so tired. If I got him working now on the next project, we could avoid this whole mess. And then Nick would see—Nick would see *what*?

Was I giving Tyler grief over homework to prove to Nick that I was responsible? Argh! What did it matter *why* I was doing it? Tyler needed to do his own work.

He hadn't answered the question though.

"Ty? When is your next project due? What is it?"

"It's a leaf collection. I have to have twenty varieties of leaves or something like that. I don't know when it's due."

"Well, we're going to get started on it tomorrow. No sense putting these things off until the last minute, right?"

"Sure, Mom."

I wasn't sure he had really listened or had even heard me over the headaching noise of the television. I made a move toward the remote, but Tyler's whine stopped me from picking it up and flipping the TV off.

"The show's almost over! Just a few more minutes . . . please?"

"Fine. But as soon as it's over, the TV's off, and you go brush your teeth and get to bed."

He nodded but had stopped listening after the first word that confirmed I wasn't shutting his show off.

"You shouldn't let them walk on you."

I started at the voice in the hallway and put my hand over my heart. Nick. Shame hit me when I realized he'd witnessed the exchange between Tyler and me.

Had he heard everything? Had he heard me trying to put responsibility back on Tyler for his homework? And if he had heard, did he feel smug over the fact that he was right, once again, and I was dumb, once again?

Not knowing what he'd heard, I ignored his comment about the kids walking all over me. *He* walked all over me and didn't have a problem with that. Why would he care who else walked on me? Arguing the comment wouldn't do me any good, and besides, I really wasn't in the mood. It had been a nice evening, going out and doing something new with people who weren't judging me every second for how well or not well I did things.

I squeezed past him in the hallway, since he stood in the middle and didn't move aside to let me by.

He followed me to the kitchen. "Nice of you to come home," he said.

I halted. I had my back to him. Was this a sincere comment? Was he glad to see me? Or was this sarcasm? I didn't move, paralyzed by the millions of words I could have hurled back at him. I finally settled on, "It's nice for you to come home too." Not the most clever or stinging remark I could have made, but I didn't have anything else. I *was* glad he was home.

I moved into the kitchen, finally forcing my feet forward, and rounded the island, keeping it between us. "So where did you go tonight?" I asked, waiting for and fearing the answer.

"The office."

I nodded. Of course. The office.

Was it an affair? If it was, what would the woman's name be? Something like Candi or Destini—something that ended in *i*. Yes. A name that gave the home-wrecking female the means to use a little heart to dot the *i*. Cutesy, cheap, absurd.

I forced myself to look him in the eye. Small smile wrinkles outlined those perfect sand-brown eyes, even when he wasn't smiling. He wasn't smiling now. But he didn't glance away like I'd expected.

No.

Those were not the eyes of an adulterer. There was no other woman. No simpering doll with too much lipstick and not enough clothing to cover her.

There was simply *the office.*

Instead, Nick would get silent and unresponsive and critical and moody and *office visiting* and—*Stop it!*

Think of glad things. Nick had good points. He was still a handsome man; even at seven years older than me, he was a good catch. He provided for the family. Things were tight because he wanted to live extravagantly, but we did always live within our means—even if it was *just* within our means. And once upon a time, he'd actually loved me.

Yes, those were glad things.

And I'd been able to come up with them all in the space of an eyeblink.

He finally looked away, an act that gave me a sense of triumph. I hadn't looked away first. It was a small thing, but small things were all I felt I had anymore.

"Where's Chad?" he asked, moving around the island I'd purposely kept between us. He tapped me aside so he could get into the drawer and get the can opener.

"He's running lines for the play audition with his friends." I didn't remind him that these were things I'd told him before the book club. It didn't matter.

"Oh, that's right." He opened a can of kidney beans, drained the liquid, and ate the beans right from the can. He'd picked up the habit while in college. Kidney beans were a cheap source of protein. "If you can't buy steak, buy little red beans and pretend," he used to say.

He didn't bother breaking the habit because he'd come to actually enjoy it. Nick's personal comfort food.

Why would he need comfort food now?

He leaned against the island next to me, his arm brushing against mine as he scooped spoonfuls of beans into his mouth.

The touch was like water filling a long-dry well. Not that I thought he meant anything by it, but it gave me joy regardless. It tamped down the ever-present scream and replaced it with the want of his arms around me.

He relaxed into the counter, his feet crossed, his arm continually brushing against mine as he ate. I couldn't help it. I leaned into him, wanting to feel him close to me, wanting to snuggle and be enclosed in the safety that was *him.*

But because he held the can in one hand and the spoon in the other, I only ended up impeding his ability to eat, so I backed up just a little.

There was a time he'd put down whatever he held because he preferred holding me, but I didn't dwell on that.

Pollyanna didn't dwell on anything. She couldn't.

Or she'd disappear.

Mandy tromped into the kitchen and stopped on seeing us standing so near each other. She raised a single eyebrow—something I'd never been able to do but that Nick did all the time. A confused half smile crossed her face, and she backed into the hallway.

"Did you need something, Manda-bear?" I asked.

"No, not really. Just coming to see what's in the fridge."

"Carrot sticks," Nick said, a smile on his face because he knew she hated carrots.

The smile and little joke were rare enough that we both blinked at him. Mandy recovered faster than I did. Her immediate forgiveness of slammed doors given for the sake of a little personal teasing from him—a little proof that he still knew her well enough to tease.

"Carrot sticks, huh? Sounds awesome. Since I'm snacking on carrots, you should get a snack too." She went to the cupboard and pulled down pretzels. She shook the bag at him. "Wouldn't want you to feel left out."

His smile widened. "Do you know where those pretzels would be best?"

He put his can back on the counter and shot his hands out to grab at Mandy and the bag before she could respond. He tackled her, nearly knocking her over while she squealed and laughed.

"No! Not in the hair!" She giggled, half snorting as she tried to catch her breath.

While keeping her locked under his arm, he reached in the bag and pulled out a handful of pretzels and smashed them between his fingers before drizzling pretzel crumbs into her hair.

"No! Daddy, no!"

My breath caught. She hadn't called him Daddy in forever. She hadn't even called him Dad in the last several months. She'd reduced him to a pronoun. *He, Him, His.*

In less than a heartbeat, the night had gone from irreconcilable to her calling him Daddy. It was a reminder that things could change.

Being alone is better than being lonely . . . Maybe I was too quick to come to the conclusion that those were my only choices. Watching Mandy with her dad gave me hope that there might be a third option.

I continued watching and smiling, and the squeezing pain inside my chest as my heart had felt heavier and heavier through the last several months of marriage eased up a little. I took a deep, cleansing breath. The whole episode before I left to the book club meeting had to have been my fault. I'd been reading more into his reactions than he'd meant. I was indulging in self-pity. It had to be me because the man tickling his daughter in the kitchen was not the same man who'd yelled about a simple oven timer earlier that evening.

But even as I thought those words, I had to blink back the memory of the uneaten dinner and the plates against the wall and the lack of an apology and the walking away when I brought up Kohl.

That *hadn't* been my fault. That had been 100 percent Nick.

Don't dwell in dark places, Livvy.

My mom had told me that several weeks before she'd died. I'd been complaining about the kids and Nick and the overwhelming feelings of failure I'd had on all counts as a wife and mother.

"I just wish I were more like you," I'd told her.

She'd laughed. "Right. Because I was such a pearl of an example. I was the mother who let you guys have cold cereal for dinner some nights simply because I wanted to finish reading whatever new book I'd bought. I wasn't perfect, but I'm glad you're only remembering the good things.

It's better that way. You should do that with the way you're thinking about your own motherhood and wifehood. You do lots of good things, Livvy. Think about those things. Don't dwell in dark places."

Ty must have heard the noise and come to the kitchen to investigate. When he found Mandy in a vulnerable state, he joined the fray, helping his dad hold Mandy down until she begged for mercy and insisted she'd wet her pants if they didn't let her up. They were all laughing while I battled not to dwell in dark places—not mine and not Nick's.

Not tonight.

Not when everything seemed to be exactly as it should.

Chapter 5

Nick stayed downstairs for a while when I mentioned I was going up to bed. He said he had a couple things to work on and told me not to wait up. His voice had been soft and pleasant—enough that I didn't feel he was running away from me by getting those few things accomplished before he came to bed. He just had things to do. I could understand that.

I detoured to the garage on my way to bed so I could retrieve my copy of *The Poisonwood Bible*. Might as well get started immediately on the reading while I had a little time to myself.

As before, the weight of the book felt good in my hands—a solid substance to anchor me back into the harbor of *me* again. I rushed through my nighttime rituals of changing clothes, brushing teeth, washing face, lotioning hands and feet before turning down the covers and climbing inside.

I opened the book with all the excitement of a small child at her own birthday party.

I started at the beginning, though I'd read the first bit before, savoring the beauty of the words and the lyrical way the author wove them together. On page eight, I came across the paragraph that had haunted me since reading it, where the mother in the story had declared herself washed up on the riptide of her husband's confidence and the undertow of her children's needs.

I read the words again and again, tasting them from all sides and feeling the kinship to this fictional woman who seemed to understand how I'd been feeling lately. The book went on to say:

I married a man who could never love me, probably. It would have trespassed on his devotion to all mankind. I remained his wife because it was one thing I was able to do each day. My daughters would say: You see, Mother, you had no life of your own. They have no idea. One has only a life of one's own.

I wondered how Mandy would take that. Would she think me the sort of mother who had no life of her own? And were she to think that . . . would she be right?

I frowned, worried about Mandy. Worried because she watched me, taking cues from my attitude and my happiness or lack of happiness. She'd been angry with her father, but when she saw us standing close, her attitude had changed. Would she follow in my footsteps, assuming that was just how things were done? Would she become the sort of mother and wife I had become? Would she become so lost to herself that she would one day wake up and not know herself anymore?

You're reading too much into this, Livvy. It's a book. Only a book. It isn't a blueprint of your life's failings.

I took several deep, calming breaths. It was only fiction. But I didn't want it souring my attitude toward Nick when he was in such a good mood. Best to put it away and read it during the day when no one was home. I had just decided and was about to close the book and set it on the nightstand by my lotion bottle when Nick's voice said, "So you're serious about this book club thing . . . as busy as you are."

My fingers froze as I was shutting the book. I glanced up to meet his gaze. His mouth had a slight turn to it . . . a sneer, I decided after a moment.

A response wouldn't form in my mind.

"So your new club is going to come between us at bedtime too?"

I opened my mouth to try to salvage the good feelings from before, to tell him I had just finished up for the night, when he continued. "I can't believe you're actually going to keep on with that. You should just call them and tell them you don't have time for one more thing to do in your life. There's no reason to meet with a bunch of strangers to hash over whether or not a book is any good. They won't miss you if you stop coming."

My mouth still hung open. Did he just call me too unimportant to miss? Did he dismiss the one thing that I was doing for myself as if it were no big deal?

I kept the book open and focused hard on the pages, not responding to his remarks and turning the pages every few moments so it looked like I was actually reading them. He didn't add any further cutting remarks but instead drifted off to the bathroom to get ready for bed. I made it to the end of the chapter before actually closing a bookmark between the pages. He wasn't out of the bathroom yet.

I turned to my side so my back faced him when, and if, he ever actually showed up. If he saw my face, he'd know he'd upset me. It was better to move on and forget about it. My mom had once told me not to dwell in dark places.

But I'm not trying to dwell in dark places, Mom, I thought. *Dark places are just where I happen to live.*

I'd actually come close to drifting into sleep when Nick's cold toe touched my foot. The touch was hesitant and brief. It was gone before I could really process that he'd touched me at all. How many nights would he torture me like this? Had our relationship really been reduced to random glances of his toes against my ankles at the foot of the bed?

I squeezed my eyes shut more tightly, determined to not care and just get some sleep. The last words I really remembered reading returned to me: *One has only a life of one's own.*

Was that the truth?

It didn't feel like the truth.

Or maybe it was the truth, but the life that actually belonged to me was so insignificantly small as to not be noticed—not even by me . . . Or maybe I needed to get some sleep and stop overthinking everything. Something glad . . .

The day is over, and I won't ever have to do this day again.

That was a glad thought I could sleep on.

* * *

Nick got up before I did, which was a surprise all of its own. Not that it was a welcome or pleasant surprise but more of a what-in-the-heck-is-going-on surprise. Confused and even a teensy bit alarmed by this, I wandered the house in search for him. He was in the kitchen watching a Lakers game on his phone.

"Hey, Liv," he said without looking up from his phone. His eyes bounced slightly as the game progressed on his tiny screen. He wore khaki pants and a golf shirt. He even had shoes on.

"Hey." I peered over his shoulder. "We winning?"

"Doesn't look like it, but there's still time on the clock. They might be able to pull it off. I didn't watch the news last night so I don't know the final score."

I watched over his shoulder a second longer before having to move away and rub the strain out of my eyes. "We have the projector for that sort of thing, you know," I said. "You're going to ruin your eyesight trying to track a ball the size of a needle point."

He didn't comment. He groaned at something happening on his screen, grunted, and shook his head. Without lifting his eyes from the screen, he said, "I was thinking of taking the kids to Knott's Berry Farm for Halloween . . . They've got that Knott Scary Farm thing going on."

I felt sudden sympathy for yo-yos. From one moment to the next, he seemed a different person, one minute silent and sulking, one minute cutting and sarcastic, another sweet and friendly. *Who are you, Nicholas Robbins?* I wondered.

"The kids would probably really like that," I agreed. I wasn't sure Marie would really like it, but the others would definitely be on board for a day at an amusement park—especially if it meant they'd have guys in hockey masks and chainsaws chasing them. Marie could hang out with me while the others did the really scary stuff. They'd have to miss church, which bothered me, but I didn't want one more thing to fight over, so I didn't mention it.

Nick nodded, still looking at his screen. "Yeah . . . I think that'll make for a good day out." Then he tore his eyes from his screen and glanced around as if realizing he was still at home. "Oh, hey . . . I better get going."

"Going?"

He paused and seemed to be searching for a response to this question he hadn't anticipated. "I've got some work to do."

"On Sunday?"

"Lots to do . . ." was all I got in form of apology.

I maneuvered myself to be on the way out the door so he could kiss me good-bye, but he turned his attention back to his screen as he grabbed his laptop bag and left the kitchen.

I stood there, blinking for several moments. It stung that he hadn't kissed me, even though I stood right in his way—stung that he'd left on Sunday for the enigmatic *stuff to do*. "Don't take it personally," I said out loud to the empty kitchen.

Because taking it personally would be stupid. He was trying to change things, trying to spend more time with us. He'd tried last night, and what had I done? Gone to a book club. And now this morning he suggested doing a family outing to Knott's Berry Farm for Halloween. For him to carve out time from the office was huge, and how stupid would I be if I just ignored that he wanted to be with us?

It didn't occur to me until the next day, while driving to Chad's school to deliver an old peacoat Chad had forgotten to take with him but still wanted to use as part of his costume for play tryouts, that Nick hadn't said he wanted *me* to go to Knott's Berry Farm. He'd said *he* wanted to take the *kids*.

Nowhere in that plan had he mentioned me.

Of course, I assumed he'd meant me. He *had* to have meant me too. I'd have liked to see him try to steer four kids around an amusement park without me there to help. He'd be chewed up and spit out like old gum.

No. He had to have meant for me to go too.

But what if he hadn't?

I spent the rest of the day fretting over who he would take instead of me. Because the Nick I knew would rather show up at work driving a 1981 Ford Pinto than to have to spend a day dealing with four kids asking for stuff, running every direction but the one they were supposed to go, and being grumpy from overexertion at an amusement park.

And then I'd chastise myself for being so dramatic and imagining all this craziness. Time to read the book club book never manifested itself as I worked through keeping the house in order, running errands, and then dealing with the kids when they arrived home from school. I was afraid to open the cover again—afraid it exposed Nick to be as monstrous as the man found within its pages, afraid it exposed me for the fool who covered for that monster.

"He isn't a monster, Livvy," I muttered while I scrubbed down the sink after the dinner dishes had been put away. And he wasn't. He didn't get into drunken rages that left bruises on me or the kids. He didn't neglect his duty as a provider for the family. We had food, shelter, clothing . . . I glanced at the clock.

He hadn't made it home for dinner, and an hour after it was done and kids were settling into the night, he still wasn't home.

He provided us with everything with all those hours he kept at the office—with everything *except* him.

When the garage door grumbled open, I scrubbed the counters harder, trying to look intent on my work instead of intent on the fact that I'd been clock watching.

"Do you want dinner?" I asked when he showed up in the kitchen. "I saved some in the warmer for you."

He glanced at the warmer as if trying to discern exactly what kind of dinner awaited him and if it was worth his trouble to eat it. "No," he finally said. "I grabbed a bite on the way home."

I pressed my lips together and nodded, noting the way his shoulders sagged, the way he seemed to shuffle instead of walk. Nicholas Robbins wasn't a sagging, shuffling sort of man. What had happened during his day to produce *this*?

I didn't ask.

He didn't offer.

Instead, he trudged to his office, looking tired and beaten.

I watched him go, wondering if I should offer a shoulder massage or if he would just think me in the way.

I stayed in the kitchen—feeling guilty and angry and sagging.

Then I turned out the kitchen light and shuffled to the bedroom. I finally reopened the book. The only companionship I'd find tonight would have to be in paper and ink. There would be no human company.

* * *

I gently mentioned the subject of Kohl's upcoming farewell party again, but Nick bristled, went silent, and distanced himself even further over the next two and a half weeks, though I'd never have believed it possible that the man who felt as far away as China could make himself seem less reachable. I should have realized there was still the moon and Saturn behind that and whole other galaxies behind that. He only spoke to me to make some random judgment on the housekeeping or the kids—picking at me until I felt raw and red.

The children kept me from throwing myself off the end of the pier. And oddly enough—reading helped too. The situation of the mother, Orleanna, and her own four children was nothing like mine. And yet I understood her. Understood why she stayed with her husband even though he was a tyrant, understood why it took losing a child to make her leave.

She was a mother.

She had her head down and worked tirelessly just to keep her children alive and growing. She wasn't able to leave until she'd lost one of those children. She wasn't able to leave until then because that was the first time she looked up to really see beyond her children—to see the man who'd become something less than human while she hadn't been paying attention.

"So what do you actually hope to gain from this little club of yours?" Nick had asked me one night while I sat curled up with a lap blanket on the couch and my book in hand.

I peered over the pages at him, wondering if he wanted to know because he was taking an interest in my life or if he wanted to know because he wanted to shoot some holes in my hopes. "I'm hoping to expand my mind through good books while making good friends who like good books." I turned my eyes back to the page, my breath a little shorter than it had been the moment before he'd interrupted.

"Friends . . . you haven't had friends since college."

I opened my mouth to argue but closed it again. On a technical level . . . he was right. By the time I'd married Nick, I'd stepped away from the friends I'd had. When I needed someone to talk to or a shoulder to cry on, I'd depended on Nick and my mom.

But my mom was gone.

I peeked up at him; he still regarded me levelly.

Somewhere along the way, Nick had gone too.

That was why I needed friends. I had no one left.

"If it's really been that long, then it's about time I make some new friends," I said simply—keeping my tone light—not wanting a fight.

"Women in their forties don't usually find true friends."

I held in my grunt of irritation as I finally lowered the book to meet his gaze fully. "Is this some statistic you read in a magazine somewhere?" I finished the sentence in my head. *Or is this something you just made up to needle me while I read because I'm doing something that isn't about you and you hate it?*

He shrugged. "Just an observation."

"Well, I am making new friends. They're good friends too."

"Okay." He wandered away, leaving me feeling insecure and stupid. I'd exaggerated a lot. I had met these women exactly once. They likely wouldn't recognize me at the supermarket.

The whole next day, I could barely function. His words followed me through my entire morning routine, trailing after me like a poltergeist, reminding me that my only close relationships came in the form of my husband and my children.

"Mom!"

I jumped at the front door slamming shut, and Chad bounded into the room with all the energy a nearly seventeen-year-old boy could muster. Which was quite a lot—especially when that boy had already crossed the six-foot mark.

He wrapped me in a bear hug, lifting me off my feet. "I got the part! I got the part! You are looking at the new Professor Higgins in *My Fair Lady*!"

I tried at a cockney accent after he'd set me on my feet again. "Well, I'll wash my face and hands before I hug you, I will."

He lifted his eyebrows and screwed up his face in the way that made him seem like the little boy instead of the man his height gave him the right to be. "I don't get it."

I smiled and patted his cheek. "A quote from the movie, but never mind. I've never been good at stuff like that. This isn't about me. Tell me about the part. I am so proud of you! What will you need? Do you need help running through your lines?"

The red flush he'd inherited from me crawled over his ears. "No. I already have someone . . . Well, the girl who's playing Eliza Doolittle is coming over in a little while."

"I see. And this Miss Doolittle . . . she's pretty?"

The flush deepened. "Don't *say* anything or *do* anything!" he insisted. "If you tell her I like her or anything, I swear I'll—"

"Go live on the moon," I finished for him. It was a little joke between us. When he'd been six and I'd made him do his homework, he told me he didn't want to live with me anymore, that he was going to live on the moon so he didn't have to talk to anybody ever again because people were dumb and homework was dumber. On the moon, no one had to do homework because there weren't any teachers to give homework and no mean moms to make homework get done.

Chad grinned. "Exactly. The moon. Seriously, Mom—nothing embarrassing. Promise me. I really like this girl."

"Well then, I promise not to pull out the baby books with pictures of your bare naked baby butt on the beach."

Chad gave me the look—the one filled with disapproval and warning—the one that made Chad seem a duplicate of his father. "Mom . . ."

"What?" I smiled. "I already said I *wouldn't* do that. Honestly . . . the paranoia of some people." I walked to the fridge and pulled out a mini Babybel cheese wheel and tossed it to him. It was one of the kids' favorite snacks, something my mother had started when the kids were all small.

He sat at the barstool at the island and unwrapped his miniature cheese wheel. He removed the wax around the cheese and popped the whole thing into his mouth at once.

Feeding him was like feeding an elephant. I doubted he even tasted the cheese as he basically swallowed it whole.

Mandy showed up, saw the cheese wheel wax and wrapper on the counter, and foraged in the fridge until she found the net bag with the rest of the cheese wheels. She took out three and sat next to Chad at the island. She set two of them in front of her while she unwrapped the third. While she was busy with that, Chad swiped the other two.

"Hey!" She reached to take her stolen goods back, but Chad's long arms kept them above her head.

"Mo-om!"

"Chad, if you want me to behave with your little girlfriend, then you have to behave with your sister."

"But she got three! I only got one!"

His protest came at the same time Mandy said, "Girlfriend?"

"She's not my girlfriend; we're just in the play together, and we're practicing some lines. That's it. It isn't anything else," Chad insisted, but his flaming eartips confessed his lie.

"Sure it isn't. What's her name?" Mandy asked.

Chad handed her cheese wheels back to her. "It's none of your business. And you have to act human. Mom promised."

Mandy took her cheese wheels and scooted off the barstool away from Chad. "Mom promised, but I didn't."

"Mandy . . ." Chad's growl carried the warning Mandy pretended not to hear. He looked ready to pounce.

The front door slammed. Mandy smiled. "The kids are home!" And she bounded out of the kitchen as if she actually cared that Tyler and Marie were home from school. Chad bolted after her. "I mean it, Mandy!" he yelled.

"I'm so glad to have them all home," I said to the empty kitchen.

The squeals and calls for motherly intervention came after a short delay. I'd expected those noises sooner and was impressed with their restraint in waiting an actual thirty seconds before beating on each other.

From the various voices, it was readily apparent that Marie and Tyler had taken sides and involved themselves in the argument. By the time I made it to the entryway, Chad had Mandy in a headlock. Marie was hanging off Chad's arm, trying to force him to let go, and Tyler was yanking on Marie's legs to make her let go of Chad.

I took a mental picture. These were the things they'd laugh about around the Christmas tree when they were adults and their own kids were fighting over things that made no difference.

"Guys! Knock it off. Chad, let go of your sister. You two!" I pointed at Tyler and Marie. "This isn't any of your business."

"She started it!" Chad insisted.

"It takes two to fight." *Or four*, I thought, rubbing my hand over my face in agitation. These might be the moments they'd laugh over, but they were moments that gave me gray hairs. Not that anyone would notice those gray hairs under the stupid blonde dye job.

The kids completely ignored my protests and demands as they wrestled. "Chad stole Mandy's cheese!" Marie shouted as if that small act were enough to justify any retaliation. Chad's white-knuckled grip on something inside his fist verified that Marie's report was accurate. Pieces of the third cheese wheel were smeared on the tiled entry way.

I rolled my eyes. Great. Something new to clean.

The noise from the four writhing bodies made me cover my ears with my hands and groan inwardly. How did things go from a light tease to the apocalypse in so short a time?

Nothing I did made a difference, so I started to walk away, figuring they'd run out of steam eventually.

That was when the doorbell rang.

"Crap!" Chad said as he immediately released his sister with a small shove. "She's here!" He looked at me wildly, his eyes begging for the interference he wouldn't accept just two seconds before.

I smirked. *Now* he needs me. "C'mon guys. We've got more cheese wheels in the kitchen." Distracted by company, the younger two gave up defending their older siblings and Marie ran to the door before anyone could stop her. She swung it open wide to reveal everyone in their varying stages of unready.

Chad ran his fingers through his dark hair to straighten out the places where Mandy had managed to ruffle it.

"Hey there, Selena." His voice had lowered into that sultry tone of a guy trying too hard to impress a female.

The girl on my doorstep was absolutely gorgeous. Her long, dark hair and her naturally tanned skin testified of her Hispanic ancestry.

Did she just bat those dark eyelashes? She ducked her head, and her cheeks flushed slightly. "Hey, Chad."

So she liked him too.

That meant it didn't matter that three of my children were hanging around the doorway like gawking orphans. The only one she would actually remember seeing was the one who made her cheeks darken.

"Hey," Chad said again, as if his vocabulary consisted of only that one word.

So cute.

Time for me to take over. "Would you like to come in, Selena?" I asked.

She flashed a radiant smile, though she directed it at him, which made him give a nervous laugh. "Yes. Thank you."

She entered our home. Marie shut the door with barely less than an enthusiastic slam, and we all continued to stare at each other inside the house. When I realized the conversation was unlikely to move forward with an audience, I herded the sibling group out of the entryway and into the rec room while saying, "It was nice to meet you. If you guys need anything, let me know."

Gratitude filled me that Mandy hadn't been obnoxious to her brother in front of his guest.

She was coming up on dating herself and likely recognized that revenge would be painful.

Revenge usually was.

I hadn't finished cleaning the kitchen, where Chad had taken Selena, and was a bit at a loss as to what to do when I remembered Tyler's leaf project.

I grabbed the remote before any of the kids could. "No TV. We're going for a walk."

"A walk?" Mandy's tone indicated that she thought the idea of walking with her mom and siblings would humiliate her to her toenails.

"Tyler has a leaf project. We need to collect leaves. It's a nice day—so let's go for a walk and get it done.

Tyler groaned louder than Mandy. "I thought you'd forgotten about that," he grumbled.

"You're not that lucky. And we've already got shoes on."

Tyler and Mandy trudged back to the front entryway. Marie took my hand and smiled up at me. "We never go for walks anymore," she said happily, as if I'd suggested we go to Hawaii.

We'd stopped going on walks when Nick had stopped going with us.

"You're right, baby girl. We don't. But we should. We're all we've got, and we should spend more time together." I thought about the friends I didn't have and about Jessica and Kohl and determined to make my words true. We would spend more time together. I couldn't let more of Nick's children dangle off the ledge of his waning devotion. I didn't have a say in what he did to Jessica and Kohl, but these? These were my children.

And we would go on walks.

Once we were outside and Mandy had boosted Tyler up to reach the exact leaf he insisted he had to have from our neighbor's tree, I made an announcement. "We're going to the beach next Saturday . . . and having a picnic."

"We don't ever do picnics anymore," Tyler declared as Mandy oofed because he'd ground his tennis shoe into her arm, but he looked excited by the idea of starting the picnics up again.

We'd stopped picnics at the same time we'd stopped taking walks.

I smiled at them. "Well, we do now."

Chapter 6

It didn't take all that long to collect the leaves. I refused to pick any of them and refused to let Mandy or Marie pick them. I'd be there to offer advice, but this was one project Tyler would do all on his own.

He actually seemed excited to classify all the leaves and arrange them in the notebook his teacher had provided. When we arrived back at the house, they all made their way to the rec room, talking excitedly about the upcoming picnic and still laughing about the crazy neighbor down the street who'd shaken a garden-gloved fist at Tyler when he'd asked if he could pick a leaf off the sycamore tree in front of the house.

My heart swelled listening to them laugh together—and hearing them communicate like they were best friends. I smiled and wandered to the kitchen to check on Chad and his new girlfriend.

"Hey, kiddos. Just checking to see if you guys need anything."

Their heads, which had been bent close to each other, swung back in a crazed sort of hurry. I hid my smile and tried to look like I hadn't intentionally busted up the romantic feelings in my kitchen.

"Nope. We're okay, Mom." Chad glanced meaningfully at me and then the door as if he thought he could will me away with just a glance.

Fat chance, my boy.

Selena scowled at him, and he blinked and said, "Oh, that's right. We . . . could use some costuming help, I guess."

"Ah, see! Now we're talking. I knew I could help." I grabbed his arm and pulled him up from the barstool. "Come help me get the costume buckets down."

We went out to the garage, where Chad and Nick had built a storage area in the dead space near the ceiling. I pulled the ladder down and pointed up. "All the yellow ones have the costumes in them."

Chad climbed the ladder and groaned. "That's a lot of yellow I'm seeing, Mom."

"Yeah, I know. Bring them all down. I've been meaning to go through those for a while now to donate the extra stuff. And get the orange buckets down too. It's almost Halloween. We can have Tyler and Marie decorate." I hadn't thought about the season much at all with the varying degrees of worry I'd had over Nick and all the trouble that came with him. It would be good to not ignore the holiday entirely. It seemed strange that none of the kids had mentioned it to me before now. There had been no requests for costumes, no asking for certain kinds of candy to be in our personal candy bowl so they could eat the leftovers themselves.

Weird.

I actually liked Halloween, liked little kids dressing up, liked handing out candy and the words *trick-or-treat*—not that many kids trick-or-treated anymore with all the safety concerns and parties they went to, but the idea of Halloween was fun for me. I didn't get into the gore and haunted houses, but I liked the cute little ghosts and the happy-faced pumpkins. When the kids had been much younger, we'd used our annual Disneyland passes just to go see the Haunted Mansion decorated like Jack Skellington's house every October. It had been tradition . . . until it wasn't.

I sighed and directed my attention to Chad bringing down various tubs of orange and yellow.

"That is so cool that you have all these," Selena said once Chad came down from the ladder with the last yellow tub and I'd unveiled the costumes in their individual boxes underneath the plastic lid.

I'd kept each costume in its own separate box to keep the accessories, like gloves or eye patches, from turning up missing and rendering the costume uselessly incomplete.

In our younger years, Nick and I had dressed up with the kids and gone out to trick-or-treat with them. Nothing too weird because Nick didn't want to be absurd. But that meant there were adult-sized costumes from Victorian and Renaissance times, things that were Gothic, things that were silly—Chad totally cast aside the clown costume I'd worn but didn't seem to mind the circus ring leader costume.

I smiled fondly at the costumes as Chad pulled out each one. "They really are great, aren't they?"

Selena nodded and held up a miniature Captain Hook. "Where did you buy them?"

Chad laughed. "Buy? My mom would never buy any second-rate, plastic-masked piece of garbage—not for her kids. Oh no. She designed and handmade each and every one. Nothing but the best for the Robbins children."

Selena grinned at him. "And you say you're not spoiled." It was a cute, flirty sort of remark, and they had a little argument about who was spoiled and who was not. But I stopped paying attention to them.

My cheeks flushed with the compliment from my oldest son. There wasn't even a trace of sarcasm in his voice, but instead he spoke with *pride*, of all things. I hadn't ever heard him talk about the costumes like that.

I'd made all the costumes back when I'd used sewing as a way to relax when the kids were down for naps. Sewing was fun and gave me a sense of accomplishment. It kept me connected to their lives. It never occurred to me that the kids might have received as much as I had from the experience.

I looked away—sure my eyes had the shine of tears in them. I blinked them dry and turned back to the flirting teenagers. "Have you guys picked out what you want?"

Chad held up a small pile of stuff that Selena took from his hands. She stood. "I'll go put these things in the kitchen. Then I'll come back and help Chad put everything away. Thanks for letting us use all this. It's great!"

"No sense in putting it away yet," I said. "Chad, help me bring these things inside."

Chad lugged the buckets into the rec room, where Tyler and Marie had a good time taking what was left of the organization inside those buckets and turning it into a tangled array of colors.

They immediately picked out what they wanted to wear for Halloween and then set to work on the orange buckets with the house decorations, dragging cobweb fluff over the light shades and dangling spiders from various handles and fixtures. Before long there were skeletons, witch hats, and cauldrons filling up every spare inch of space in not only the rec room but throughout the entire house. They had a great time.

Amanda even helped the little kids a bit.

But mostly she helped me arrange the costumes into piles—ones that my children still might have use for, ones to offer to Jessica and the grandkids, and ones I planned on saving for other grandchildren who might come along. I set aside several little boy costumes—thinking about baby Kohl and how cute he'd look in them when he was big enough.

Then there were the ones I would have to donate to Goodwill or whatever.

Just as I was arranging and then setting everything up to either be delivered to Jessica or shoved back in the dead space in the garage until I could get to Goodwill, Paige's name came into my mind.

Paige . . . from book group.

It occurred to me that she might like some of those costumes for her own little boys for Halloween.

But that was ridiculous. I barely knew her. We'd not even really talked for more than a few minutes. She'd think I was insane if I showed up at her house with a bunch of homemade costumes.

"Hey, Manda-bear? Help me get these back in the garage."

"Do I have to take them up the ladder too?" she asked, looking doubtfully at the ladder, as if she could already see herself falling off the rungs and landing on the cement floor of the garage.

"No. We'll get Chad to help with that."

She snorted. "Good plan! He might even help without arguing because he has a gi-irl to impress!"

I cut her a look that told her to give her brother a break, but she only smiled wider. "I'll go get him!" And she dashed out of the room before I could protest.

I sighed. Kids. Best friends, mortal enemies.

Chad came much more quickly than he ordinarily would have, which meant Amanda had been right about him trying to impress the girl with his sense of family duty. I hid a laugh in a cough and showed him the tubs that needed to be put back.

When he got to the one I'd set aside for Goodwill, I stopped him. "Wait . . . Not that one just yet."

Paige's face, so alone and sad in spite of her trying to put on a smile, came to my mind again. What if she could use these? But seriously? Halloween was barely more than a week away. What were the chances of her not already having it taken care of?

But what if she *didn't*?

You're being silly, Livvy. She'll think you're a lunatic.

Chad hovered over the tub. "How about now?" he smiled and lifted his eyebrows.

I grunted. "No, not now either. Let's leave that one down. I'm not sure what I'm going to do with it yet."

Chad shrugged, straightened, and stretched. Did he really just flex his muscles in that stretch? I rolled my eyes. Oh brother. He really was in a crush situation.

Everyone left me alone in the garage to contemplate the tub on my own.

What if Paige had little girls too? I tried to remember what she'd said the night of the book club. I didn't remember her saying anything about any little girls. Just little boys.

What would I say if I called? *Hi, I'm the crazy lady with the cookies at book club, and I thought you'd like some old costumes from my attic, even though you probably already have your own.*

I groaned at my own stupidity, turned, and went to the garage door. I'd need Chad to come back and put the tub away.

But I stopped with my hand on the doorknob.

I bit the inside of my lip, the feeling of needing to offer this small token of friendship intensifying until there was no way to ignore it.

"That's what it is," I said out loud. It wasn't offering old homemade costumes. It was offering friendship—friendship to a woman who was pretty much alone in a new town.

I could relate to that in spite of having lived in the same place for as long as I had.

Loneliness had all kinds of levels.

That decided it. She might think I was a wacko, but then again—she might think I was a friend.

I put off calling her for a long time—making dinner for the kids and making sure it was a nice dinner, since Chad invited Selena to stay, and then cleaning up after the dinner and tidying up the decorations so they didn't look so completely random.

By then, the idea of calling Paige had started to sound ridiculous enough to not bother at all.

But the nagging niggle in my stomach persisted every time I decided against it.

"Fine!" I said to the empty kitchen. "I'll call."

After a few moments of digging through my purse, I located the slip of paper with the numbers of the other book club members Ruby had given me and ran my finger down the short list until I came to Paige's name.

I almost hung up as it rang, feeling dumb for a number of reasons I couldn't exactly explain, but before I could pull the phone away from my ear, a female voice answered, sounding like she'd run to grab the phone. "Hello?"

"Hey, Paige? It's Livvy . . . Livvy Robbins? From book club?" I figured I'd better get specific so she'd remember me and not assume I was a telemarketer trying to sell her a time-share.

"Oh, of course. Livvy. Hi. What's up?" Though she tried to make it sound like she knew exactly who I was, I could hear the wheels of confusion turning in her head, which was understandable. We'd met one time for fewer than two hours. It wasn't like I'd said anything brilliant or amazing enough to be outstanding. And even if she remembered me, she had to be baffled by my interruption of her life. For all she knew, I *was* selling a timeshare. Better get to the point fast before she called Ruby and told her I was a menace to the book club.

"So I was cleaning out stuff today and came across a plastic tub full of old costumes I made for Chad and Tyler forever ago. They've both outgrown everything, and the costumes have just been gathering dust. I hate to throw them out since they're still perfectly good, and well . . . I know not everyone likes hand-me-downs, so feel free to just say no, but I just wondered if I could swing by sometime and let you look at them in case there's something in there one of your boys would like."

There was a short pause on the line before Paige answered, "That would be great," though she didn't sound exactly excited.

She just didn't know what I was offering and likely hadn't ever seen a good homemade costume before. No one sewed anything anymore. It was a dying art. Because of this, most homemade things ended up *looking* homemade. Paige was letting me come over. She'd see I wasn't offering costumes made out of toilet paper tubes and duct tape. And the fact that she agreed to let me come meant she really hadn't bought costumes yet.

Chances were good she could use them.

"I don't suppose you could come over tonight, could you?" she asked. "We could wait until the next book group, but Halloween will be over by then."

I glanced at the bucket and then the clock. It would be best to have it gone and everything put away before Nick came home from his dinner meeting with clients. "Tonight's great. I have to run to the grocery store tonight anyway. I could be there in about a half hour."

She seemed to be warming to the idea and gave me directions to her apartment. I wrote them down on the notepad I kept in the kitchen drawer by the fridge.

Once we'd hung up, I lugged the bucket to the car and stuffed it into the backseat. I almost felt out of breath from the exertion and felt stupid about being so out of shape that carrying one object the thirty steps to my car could make me wish I had a glass of water and a hand towel to mop up my forehead. Hitting forty had not been kind to me, which made the idea of taking the kids on walks and to the beach where I'd be forced into exercise seem better and better every minute.

I found Paige's apartment relatively quickly. It wasn't elegant or even really very nice, which led me to think that maybe things weren't great for her financially. But the outside of the place was tidy and sturdy looking. I took a few moments at her doorstep to put down the bucket and catch my breath. No sense arriving looking like I'd jogged the whole way there.

After my breathing had slowed to something that could be considered normal, I rang the bell and waited.

Paige answered. The door opened in a flood of light from the television, which was making the sorts of noises I recognized from when my own kids were small.

I smiled wide. "Hi there! I am so glad to have these things be useful to someone else. I really love all of them, and it seems so wrong to let them sit in an attic collecting dust when someone could actually use them."

Paige smiled back and invited me inside.

I was grateful to get in and put the bucket down. Who could have known how heavy clothing for little bodies was? I had to carefully sidestep some potato chips to keep from smashing them into the carpet even more and all but dropped the bucket in relief.

I glanced around the small room. A rumpled blanket stretched over the floor in front of the TV. The two boys sat on the blanket with empty juice boxes, potato chip crumbs, and various brightly colored candies littering its surface.

"It looks like a picnic!" I said enthusiastically.

What sat before me was a single mom allowing her children the wonder of childhood. My heart swelled with regret for all the times I'd made the kids hurry to clean up their forts before their dad came home. I wondered what he'd have done if he'd come home and found a fort there and a blanket with chips and juice boxes? He'd gone silent by that time.

My paranoia and attempt to second guess everything followed his silence.

Would he have yelled? Would he have pressed his lips together in that thin line of disapproval?

He isn't a monster, Livvy. He isn't a preacher forcing his family into the jungles.

For all I knew, he would have undone his tie, taken off his shoes, and joined us under the blanket ceiling.

I'd never let the kids keep them up long enough to find out. So was it my fault they'd never had forts in the evenings? Or his?

I gave myself a mental shake to try to focus on the scene in front of me that had nothing to do with my own family.

Having little ones was a lot of work. Doing all that work by yourself had to be a nightmare. The house was disorganized—not in a way that made Paige look like a slob or anything but in a way that showed she had her hands full.

I could have offered to help. I wanted to race to the broom closet and get the vacuum and whatever dish towels and cleaners she had and get to work. The rooms would sparkle in fifteen minutes if she gave me the chance. But such an offer could be embarrassing, or worse, rude. I wanted to be a friend. Friends didn't look at messes. Besides, when the kids went to bed, Paige seemed the sort of mom who stayed up a little longer to clean.

The two small boys barely noticed my presence and didn't respond when I mentioned the picnic, but Paige smiled.

I pointed at her children. "Now aren't they the cutest things in the world?"

"I think so." She shrugged, but her smile revealed that she didn't just think so. She knew it to her very bones. "But then, as their mother, I'm a bit biased."

"It's a good mom to be biased—at least a little bit," I said as she swept up the remote control and pushed a button. Everything on the screen froze in place, much to the dissatisfaction of the boys who'd been watching.

"Mom, why did you pause it?" the older one asked.

Paige pointed at me, and I felt guilty for being the reason they weren't watching their program. "My friend here has something for us to look at."

Which was my cue to hurry and deliver something awesome enough to be worth putting their show on pause. I grabbed an end of the tub but couldn't make it skim over the blanket to where the boys were. Paige ended up helping me, which made me feel old and out of shape again.

I *was* old and out of shape but genuinely hated feeling like it.

I followed Paige's example and sat next to her on the couch in front of the yellow tub so I could open it up. The boys sat in front of us on the floor. The little one held a juice box in between his soft toddler hands.

Seeing him like that made me think of baby Kohl and Gracie. So much would be better if Nick had allowed me to embrace the children he shared with The Ex. Then Jessica would call me for babysitting. She'd bring the kids over at holidays. Then I wouldn't be stuck in the middle when Jessica tried to plan a party for her brother. I took a deep breath and started pulling at the lid to the plastic tub. Now was not the time to worry about what Nick didn't do or didn't allow me to do.

"I used to make Halloween costumes for my boys," I said. "All kinds of fun stuff. But they grew out of them, and I thought maybe you might like to have some of them."

At the word *Halloween*, the older boy blinked and straightened, suddenly interested in whatever might be in the big yellow tub.

I finally popped the top off, which bent my thumbnail backward and hurt like crazy, but I didn't curse out loud. I remembered that Paige was Mormon, and I remembered having a coworker who was Mormon who didn't like cursing of any kind.

I set the lid aside. The top costume was one that didn't have its own box; it hadn't needed one since the accessories of the green gloves were attached by long curly vines. Chad had been a toddler and loved everything pumpkin during that Halloween season. It had been my first attempt at making costumes—the pattern was simple, and the stitching lacked embellishments, aside from the vines and gloves, but it had turned out okay. Nick had smiled and teased Chad about making him into a pie because he looked so good. Nick had taken Chad's green gloved hand and led him outside into the world of trick-or-treating.

We'd laughed and swung Chad between us. It had been a good night.

"Hmm . . ." I glanced at the blank stares on the little boys' faces. "I think this might be a bit small for you boys. You're both so tall." I shook my head, clearing it of thoughts about Chad and Nick and realizing these boys in front of me weren't interested in being pumpkins for Halloween. "Nah. I think you'll like some of these other ones better anyway."

I sifted through some of the other options, moving aside boxes labeled *Mummy* and *Monkey*, and finally pulled out one I'd been especially proud of. "This is a knight costume that Tyler wore two years ago."

The taller boy straightened even more—stretching his spine as far as he could make it go, as if he expected to be knighted that very moment by a queen's hand. "A knight?"

I wanted to hug him for being excited. "Yep. It's got a helmet, arm and leg shields, and everything. You may have to use your own toy sword though—if your mom says that's okay."

"I can't bring a toy sword to school though," the boy said. He finally couldn't take it anymore and scrambled to his feet so he could peer over the edge of the bucket. His eyes widened, taking in each piece of the costume. I pulled the helmet out. "And here's the best part. No knight is complete without a proper helmet." I helped him put it on so he didn't catch his ears. Then I strapped on the breastplate and the arm and leg shields. He immediately drew an imaginary sword to fight off an imaginary dragon and save an imaginary princess.

Which made my heart ache in that way that sent little pains through my nerve endings.

I'd always wanted to be a princess saved by a magical knight. But now I wished I'd learned how to save myself *from* the knight—just a little bit. Why didn't anyone tell princesses that knights were sometimes more dangerous than dragons?

"I think he likes the knight," Paige said. And something in her eyes looked a bit like gratitude. Coming here had been the right thing to do, no matter how absurd it felt during the phone call and drive over. My mom would have called it a Heaven Reminder. It was her way of saying she felt like God directed her to people who needed help.

"Great!" I said, fishing around in the tub for something equally as fun for the knight's little brother. Didn't want anyone feeling left out or less cool. "Okay, next one."

The dragon-fighting knight spun so fast, if he really had been holding a sword, someone would have lost an arm. "More?" All the incredulity and excitement a little boy of six or seven could muster into one word found its way into the word *more.* "Do you have a Spider-Man costume?"

Was that a sigh I heard coming from Paige? "Let's just see what she has," Paige said. "Livvy is being so nice to share some of her things with us. Isn't the knight costume neat?"

"Oh yeah!" The knight practically glowed with happiness, and his little brother had his head so far over the tub I feared he'd fall in.

I leaned closer to the little guy, wanting him to know he hadn't been forgotten. "I bet I have something in here that you'd like too."

A moment later, he looked as if I'd offered him an actual pirate ship loaded with chests of treasure instead of just the simple pirate costume.

I laughed as he clapped and giggled. I'd improved with pirate costumes as time went on. The Captain Hook one being my very best ever, but it made me happy to see the little boy practically bouncing out of his skin as I helped him pull the tattered leggings over his pajama bottoms. I strapped on the belt and the eye patch and giggled a bit myself as he stuffed his feet into the boot shoe covers and planted the hat on his head. He growled a pirate sort of noise at his brother, and before they could think about what else might be in the tub, they turned their juice box straws into swords and were calling each other names like *scallywags* and *knaves*. They obviously had access to a good education to know the proper insults of pirates and knights. From that I could guess Paige probably read to them.

She really was a wonderful mother.

"Wow, Livvy, thank you so much. They're a hit—and so much better than anything I could have provided for them this year."

I pretended to not notice the shine in her eyes and even blinked away a few tears of my own. It *had* been right to come here. I was glad I hadn't brushed aside the opportunity to help someone . . . No. Not help. To *befriend* someone. I thought of *The Poisonwood Bible*, of Orleanna and the passive way she'd lived her life. She could have made friends in the Congo. Things might have been different if she had just stepped outside herself for a moment or two.

I wanted to hug Paige—hug her and hope that perhaps in this small act of moving outside myself and my comfort zone, things could still be different for me.

A few costumes and one valuable friendship was a step in the right direction. I smiled at Paige and her shining eyes. "Oh, I'm not done yet," I said. "If they want to be a knight and a pirate, that's fine. But I have more costumes in here they can try on. And they can have them all to use as dress-ups through the year if you like." From experience, I knew that even little boys liked to dress up as something else. Even little boys dreamed of being something more.

Did Nicholas Robbins dream of being anything more?

Maybe.

Maybe not. He was king of his household. Lord over his wife and children. Was that enough? Who knew?

I pulled out more costumes to distract myself. The shiny astronaut suit made me smile, recalling how Chad, and then later Tyler, had counted down to blast off over and over and over in their cardboard box spaceships.

"Are you sure? You could probably sell these on eBay or something." Paige offered me one last out, but her heart wasn't in it. Her eyes trailed over the costumes with longing and hope . . . and relief—which I hadn't expected at all.

"Sure I could sell them, but then I'd have to figure out how to list them, and then box them all up, and then take things to the post office. I hate the post office. I'd really do anything to avoid waiting in those lines. Besides, I've got my hands full with the kids and husband. I don't need anything more to put on my to-do list."

But even as I chanted my mantra of motherly and wifely dedication, the compliment of Paige thinking the costumes were worthy of someone buying warmed me from the inside out. Which made showing her the rest of the tub's contents a delight. Paige's eyes nearly bugged out of her head when I showed her the magician outfit. The boys acted as though I were the magician; they oohed and aahed with every new costume. They changed in and out of everything until they were a hodgepodge of everything, with the older boy, Shawn, wearing an eye patch, a wizard's hat, and a Robin Hood cloak over the knight costume—which he'd refused to take off for even a minute—and the smaller boy, Nate, wearing the wizard's cloak over the astronaut costume and topping it all off with a camouflaged army man helmet. The boys looked pretty bulky by the time I'd reached the bottom of the tub.

I almost hated reaching the bottom because it meant it was time to leave. But once the tub had been emptied, there was nothing left to do but stand up and leave. I had stayed longer than intended—longer than promised. I hoped Paige didn't mind.

"Thank you—so much. This is so generous of you," Paige said as she walked me to the door. Her voice caught, which made me wonder how she was doing on her own. I wanted to ask. I wanted to know what else could be done that would help her and keep her from crying. She'd looked like she was on the verge of tears nearly the whole time I'd been there.

I fiddled with my purse and didn't ask anything. The last thing I wanted was her feeling awkward because I'd pried into a life not wanting examination. "I wanted them to be used and enjoyed, not gathering dust or going in the trash or who knows where with who knows who."

Paige nodded. "You made a couple of boys very happy."

Making people happy. That's what it was all about. Being glad, being useful, being pleasant. It's all I'd ever wanted. "It's my pleasure—and I mean that." I opened the door and stepped out into the hallway, the dim yellow bulbs offering the kind of illumination that made a person feel slightly ill.

I couldn't feel ill—not at that moment. I'd offered friendship, and it hadn't been rejected. It was good to know Nick had been wrong. Friends could be found at this late stage in my life. "If there's anything else I can ever do, just holler, okay? That's what friends are for."

Paige blinked, looking surprised by the word *friend.* Had I overstepped myself? Had Nick been right after all? "O—okay," Paige said, and a smile spread over her features, one that said she *would* be my friend—surprised by it, maybe, but committed to it just the same.

It was like being an old, dusty, cobweb-filled cup—taken, washed, and refilled with clean water. I made my way to the elevator, stopped walking, and turned back to her. "I mean it."

"Okay." The grin on her youthful face promised she trusted me enough that if she were in trouble, she'd call me.

The elevator door closed, and I took a deep breath—filling my lungs completely.

I had a friend.

Mom would have been so proud of me.

And Nick?

He could eat sand for all I cared. What did he really know about me or what I was capable of?

Nothing.

Nothing at all.

Chapter 7

Nick had informed the kids they were all going to Knott's Scary Farm for Halloween. Chad had already made plans but was so desperate to do something fun with his dad he cancelled the plans immediately. All of the kids were thrilled at the surprise.

But Nick still failed to mention whether or not he wanted me to go. He never said he *didn't* want me, but whenever he spoke of it to the kids, he never mentioned me as being part of the day's activities.

It was a strange sort of abandonment—the not knowing.

He didn't mention the house decorations beyond a remark that he couldn't wait for the holiday to be over so we could get "that mess" cleaned up. By *we,* he meant *me.*

I stuck my tongue out at his retreating back because that's what classy, mature women did when their husbands irritated them.

I finally couldn't take it anymore. It was the day before Halloween. And happily, all kids had holiday events and parties to go to that night so I could discuss the coming day's plans without eavesdroppers.

Nick was in his home office, the door of which remained firmly closed. I crept to the end of the hallway, wondering exactly how I was supposed to approach this.

With a quick prayer heavenward, I turned the knob and rapped my knuckles lightly over the oak. "Hey, babe." *That's it, Livvy. Keep it light.*

He sketched a brief glance over his laptop at me but went immediately back to his work. "What's up?"

"Just wondering if you wanted me to pack us a lunch for tomorrow or if we were planning on eating in the park." I'd practiced this a hundred times in the kitchen, but now as I let the words out, they sounded as contrived as they actually were.

His fingers froze over his keyboard, and this time when he looked up at me it wasn't a brief glance but a scowl. His eyes went over every inch of my face. I smiled, felt stupid for smiling, and dropped my lips into a more neutral position.

I'd seen what I'd come to see. He *hadn't* planned on me for the day. It was strange that my instincts and ability to read him were strong enough to allow me this insight weeks before this moment when the look in his eyes confirmed it. It was strange that I would ever suspect not being invited on a family outing with my own family.

And what would he do now that he'd been confronted?

I held my breath . . . waiting.

He let out a bark of a laugh. "I was planning on giving you the day off," he said finally.

The little bit of hope that perhaps I'd been wrong crumbled to ash inside me.

"The day off?" It felt as though I were falling to the ceiling because the room had turned upside down. I leaned into the door frame to keep my feet under me.

"Yeah, you're always busy with the kids and stuff. I thought I'd give you a break—take them off your hands for a day so you could do whatever you wanted to do—like read your book." His eyes dropped back to his keyboard, and his fingers punched keys rhythmically, though I doubted he focused on the words he typed. He would likely have to delete everything he entered while I stood there watching him.

"I see," I said finally. But I saw nothing. Black spots caved in through my vision. Confusion fogged my thoughts. "Do you want me to pack a lunch for the rest of you, then?"

I swallowed the pain of those words, *the rest of you.* Without me.

One only has a life of one's own, Orleanna Price had said. But my life felt suddenly vacant being only my own.

"Nah. Don't trouble yourself. We'll catch something at the park. It'll be easier."

I nodded, not trusting my voice. *Easier. Easier for who?*

My feet retreated, my hand pulling the door closed again—like nothing had happened—like I hadn't just been excluded and uninvited in my own family.

Was this how Jessica felt? Was this why Kohl hadn't spoken to his father in more than three years?

I'm sorry, I thought. *I'm sorry, Jessica. I'm sorry, Kohl. I should have stopped him from leaving you behind so completely.*

Who would have known he'd leave me behind too?

* * *

I didn't bother setting my alarm for the next day. What was the point? But my eyes, out of habit, opened at about the same time everyone should have been getting ready to leave for Knott's Berry Farm.

I didn't get out of bed. Instead, I listened to Nick herding the children out the door. His temper shortened with Marie, who kept holding back and asking why Mommy wasn't coming. He tried to play it off to them the way he had played it off to me. They were all giving Mommy a break for the day. They were doing this as a special present to Mommy because she deserved a day to herself.

The other kids accepted this easily enough. Marie didn't like it though. She knew the park would be filled with Halloween-themed scares, and she really didn't like the guys with the chainsaws.

I didn't either.

I hoped the park didn't have them, or that if they did, she wouldn't have to deal with them. I hoped Nick would be smart enough to shelter Marie a little; otherwise I'd be up at two in the morning for the next three months dealing with her nightmares.

When car doors in the garage clicked and the garage door ground shut and the car rolled down the driveway, I allowed the anger to seep into every part of me.

A day off, huh?

I'd never asked for a day off.

Never wanted one.

I was the physical embodiment of the wife of *The Poisonwood Bible*—that passive woman who allowed her husband to drag her children into African jungles to find his immortality. Maybe Nick hadn't taken our kids to a different continent, but he'd led our family to a place I didn't want to be.

Yet, I had followed him here—to this place of silence and placation. And that made me guilty by association.

The clock made a tick noise as the hour clicked over into the next.

No more.

I would be passive Orleanna Price no more!

I picked up the clock, ripping the cord from the wall, and pitched it into the door. Take *that,* Nicholas Robbins!

I gasped when the door opened a fraction of a second later and Nick carefully poked his head inside. "What's going on in here?" he asked, truly baffled.

"What are you doing home?" I shot back at him instead of answering.

"I forgot my wallet. We'll need cash for lunches and dinner later on." He opened the door wider, now that he knew I wasn't under attack or anything, and crossed the floor to his nightstand. His eyes trailed over the shattered splinters of alarm clock on the carpet, over to the back of the door where the paint and wood had been damaged.

I expected him to ask after my well being—to show some modicum of concern that I had hurled his clock into a door. But he didn't.

This is my fault too. I followed him here to this place of unsaid words.

But no more.

He'd reached the door again and was turning the corner to leave when I said, "Nick?"

He turned back and leaned over so he could see into the room.

"When you come home, we need to talk. There are things that need to be said . . . about *us.*" My voice didn't crack on the word *us.* But my heart did.

"Sure." He shrugged. "Fine."

I got out of bed as soon as the front door slammed closed.

Once I'd dressed and made myself somewhat presentable, I picked up the phone. I needed to talk to Jessica.

* * *

Jessica met me for lunch—I wanted to go somewhere nice like Bayside Restaurant, but Jessica assured me we'd be better off at a fast food joint with a playland. We compromised and ended up at Ruby's on Balboa Pier so Grace could look out over the ocean and try to spot fish for us. That kept her entertained for far longer than I would have expected.

"I've been thinking about Kohl's party," I said, once Jessica and I had met at the restaurant and exchanged the typical how-are-you-doing commentary. "And it's going to be great!"

We discussed options for the location of Kohl's party and finally settled on the clubhouse in Jessica's apartment complex. If we decorated nicely, it could be really quite attractive. Anywhere else would either be too expensive or too contentious. Jessica was the only person who was neutral territory in the friction between the families.

By the time we'd ordered dessert and Grace had more hot fudge on her face than in the ice cream dish, we had settled on all the details of Kohl's party. I pushed away Jessica's credit card and used mine instead.

"I can't let you do that," Jessica said.

"Of course you can. I'm the grandma. It's the perk of being the grandma."

Jessica's eyes misted slightly. "How does Dad feel about all this?"

I hadn't mentioned anything about Nick or the amusement park or the fact that I felt I was waking up from a fog of blindly following a man who probably didn't love me anymore.

"Oh, you know your dad . . ." I said with a casual wave, but Jessica caught my hand.

"No, Livvy. I really *don't* know him. That's why I came to you. What did he say when you told him about the party?"

I met her eyes, those beautiful warm eyes that I loved so much in her father. "He didn't really say anything," I admitted finally.

"You didn't tell him, did you?"

I scowled and gave her a playful swat. "What do you take me for? Of course I told him."

"And he didn't say anything?" She let out an exasperated sigh. "Which means he thinks the whole thing is stupid and he won't come."

And she said she didn't know him . . . But I had the good sense not to vocalize my thoughts. "He'll come."

"You can't promise that."

"Okay, I can't promise it, but I can do everything in my power to get him there and to get him there *pleasant.*"

"The only event he'll show up to acting pleasant will be his own funeral, and even then he'll probably figure out a way to paste a scowl over his dead features." She groaned and buried her face in her hands. "This is all a mistake isn't it, Livvy? It's useless for me to even try."

I pulled her hands away from her face and made a gentle shushing noise. "It is definitely not useless. You are so brave, Jessica, braver than I've ever been."

Her eyebrows raised in disbelief. "Brave? Hardly."

"You want to unify a family that's come apart at the seams. And . . ." I swallowed hard before continuing. "And some of that coming apart is my fault."

She slapped her hand down on the table. "Your fault? How is any of this your fault? You weren't the first wife sleeping with her husband's best friend. And you weren't the demon dad ignoring his kids. This isn't your fault. This is *their* fault. You just got stuck in the middle of it with the rest of us."

Her anger hung in the air, as tangible and sharp as broken glass. Her tone had upset baby Kohl, and even Grace had stopped scouting the churning water for fish so she could, instead, seek out what had hurt her mom's feelings.

"But I didn't stand up for you and Kohl. I didn't insist on spending time with the two of you. I should have done more, Jessica. I was . . ." So many things could be tacked on to the end of that sentence. *I was stupid . . . scared . . . blind . . . selfish.* "Well, I just want you to know I'm sorry. I'd do anything to go back and change it."

"I used to think you didn't like us," she said softly. "Everything started out okay enough, but then he started liking his new family better—at least that's how it seemed. I thought Kohl and I had done something wrong—that we'd made you mad or something . . . I thought that was why he didn't like us. I watched him play with his new kids, and . . . it felt like . . . he didn't just divorce Mom. He divorced us too. I don't know what I was thinking. But I'm sorry I blamed you. I know now that it wasn't your fault. I understand his feelings toward Mom, but the rest of us? We're like a whole family of *not enough* to please Nick Robbins."

I tried to smile, tried to keep the words *not enough* from sinking into my bones and settling there. Since the smile failed, I leaned over and hugged my stepdaughter—hugged her so tight she likely had a hard time breathing, and even that didn't feel like it was tight enough.

Jessica had to get on with her day, which meant lunch ended far sooner than I would have liked.

She walked me back to my car, but I didn't get in—not even after she waved and drove away with Grace and Kohl tucked into their car seats.

I couldn't return to the tomb of my house. I turned away from my car and walked to where the cement met the sand. I removed my shoes and left them there—not really caring if anyone took them. They were old, frayed, needing replacing. My feet dug into the surface warmth of the sand, reaching the cooler sand underneath.

I walked to the left, away from the pier, following the dark sand—tamped down from fresh waves. When the first wave crept high enough to flow over my feet, I didn't pull away. The shock of cold water felt as good as the sand itself. My pants were soaked because I'd forgotten to roll them up, but who cared?

Nick didn't care. He was off on rides with my children—off without me.

Find something to be glad about, Livvy.

I thought about Jessica and Kohl and felt glad that even though Nick had been easing himself out of my life, he seemed to be stepping forward in the lives of my own children.

That was a good thing. I prayed Tyler or Chad never became estranged from their father so that he refused to communicate with them. I prayed Marie or Amanda never felt as if they had to tiptoe around him.

More waves washed up over my feet, slammed into my ankles. The water displaced the sand underneath me, unsettling my balance, tugging me back to its deeper places. The scream that had lived inside my throat bubbled up, but I still didn't release it. Instead, I swallowed it back down and lifted my face to the ocean spray.

I stood my ground in spite of the pulling tide and the sand shifting and caving under me and stared out to where the sea touched the sky.

I'd been living inside my own head for far too long—asking questions that I answered—having full conversations when no one else was present. I needed someone else.

Mom. I miss you so much.

She would've known what to do. She could've told me what to say and how to say it because I meant what I'd said to Nick before he left me alone in his house.

I meant to talk to him tonight.

And if that didn't work, there were always the options of shaving my head bald and filling his shoes with oatmeal.

Chapter 8

I WALKED THE LENGTH OF the beach and then settled, letting the sun dry my pants to something stiff and white with salt residue. I sat for a long time—long enough to watch the sun melt into its watery bed.

My shoes were gone when I traced my way back to my car.

I shrugged and opened my car door.

The brake and acceleration pedals felt cold against my bare toes, forcing me to suppress a shiver when I moved from one pedal to the other. Nick's car was already in the garage when the door rose.

I entered the house through the mudroom and the kitchen. "Hey!" I said, upon finding Mandy and Chad sitting at the island with a pizza box between them. "Did you guys have fun?"

"So awesome!" Mandy said through the mouthful of pizza she must've bitten off right before I walked in. "Dad nearly threw up, but he went on everything!"

"Really? How did you get that to happen?" Nick's stomach had always made it so halfway through a day at an amusement park he was sitting on benches waiting for us to get off rides.

"Marie." Chad interrupted his sister's explanation, even though he also had a mouthful of food. "She was scared. So Dad made her a deal that if she'd go on everything, he would too—no matter what."

In spite of everything, that made me smile. He'd taken care of Marie and helped her stretch herself a little by doing things that scared her. For the briefest moment, it seemed like a good idea to have left me behind. I would've let her wait for the others instead of going on a ride that scared her.

But the moment was only brief because my smiling, happy teenagers were happy because of a family activity without me. Was I so unmissable? Was I really such an unnecessary component in the family?

"Where are Marie and Tyler?" I asked.

Mandy looked at me as if really seeing me for the first time. "What happened to your pants?"

My jeans were still damp in places and caked white in other places from the salt water. They were stiff and uncomfortable and dripping sand with my every movement. "I walked on the beach. Where are Marie and Tyler?"

"Marie's asleep already," Mandy said. "She didn't even want dinner. We wore her out running from ride to ride. Tyler's in the shower. He spilled his entire slushie on himself on the way into the house. He's hopeless."

It was then that I noticed the blue spots trailing from the mudroom, through the kitchen, and out into the hallway. The spots likely ran up the stairs and all the way to the bathroom. Blue slushie-stained carpets forever.

I bit back my sigh.

"Where's your father?" I asked, hating the coming confrontation.

Chad socked Mandy's shoulder in response to something she'd done that I'd missed in my inability to focus. "In his office," Chad said, dodging Mandy's tiny fist and laughing so hard he almost choked on his pizza. "He said Selena could come for dinner tomorrow. Just thought I'd let you know."

I uh-hmmm-ed absently, not really listening. I'd already mentally moved on to the conversation with Nick and was steeling myself for the occasion. Putting off this talk would accomplish nothing. Jessica would be calling tomorrow to find out if he'd agreed to come to Kohl's farewell party.

He was at his desk, his stockinged toes peeking out from underneath, where he had his legs crossed and stretched in front of him.

"Hey, Liv! How was your day?" he asked as soon as I cleared my throat to warn him of my presence.

I blinked. His tone . . . casual, happy, almost with a singsong quality, as if he'd been humming a tune and greeting me had become an extension to that tune.

"Hello."

The man in front of me was one I barely remembered. His shoulders weren't drawn up around his neck as if he held in some hidden tension. The crease in his forehead wasn't all bunched up and tight over his eyebrows and bridge of his nose. His eyes weren't squinting into that perpetual look of irritation.

I knew this man. *This* was the man who'd kissed my hand good night at the end of nearly a month's worth of dating because he'd wanted to take things slowly. This was the man who'd stuttered and stammered while he fumbled and dropped the ring box when he asked me to marry him. This was the man who'd admitted to liking chick flicks and who'd massaged my feet when we'd watched them together.

"Where've you been?" I breathed.

A half smile quirked up on his lips. "Knott's Berry Farm." His eyes trailed down to my pants, which were shedding sand and salt the same way Tyler's slushie had dripped blue spots. "I take it you went to the beach . . . and were nearly dragged in by an angry seal?"

A joke. Nicholas Robbins had just made a joke. On a different day and with a different tone, that would have been an insult, a cut to me for being too careless to roll up my pants like normal people walking next to the surf. But this was something else. Interest in *why* I'd been dodging waves fully clothed shone in his eyes. When had he last looked at me with interest?

"It was actually a seagull," I clarified. "We were fighting over a chicken nugget."

"Seagulls are such cannibals—eating other birds like that!" he declared, warming to our made-up version of events. "But wow, he must've been a huge seagull to have dragged you so far in."

"Actually he didn't drag me. He got the chicken nugget from me, so I decided to settle for the next best thing and catch him and bake him up on the beach. I had to dive in to catch him before he took off too far."

"Did he taste good?"

"As good as a trash bird on a beach can taste—a little greasy. He apparently ate a lot of chicken nuggets." I couldn't help myself. My smile muscles took over. This absurd little conversation of meaningless nothing, that felt like *everything*, was certainly not the conversation I'd been expecting.

I rounded his desk and wrapped my arms around his neck—kissing the back of his ear. "I'm glad you're home." I meant so much more than just being home for the day. The man I held in my arms hadn't been home in a long, long time.

"I'm glad *you're* home," he returned. He swiveled his chair and pulled me down on his lap.

I could've curled up there and wept with gratitude. *Where have you been, Nick? I've missed you so much!*

His arms wrapped me up close to him. "We haven't done anything together for a while."

I bit my tongue to keep from snorting at *that* understatement.

"Let's go on a cruise."

I pulled back in shock. "What?"

"Yeah, a cruise. They leave out of port every day. Let's say we get on one of them and have a kind of second honeymoon."

I laughed, which sounded like a bark because of the emotion swelling beneath it. The scream in my throat dissolved. Maybe I'd read too much into him leaving me home today. Maybe he really had intended to give me a day off. Maybe, just maybe, the man I married still actually loved me.

"I love the idea of going anywhere with you." No words falling from my lips had ever been more sincere. I would go anywhere . . . do anything . . . for *this* man.

"Great! It's all settled then. I already bought the tickets."

I was certain my eyes had the shine in them. "Truly?"

"And honestly."

I stood up, now too excited to stay sitting—even if it was sitting on a lap that hadn't welcomed me in years. "What'll we do with the kids? When are we going?"

"We'll leave January third. And we're not coming back until January seventeenth. It'll be a full two weeks, with nothing but you and me and the fishes."

My heart sank into my toes.

"You . . . already bought the tickets?"

"Yep. Happy—"

"That's a bad time for us to be leaving." I cut him off before he could say the words I'd been waiting to hear since the night of the failed dinner. He was going to finally tell me happy anniversary.

At seeing his face fall into confusion and not wanting to lose this important moment where things were good, I hurried on to explain. "We could change the date. Cruises are so flexible with things like that." I didn't know if they were or weren't, but I would say anything to slow the creases in his forehead from crawling up over his nose. "But we already have plans on January fourteenth—plans we just can't miss."

"What plans?" His head gave a little shake of confusion.

"Kohl's party." The words came out like a plea for understanding. "Kohl's being deployed clear to Africa soon. I've told you about it. Jessica and I went through our schedules today, and the fourteenth of January is the only day everyone would be able to come to his farewell party. It means so much to her, to me, to our family. I gave my word that we'd be there."

His face roiled with a tumult of emotions I couldn't read. I waited for what would settle there when he'd tasted each emotion and cast them aside for a different one, waited and wondered which one he'd keep and use against me. "Send him a card," he said finally. "Write him a check. Tell him congratulations." He turned back to his laptop. "We're going on the cruise." He punctuated the words with finality. He made the choices in the Robbins household. He didn't require anything from me but silent obedience. This was his jungle of unsaid words. He'd led me here. But being led to a place didn't mean I had to stay. I was done being silent.

I slapped the lid to his laptop closed, nearly catching his fingers in it. He had to move fast to get them out of the way. "I will *not* send him a card!" I shoved his rolling chair away so he couldn't reopen his laptop and go back to ignoring me. "Do you have any idea how many cards I've signed your name to over the last eighteen years of our lives?"

His lip quirked up at the same time his eyebrow lifted with my outburst. "Eighteen?"

"Don't you dare try to be cute about this. This is not cute. I have sent thirty-nine birthday cards, thirty-nine Christmas cards along with presents you wouldn't even help me pick out. I've sent thirty-nine valentines and thirty-ni—"

"Wait a minute. Why the magic number thirty-nine? Your math is a little off, Liv. We've been married eighteen years. There were only two kids from the previous marriage. That's thirty-six."

I took a deep breath and released it. I said quietly, "You have two grandchildren. A one-year-old and a two-year-old. Remember?"

All of his humor died along with the smile. A part of me died to witness that show of playfulness disappear. I'd taken a great moment and ruined it. He'd wanted to go away with me . . . but now? What did he want? What was that crossing over his face? Was it pain? Did Nicholas Robbins feel pain? The idea seemed insane. Nicholas didn't feel anything.

"I remember," he said, just as quietly. His shoulders slumped a little, all light in his eyes blown out like the candles on the farewell cake he'd never see if he chose to ignore this invitation.

Desperation laced the pleading. It would crush both Jessica and Kohl if he failed to show up. "Please, Nick. You have to go."

His body jolted—his shoulders straightened. "I don't have to do anything."

"He's your *son!*" I couldn't believe this. How could he be so stubborn?

Nick bristled. "What do you care? He isn't *your* son. He's just another kid to you."

I jerked back as if he'd struck me and lowered my voice to a whisper. "And do you think that's how I wanted it? When we were dating, right from the beginning, you told me you had kids, and not only did I not mind, but I was excited to meet them, to be a part of their lives. And you, who are their father, who should be excited to be a part of their lives, you don't care at all. What's the matter with you?" Somewhere in all those words, I'd ended up shouting again. That baffled me. I wasn't a shouter. This was something new.

"The matter with me . . ." His voice remained quiet. Nick leveled his gaze at me. "Now there's a question. I'll bet you have an answer too. I'll bet you have a list somewhere of all the things that are wrong with me."

He retreated to somewhere within himself. His eyes had taken on that haunted look I'd caught a few times throughout our marriage. The faraway sadness that seemed to seep from his every pore. It only happened when I pushed too far about his kids. I'd always backed away when it showed up, never wanting to cause him pain.

But frustration from his continual emotional neglect of his two oldest children shoved me forward to territory I'd never dared enter before. "There *is* something the matter with you," I continued. "They're good kids, and you think you've done your duty by them simply because they had new clothes at the first of every school year and braces and an education. But you're a bad father, Nick Robbins. You haven't done your duty at all because a father's duty is to be there for his kids, to be *present*. You've been hiding behind your computer and your office and even us, your *other* family." I curled my fingers into air quotes around the word *other*. "You hide from them behind us and hide from us behind work. You're nothing but a *hider*, Nick!"

"You don't know what you're talking about, so just leave it alone, Olivia."

I took a step back, bumping into his desk. He hadn't called me by my formal name since the day he'd met me.

His face had reddened with rage. "*I'm* a hider? What are you, Olivia? What are you—running around attending school functions, Junior League, fixing, mending, cleaning, cooking, fixing some more, cleaning some more, cooking some more? You're so busy *doing*, I don't even know you anymore. You're like that stupid book you used to read to the kids when they were little—*The Giving Tree*. That's what you are, Olivia—a stump of a tree. You keep giving, and now there isn't anything left."

I gasped at his words and felt my head shake *no* as if to deny that he'd said them.

He stood from his chair, making him closer to me, but he didn't close the gap between us. "Those kids aren't your concern. Send a card, don't send a card, I don't care."

He moved around me and took quick purposeful strides to the door.

"Nick?" I called out before he could disappear beyond the door frame. He turned, almost grudgingly, his jaw set, his eyes flaring with a cruel light I'd never seen.

I lifted my chin. The place of silence where we'd lived all those years was gone. In its place was something else—something animal, something cruel like the fire in Nick's eyes.

"If I'm the Giving Tree, then that makes you the little boy—the one who took everything and gave nothing in return."

The fire in his eyes gave way to shock. His lip trembled, but he tightened it into a thin line and gave a quick nod, as if conceding the words might be true.

Then he was gone, and any opportunity for fixing things between us had gone with him. I had hurt him. I had finally said the words I'd only thought in my head before now. Only . . . where was the liberation that came with speaking out?

My body shook, my teeth chattered, and I pulled my arms in to hold myself together.

I sank into his chair, the wheels shoving back far enough that I almost fell out of it, and buried my face in my hands. I had hurt him. In the moment I'd *wanted* to hurt him, to twist those dagger words deep into his chest so every heartbeat would pump the pain through him. But that moment was gone. And now it seemed that I'd twisted the words into my own heart.

What have I done?

Chapter 9

Nick didn't sleep in our room that night. After three in the morning, after waiting for the inevitable touch of his feet on my ankles, for the inevitable energy and warmth that comes from another person, I realized he really had no intentions of coming to bed.

And then I wondered if he was even still in the house. Had he gone to the office to sleep in his leather chair with his feet propped up on the desk? Had he gone somewhere else?

The hurt in his eyes . . .

I finally threw aside the covers, slipped my arms into my bathrobe, and carefully moved out into the hallway, trying not to disrupt the children—or Nick, if he actually still existed inside the walls of the house.

"He's at Grandma's house," Mandy said—shattering the silence of my search when I entered the kitchen.

I let out a squawk and grabbed at my chest to make sure my heart hadn't leaped out entirely.

"Scared you," she said. But her voice lacked any amusement it might have had in startling the wits out of me.

"How do you know he's at your grandma's?" I asked, sinking onto the barstool next to hers.

"I heard you yelling at him. It's been a little hard to sleep. I was sitting here when he left. I asked him where he was going, and he told me." It was hard to read her expression when her hair shadowed her face from the moonlight coming from the windows.

I said nothing. Chad had to have heard as well . . . maybe even Tyler. I could be glad that Marie had already gone to bed. What happened after the fight still fuzzed in my head. I didn't remember going to my room, changing into my nightclothes, or getting into bed.

"I'm sorry," I said to Mandy. I'd affected my children. The day had been a good one for them—a day where their father was really available to them. And now he was gone—not available to anyone. And the fault of this new drama fell completely at my feet.

"Are you okay?" she asked.

"No." Why lie now? And why should I be okay? Nick wasn't. Amanda wasn't. Tyler and Chad likely weren't either. Marie would figure out something was wrong in the morning. I'd failed them.

But I wasn't alone. Nick had been there—accomplice to the crime of family failure.

Mandy's shoulders shuddered. I leaned over and pulled her close while she cried over the mess we called the Robbins family. I didn't cry, not then, not yet. This moment didn't belong to me but to Mandy as she processed, worried, suffered, feared.

I would have moments later when the house was empty. Those moments would be mine.

My daughter needed to be comforted. That couldn't happen if I fell apart on her. She'd been getting moodier and more distant with me. I needed to let her have right now.

What was it Nick had called me? The Giving Tree? He'd meant it as an insult, but as I considered my life, the soup taken to sick neighbors, the meals cooked and cleaned up, the time that belonged to everyone but me, the giving . . . him calling me the Giving Tree was likely the greatest compliment he'd ever given.

And in that unintended compliment, I learned something about myself. I learned that I liked myself that way.

* * *

Nick finally came home after being at his mother's house for three days. I was relieved to have him back, though I knew he likely only returned because he needed fresh clothing. The kids managed well enough during his absence because I'd used the excuse that Dad had a lot of work and needed to be able to focus night and day.

The excuse worked for Marie and Tyler. Not for Chad or Amanda.

Amanda stomped around, slamming cupboards and doors, casting the evil eye on anyone who dared look her direction.

It worried me that she took it the hardest. Chad was so wrapped up in the play and Selena that he barely noticed Nick's absence. But Mandy hadn't *ever* really connected with Nick. They fought about everything. This drastic reaction from her made little sense to me. It felt as though she held me accountable for his absence.

Mandy's anger tempered a bit when Nick returned home.

Nick talked and joked with the kids but not with me. Not at all. The unbearable silence from before was nothing compared to this new form of ghostly existence. For that is the role to which I'd been relegated. His conversations with the children happened like breezes through a screen on the window. They moved around me and through me, but I was not, and never could be, a part of them.

I shadowed from room to room when Nick was home—keeping out of the way but never worth his notice when I did happen to stretch out my hand to get a roll from the basket at the same time he did.

Never in my life had I felt such gratitude for anything as I did the book club. An escape existed—an evening where I could plant a firm step instead of tiptoe across the floor. I didn't make cookies for the second book club. I ached to make cookies but didn't want Nick asking what they were for. Better to leave it alone and simply go without anyone asking anything. Mandy agreed to watch the little kids. Chad was at play practice. And Nick wouldn't arrive home until I'd already left.

A deep breath escaped me upon slipping into the driver's seat of the car. Logic tormented me. Leaving home when home had so many issues that needed to be dealt with was likely beyond the stupidest thing I'd ever done. "What am I doing?" I asked the windshield, but this time I didn't bother answering myself. I didn't have an answer.

I turned the car off in front of Ruby's house and just sat for a moment staring at it. Maybe if things grew too unbearable at my house, Ruby would let me move in with her. I rolled my eyes at myself for thinking such absurdities and exited the car. As I walked up to the front step and rang the bell, headlights swept over the lawn. I turned and squinted into the light—catching a glimpse of someone whom I assumed to be Daisy.

Ruby opened the door and gushed a warm hello while enveloping me in a tight hug. I leaned into the embrace, feeling like I was with someone who genuinely cared about me. Ruby had seen me one time, and yet here she was—acting like she was my long-lost aunt. I almost broke into sobs and started spilling all that had taken place over the last month between Nick and me, like I would have if it had been my own mother who held me, but I refrained. No sense in making myself utterly ridiculous in front of the only people I had in my life to escape to. Ruby released me.

"Welcome, welcome! We're just waiting on the others." She led me into the living room.

"I think I saw Daisy's car pull in after me. She should be here any second," I said before looking up to see who'd arrived before me. My eyes immediately fell on Paige, and I couldn't help but smile. She looked less frazzled this time around. I hoped the move to California was going well for her. "Hey, Paige!" I almost asked how Halloween went when I realized there was someone else sitting in the living room with her.

She sat on one of the folding chairs, wearing navy blue dress pants. Her pale pink blouse looked nice with the blue pantsuit. I'd never be able to pull off that outfit, but then . . . there weren't many outfits I felt I could pull off.

"Hi. I'm Livvy," I said and scooted next to Paige on the love seat.

"Ilana." She said it with a short nod, her eyebrows rising slightly as she inspected me. What did that eyebrow raise mean? *Did I pass the inspection?* I wanted to ask but didn't. Speaking my thoughts out loud to Nick had been enough drama for one lifetime. I certainly didn't need to get into a catfight with some uppity silk-wearing woman in Ruby's home.

Maybe I should've gone walking on the beach instead, I thought, but then Paige spoke up next to me. "Thanks again for the costumes. You are an amazing seamstress. The boys had the Halloween of their lives."

I smiled my gratitude. Nope. Going to the beach to walk off my frustration would never have filled the hole in my soul the way making good friends would.

Paige.

Seeing her in her own home had left a lasting impression on me. She really was a good mom—a Giving Tree, as Nick called it. I liked her a great deal.

"The boys have been playing with the costumes every night before bed," she continued. "You were a lifesaver. I don't know what we would have done on Halloween without you."

She would've come up with something without me. She was that kind of mom, but I was glad to be able to take the stress off of *needing* to come up with something. "It was my pleasure, really." I waved my hand like it was nothing, but really, the way it had all come together still astonished me a bit. Definitely a Heaven Reminder. My mom had a knack for knowing when neighbors needed a sitter or a meal brought in because they'd fallen ill. *I got another Heaven Reminder*, she would say and then bustle out of the house with a pot of stew. Paige would think I was some nutcase if I mentioned that to her, so instead, I smiled even more and said, "I just wanted the costumes to be loved. Halloween isn't nearly as fun now that my boys have outgrown it." I turned to Ilana the Nodder. "Do you have any kids?"

Ilana stiffened. "No, I don't."

Oh boy. That had been the wrong question to ask. She either hated kids or all of hers had run away and joined the circus or something because the question had obviously hit a nerve. I almost felt disposed to not like this newcomer all that much until it occurred to me maybe she couldn't have any kids.

Don't judge, Livvy. You don't know anything about this woman. I needed a safe topic, so I picked up my copy of *The Poisionwood Bible* from off my lap and held it up a little so everyone would know what I was referring to. "Did you like it?" I asked Paige, but I addressed Ilana too, in case she'd known the reading assignment and had actually read the book.

Paige nodded in absolute approval. "It's one of my all-time favorites."

I was glad to hear that. It would make the discussion more fun to have someone else who liked the book as well as I did.

"It's a beautiful work," Ilana agreed, and I tried to loosen up. She had read the book and liked it. This meant she had good taste. Of course, I could see she had good taste just by eyeing the pantsuit.

Since she was agreeing, I kept the conversation going so she would feel more comfortable. If she felt comfortable, I would be able to relax around her. "It was beautiful, but more than just being beautiful, there was a lot of raw humanity emanating from the characters."

"Especially from the husband," Ilana replied. "He was the epitome of raw humanity."

I groaned. "You aren't kidding there. You know, at times I wanted to bust Nathan's kneecaps. What a jerk." The comment flew from my mouth before I could stop it. Busting kneecaps was likely the least intelligent thing I could have said. The flush crawled up my neck when Ilana's lips twitched in what might have been amusement.

Did she find humor in what I'd said, or was she merely amused by the ignorance of a middle-aged woman who didn't own silk because it was too expensive and bothersome to dry-clean?

The bell rang, which I found odd, since Daisy had been right behind me and several minutes had already passed. Maybe she'd sat in the car to spend a moment being glad to be at book club too. Ruby wasted no time in opening the door and ushering Daisy inside.

"I'm glad I could make it. Things have been a little crazy," Daisy said as she walked with Ruby into the living room.

Daisy and Ilana said hello to each other. Ilana's chilly sort of greeting didn't bother Daisy at all. Daisy's confidence carried her through petty things that *did* bother me. I worried Ilana didn't like me, wouldn't be pleased by my words and thoughts. Daisy couldn't care less. I admired that quality. Caring too much made me the sort of woman who was called a Giving Tree by her husband before he stormed out of a fight.

I noted the éclairs on the coffee table and felt gratitude in having not brought cookies. I didn't want to detract from the dessert someone else had done.

Ruby called us to order by letting us know Athena and Shannon wouldn't be able to come this month. "Shannon had to work a later shift, so she'll be here next month, and then Athena called me about an hour ago and said she couldn't come." Ruby shifted her shoulders in a worried sort of shrug. "Something came up."

My Heaven Reminders kicked into gear. Something about the crease in Ruby's brow and the tone of her voice made it seem like Athena had some real trouble that prevented her from coming. "That's too bad," I said slowly, trying to gauge the level of worry in Ruby. "I hope it's nothing serious. Did she give any clue as to why she couldn't make it? I feel bad she's missing her own book suggestion."

Ruby shook her head. "None." She took an éclair from the tray. "But that's why I ended up making these—Athena was supposed to bring the treats this time." She took a big bite and closed her eyes as she chewed. Another reason to love Ruby—she loved food as much as I did.

Daisy helped herself to an éclair and said, "Could be a work deadline or something else with her magazine."

While Daisy's suggestion seemed like a possibility, the way Ruby frowned at her éclair made it seem unlikely. Something else was wrong. "I'll give her a call later to see if she's okay," Ruby said, giving herself a little shake as if to remind herself where she was and what she was doing. She picked up her copy of *Poisonwood* from where it sat next to the éclairs and smiled big to let us know it was time to get to the business at hand: books. "Since Athena picked this month's book, she was supposed to lead the discussion, but I suppose I'll have to do." She squinted at some papers in her hands. She gave some facts on the author's life. And then smiled and looked up at us. "Isn't that interesting? She had a degree in biology. She's lived just about everywhere."

I hadn't read the biography of the author at the back of the book. I had been so caught up in my own troubles and the story itself to remember the person behind the words. She sounded like someone I could be friends with. "She sounds lovely," I said.

"She does, doesn't she?" Ruby responded. "Okay, so my first thought was about the nature of religion and how it impacted the lives of the five female voices in the book. I believe in prayer and Jesus and all that, but I'm not much for organized religion, and books like this kind of make me glad I'm not—especially as a woman."

I couldn't help it. I looked toward Paige who had talked so much about her religion when we were all here last. I *was* religious. My mother had taught me that God is in the details but only if you ask Him to be. I wasn't exactly vocal about religion, but I believed in God and felt there had to be something more than just *this.* My mother was gone somewhere beyond my reach. If I hadn't had faith in God, I would never have survived losing my one true friend.

Paige readjusted herself in her seat. I realized everyone had turned to stare at her—even Ilana, who didn't know Paige was a devout Mormon. Ilana simply seemed curious about why the rest of us had turned to the same person to comment on this topic.

Paige started slowly, as if sifting through her words and casting out the ones that wouldn't be quite right. "I don't think the problem is with organized religion, per se." She paused. "Throughout history, people have used religion and God as an excuse to do all kinds of terrible things. But religion was just that—their excuse. Religion has done as much to bring people together and accomplish amazing things as it has to destroy. It's powerful."

I agreed. My mother once told me that both good and bad people could be found in any walk of life—religious, nonreligious, intelligent, foolish, educated, laborer. Every day, the people who I came in contact with proved Mom right. I watched Paige take an éclair. But instead of eating it, she glanced nervously at the rest of us. She took a napkin as well and settled the éclair down onto the paper as if recognizing she wouldn't be able to eat for a while longer.

"You all know I'm a Mormon," she started. Everyone nodded, except Ilana, who actually looked surprised. "Something you might not all know is that my church helps people all over the world. One of its missions is all about reaching out to those in need. In that way, I think organized religion is a really good thing, not just for its members but for the people they can help."

Ruby leaned forward. "When you say help, don't you just mean the boys in suits that teach about your church?"

"The Church provides food, clothing, shelters, schools, and clean drinking water for communities around the world—even in areas where there aren't any Mormons, even in areas where we don't have missionaries, so they don't have any ulterior motive beyond simply helping people just because it's the right thing to do. Other religions have this same sort of policy. Mother Theresa is definitely not a Mormon, yet look at all the good she did."

She mentioned a few other names—some I'd heard of, others I hadn't, but they were all good examples of how organized religion can uplift humanity. "Even Christ Himself," she continued, talking faster—the way she seemed to do when excited or nervous. "Even if you don't believe He was the Son of God, like I do—you can't dispute that Jesus' teachings were revolutionary for their time or that He did a lot of good."

I nodded and gave an encouraging, "Absolutely."

Ilana spoke up. "He was a good man." She paused. "I'm Jewish, so, well . . ."

At this point, Paige looked like she could have started a forest fire by standing under a tree with her cheeks flaming red the way they were. It was another thing that endeared her to me. The telltale flush was a horrible curse. I envied people who could feel the same sort of emotions that roiled through me and yet never have their cheeks stain red or their neck splotch up with heat.

Paige cast a frazzled, desperate sort of glance around to see if we were going to mob her and have her stoned as a heretic. I smiled and nodded some more. *You're doing great, kid.* I considered interrupting, but she said it all so much better than I would have that it seemed pointless to try to add anything more.

"I guess what I'm saying is that some people get so wrapped up in one thing—and it could be a good thing, even—that they lose sight of what's most important. So that one thing could be *saving* the heathen."

She did a one-handed air quote and eyed her éclair with a look of longing. "Like Nathan wanted to do in the book, at the expense of his wife and daughters. Or it could be someone working so hard on a charity that helps people in another country but totally ignoring the needy right under their own roof."

I jolted slightly. Nick had called me the Giving Tree, and I'd worn the insult with pride, but . . . I hadn't neglected him in that process . . . had I? Did *he* think I had?

Paige finished her explanation and took a huge bite of her éclair, as if indicating that she expected someone else to say something in this discussion.

Ruby took the baton and ran with it. "You make a really good point. I hadn't thought of it that way. Nathan used religion as a crutch to feel important and do what he wanted to do. Sort of took himself out of being responsible for anything—he could blame it all on God and his desire to serve."

Nick couldn't have thought I'd neglected him. Stupid man! Giving Tree? Did Nick have any idea what it cost the tree to give *everything* to that stupid boy? "Ooooh, that makes me hate him even more," I said in reference to Nathan in the book before I could stop myself. The true disadvantage to becoming used to talking to yourself was not being able to filter your outbursts in public. *Makes me hate him even more? How old am I? Thirteen? Can I not come up with one intelligent comment on this book and not sound juvenile?* I determined not to speak again unless I had something educated to add to the conversation.

I followed Paige's example and took an éclair for myself. Better to keep my mouth full of food than with foolishness.

"I'm glad your church is such a support to you." Daisy crossed her legs and looked thoughtful for a moment. The words were nice enough on the surface, but a barb—whether intended or not—lay underneath those nice words. For a moment, I thought of DeeAnn and all the "nice" things she said to me, but no . . . Daisy wasn't like that exactly. She wasn't attacking Paige. The barb existed but didn't seem aimed at Paige at all. "But not everyone gets the same kind of support from their parishes," she finished.

Ah. Definitely not aimed at Paige but at Daisy's own parish. From the faraway look in her eyes, the instance she'd thought of was a long time ago, but it obviously still hurt.

Daisy shifted slightly, uncrossing her legs, which unsettled her barely eaten éclair and dusted her slacks with powdered sugar. "What you said about good people being in churches is true. Absolutely. And I think Paige is on to something when it comes to people using religion as a crutch—an excuse. From my experience, the problem comes—and all too often—when people put church before God." She brushed at her slacks, scowling and fretting at the sugar there. How she could not devour the entire pastry defied all known reason. They were perfect. I'd have to get the recipe from Ruby.

Daisy continued. "One good thing about organized religion—at least in real life, not in the book, for sure—is how it can bond families together. But if some family members are devout and others . . . aren't . . . religion becomes a schism and something . . . something painful." Daisy paused.

That had never been my experience because I did what Mom did, and my kids did what I did. Nick did whatever he wanted, but then . . . he'd always been like that. Though he had gone to church with us most of the time until the last few years or so.

But Daisy? Daisy had been burned not just by some pastor in her church but by someone in her family. Maybe her dad was a pastor who demanded too much, like Nathan in the book. Nathan, who always clashed against his daughter Rachel.

Daisy continued. "We saw that with Rachel when she struck out on her own; she never looked back on God or her family."

I tsked softly. "But Rachel never really looked to God at the start either. She was always materialistic and vain, start to finish." If Rachel had been my daughter, I'd have grounded her forever. And not because of the religion thing. No. Not that. But because that girl was so egotistical, she couldn't be bothered to see anything that didn't orbit around her.

"She was the polar opposite of her sister, Leah," I continued. "Nathan's religion is his worshipful obsession, but Leah worships her father to the same crippling degree. She wants so much to please him that she very blindly accepts every crazy idea that man takes into his head."

Paige piped up. "She does denounce her religion though. She leaves the Baptist faith behind."

"But not God," I said. I liked that about Leah. She remained true through the entire story. She chose different means but always toward the same end. Leah wanted to be a good person. Isn't that what God wanted from all of us? To be good? "In fact, I think He becomes bigger in her mind and heart as the book progresses," I added, knowing it didn't really explain my thoughts but figuring it was better than me spurting out how much I wanted to bust Nathan's kneecaps.

Paige pointed out that Nathan's choices were bad but were certainly not the fault of his religion. "Doesn't drawing that conclusion do the very same thing Nathan did?" Paige asked. "State that one way is the right way at the expense of all other ideas?"

I opened my book, not sure how to make my point intelligently, so I hoped I could make the author do it for me. After sifting through pages, I found what I searched for and read a quote from Adah. "On page one forty-one, Adah says, 'I wonder that religion can live or die on the strength of a faint, stirring breeze. The scent trail shifts, causing the predator to miss the pounce. One god draws in the breath of life and rises; another god expires.' Maybe instead of God being the focal point of that quote, it's more like vision or belief or something a bit more ethereal in relation to God. Not one of us in this room believes in God the same way another one does, but I imagine that if Nathan had respected the god worshiped in the Congo, even as he remained true to his own beliefs, the story would have been very different."

Ruby laughed. "And probably not worth writing about. Without conflict, there's no story."

Ilana raised a hand, which almost made me laugh since she was the one wearing silk and yet acted the part of a grade school child getting permission to speak. The action struck me as sort of cute, which made me grudgingly like her. "I'm a bit split on the whole organized religion thing," she said. "I grew up with a pretty conservative family—we always went to temple on the Sabbath, we ate kosher, I had my bat mitzvah, the whole bit. My parents have always found strength in reading the Torah and following the laws, but as I've gotten older, I'm not so sure I believe any of it—even whether there's a God." She pointed at the closed book resting on Paige's lap. "As far as the story in *Poisonwood* goes, I see it as just as much about the repression of women as about religion—religion is just the vehicle the author uses to tell the story about the women and how they're kept in place and held back."

"That's a great point." I smiled at Ilana, still liking her for raising her hand. "And there are all kinds of political, gender, and socioeconomic themes throughout the book; only seeing the religious connotations is missing a huge portion of the story."

Ilana nodded, agreeing with me. But even as she did so, I considered the parallels between the book and my own world. I was one of those women . . . kept in her place.

I looked down, feeling the flush. The kinship felt toward Orleanna Price shamed me. Would Nick and I have been different if we'd respected each other's beliefs? If he could have accepted that family was everything to me? If I could have understood . . . what? What was I missing? What hadn't I understood in this silent, brooding man?

To distract myself, I took another éclair.

Daisy nibbled on her own pastry, looked like she might throw up for the briefest of moments, and then set it down on a napkin.

"You don't like the éclair?" Ruby asked Daisy. I hoped she didn't take offense. Heaven knew those éclairs were the best things I'd eaten in a while. I'd have cleaned off the whole tray if I'd been alone with no witnesses.

"I love éclairs," Daisy said. "Paul and I went away last weekend, and I haven't quite recovered from something I must have picked up down there." She apologized for wasting the éclair and looked truly sorry not to be able to eat it.

"I've been getting the darndest indigestion at night myself." Ruby patted her midsection. "Don't know what's causing it. I don't dare see a doctor in case it's an ulcer—or something worse." She ended in a whisper, as if in saying the word *worse* too loudly, fate would take her up on it. "I hope your situation isn't serious," she said to Daisy.

Daisy immediately protested. "I don't think it's anything like that. It's probably just a bug or maybe some food poisoning. I've just been a little sick to my stomach ever since, and sweets are especially unappetizing. I'm tired a lot too—probably from not eating like I usually do. I'm sure I just need some extra sleep to kick it."

Paige glanced up. "Nausea and fatigue? Maybe you're pregnant."

Tense silence followed the words. Ilana, Ruby, and I darted glances between Paige and Daisy. I half wondered if Daisy would tell Paige off despite the fact that her diagnosis made sense considering the symptoms.

Daisy's mouth quirked up in what was meant to be a smile but was anything but. "That's quite impossible. I took care of that fifteen years ago." She smiled wide then, but even that curve upward left a chill in the room that didn't seem likely to dissipate on its own.

Paige's eyes widened in understanding. She'd accidentally moved into the territory of too personal. "I'm . . . sorry . . . I didn't mean . . ."

Poor girl hadn't meant anything by it. And poor Daisy—looking so horrified to be put on the spot with such an idea. Time for a change of topic. "Adah's character fascinates me," I broke in. "I find it interesting that she discovers at the end that she limps out of habit more than anything really wrong with her and that throughout the whole book she's silent and detached from the world she lives in, but then at the end, when she decides to speak, she . . ." I thumbed through to find the right page so I didn't misquote. "'She finds she's afraid because she has begun to love the world a little and may lose it.'"

By the time I'd finished the quote, no one seemed to remember Paige had accidentally called Daisy pregnant. But more than that, I saw something in the book I hadn't seen before.

I'd constantly compared myself to Orleanna Price, the browbeaten wife. And I'd compared Nick to the husband doing the beating. But Nick wasn't anything like Nathan Price—not really.

Nick was more like Adah—silent, detached, which led me to wonder if he feared loving his children from his marriage with The Ex because he'd lost them in a way? Was that the reason for his apathy?

Ilana warmed to the discussion now that Adah had been introduced. Adah was brilliant. On that, everyone agreed. I warmed to the conversation as well, now that I'd stopped burbling out emotional responses versus the intellectual ones. Not using my college education for a job didn't mean I hadn't used it for my life. I *was* capable of intelligent conversation.

Ilana and I had a lively chat, comparing quotes that interested us both, dissecting the characters until they lay bare on the altar of our curiosity.

What better measurement could be taken to gauge the intelligence of these women than to bring politics and religion into the conversation and then see how they responded?

Respect was the outcome.

It was at the end of the evening that I brought up the one quote from the book that had stayed with me from the beginning.

"'I had washed up there on the riptide of my husband's confidence and the undertow of my children's needs.'"

I hadn't meant to say it out loud. Hadn't meant to confess how much and how often I felt like this—washed up.

Thinking out loud again, Livvy?

But no one seemed to recognize the confession in that quote.

And the conversation spun another direction.

"Well, it's getting late," Ruby said once we'd moved off the topic of books and a little into our personal lives. "Does anyone have a suggestion for next month's book?" She looked at Paige, who didn't notice because she was texting on her phone. "Would you like to choose it, Paige?"

She still didn't notice anyone had addressed her.

"Paige?"

She looked up suddenly, as if startled to find there were other women in the room. She dropped the phone into her lap and covered it with her hands like Marie did when she was trying to hide the gum she'd sneaked out of Mandy's purse. "I'm sorry, what?"

"Ruby was asking if you'd picked out the book for the next month. It's your turn," I said gently.

"Oh, um, I'm not sure right off the top of my head. Do any of you guys have one in mind?"

No one answered immediately, likely because no one wanted to be singled out to make the decision for everyone else. But the book club offered me the chance to be something more than the woman who only had conversations with herself. I cleared my throat. "Actually, *The Poisonwood Bible* reminded me of another book—very different, of course—that I read a long time ago. It's called *My Name Is Asher Lev*. Have you guys ever read it?"

"I have," Daisy said. "Or at least, I read part of it when I was dating a guy who was Jewish." She grinned in a way that looked both mischievous and playful at the same time. "I stopped reading when we broke up though, so I never finished it. It's by Potok, right?"

"Right," Ilana said.

Yes.

Intelligent women. Half of them had already heard of the book and read at least parts of it.

Paige piped up. "We don't have to read something Jewish your very first month."

I'd actually forgotten Ilana's religion. *Good thinking, Paige, for making sure Ilana is comfortable.*

"I don't mind," Ilana said. "I've read *The Chosen* and really liked it."

Good! I scooted forward, excited to be able to discuss the book with a group of women who were as well spoken and interesting as these.

"Not that we want religion to be a theme or anything, but I just loved the way Potok delved into the interpersonal relationships, into specific practices of his orthodox life and found himself within those things but also outside of them."

Ruby clapped. I loved that she clapped. "Sounds delightful. I've never read that one, but I visited Israel many years ago, and it was wonderful." She turned to Paige, who had yet to go back to her phone, though it looked like her eyes were going to start watering from the effort it took to not check for another text. "What do you think, dear?"

Paige looked pleased with the choice. "I've read something by Potok, but I don't think it was that book. I'm totally up for it."

We gathered our things; I snatched one of the few remaining éclairs before getting to my feet. I really needed the recipe.

"Until next time!" Ruby said, walking us to the door.

I stopped and offered her a brief hug. "Thanks for everything, Ruby. You really are a lifesaver to me."

She hugged me back. "As you are to me, darling."

"First Saturday of December!" Ruby reminded us. "Don't let anything Christmassy get in the way—or Channukah-ish," she added as Ilana walked past. Ilana laughed at being singled out. She really was a good sort of woman underneath the intimidating facade of silk and propriety.

Ruby kept waving as we headed outside and to the lives waiting for us at home. "Oh!" she said. "Maybe I'll find a latke recipe so our refreshments will be Jewish! Ilana, if our meeting ends up during Channukah, could you still make it?"

Ilana confirmed that she'd be there, and they made plans for the refreshments to tie into the book. Even though it was my book choice, the recipe ideas they had were all things Ilana said she could make in her sleep, and she seemed to want the task, so I decided not to help with the food.

As we headed down the walk, Ruby called after us. "See you gals next month."

"Thanks for hosting," Paige called over her shoulder. "I know I love coming to your house."

Ruby put a hand to her heart. "And I love having you. Book club is becoming my one bright spot each month. I'll tell Athena and Shannon about the next book. And I'll let you all know how Athena is holding up."

And the Heaven Reminder kicked in again at the mention of Athena. I wasn't anything like my mom. She'd been all things wonderful. She always knew when people needed her. I very seldom had any kind of inkling when people needed me. I tried to be there when they did, but it wasn't instinctive—not like it had been with Paige and the costumes or this feeling I had now.

Something was wrong in Athena's life. That's why she hadn't come. I was very glad Ruby would be calling her and checking in on her and glad she'd be calling the rest of us to keep us in the loop. I had the feeling Athena would need us in the loop.

Chapter 10

Nick wasn't home when I arrived back at the house, and I let out a breath of relief I hadn't realized I'd been holding. I wouldn't have to deal with him or his silence. I could walk on the floors rather than eggshells.

It struck me as sad that his absence had, over the course of a few weeks, become preferable. Chad was at play practice, but Selena had agreed to drive him home so I wouldn't need to pick him up. Mandy was playing with the little kids on the game system in the rec room. They all smiled and said hello when I went in to check on them. They looked happy and unaware of the fact that their father was late coming home yet again, but then . . . things had been better between him and them lately—even as they grew worse between him and me.

That hadn't affected them the way I thought it might. Mandy seemed angry with *me* but perfectly fine with *him*.

I thought a lot about Nick as I switched out the laundry from the washer to the dryer—thought about the relief I felt upon opening the garage door and finding him gone, thought about the idea of him being more like Adah than Nathan Price. It was hard to think of him as the riptide when I'd been the one to cause him the pain that resulted in our current form of silence. I felt guilty for speaking my mind, but what had I said that wasn't true?

And yet . . . Mandy was mad at me. That bothered me more than anything. I'd been right. Why did I feel guilty for speaking the truth?

I went to bed late, waiting to see if he would show up but gave up around midnight.

He must've come home long after I'd fallen asleep because I failed to notice his arrival. He was snoring softly next to me when I woke up.

I crept out of bed, trying not to wake him so I could move through my morning without worrying about what room he might be in or if he could hear me.

He rolled over but continued to snore, his mouth hanging slightly open and his dark hair with the fine bits of silvering all mussed up as if he'd been tugging at it in his sleep. I reached out to brush his hair from his forehead—lightly enough it wouldn't wake him.

How can I feel like this? How can I love him, fear him, despise him . . . all at once?

I watched his chest rise and fall for a moment before stealing out of the room. Watching him, *touching* him, was foolish. What would I say if he woke up?

No one else was awake. It was Sunday, and church wasn't for a couple more hours. I called Jessica, knowing no one could overhear, and asked if she could meet us at the beach later on for an evening picnic.

"Will Dad be there?" she asked.

"I . . . doubt it. But it'll be good to spend some time together. I haven't seen the grandbabies for a while."

"Okay, sure. Sounds like fun. I'll be there."

I hung up, smiling. I'd get to keep my promise to the kids by taking them on a picnic to the beach and get to keep my promise to myself that I would be an involved part of Jessica's life.

Once the kids were up, it took no coercion to get them dressed and out the door for church services because I'd bribed them with the picnic.

Nick was still in bed, so I quietly gathered my things and moved them to the downstairs guest bathroom so I could get ready. He was home when we came home, and though Mandy and Marie tried to talk him into coming to the beach with us, he maintained his need to get some things fixed around the house.

Again, the flood of relief at his refusal to go.

Chad wanted Selena to come along, and I couldn't see any reason to object, so we picked her up and then drove to Newport Beach. Jessica and Mike were already there with their kids. I lifted my hand in a wave to them as I pulled the picnic basket out of the back of my car.

Mandy's jaw dropped when she saw them. She whirled on me. "Are you kidding?"

"What?" I asked, bewildered by the fury in her words.

"You didn't say anything about inviting *them*." She said the word *them* as if it tasted bad to her.

"I thought I did. What difference does it make?"

She didn't answer but stood there silently shaking her head, her jaw working.

"Manda-bear? What's wrong?"

"Whatever." She stomped away at the same time Selena bounded to the back of the car with Chad in tow, offering to help me carry stuff to the sand. I blinked at Mandy's retreating back.

"What's her deal?" Chad asked after handing off a small cooler to Selena to carry out.

"I have no idea. She's been mad at me a lot lately." I turned to him and squinted into his eyes. "Do you know what's going on there? Has she said anything to you?" They were pretty close. She usually talked to him about personal stuff. Even though they teased and tormented each other, they were always there when one of them had things to talk about.

Chad shrugged as he strong-armed the small table I'd brought to help keep sand out of the food. "She hasn't said anything, but I haven't been around much either."

And he hadn't. Even when he was home, he was either talking to Selena on the phone or she was there at the house with him.

He'd moved into the realm of "relationship" faster than I would have imagined. But he seemed happy enough. And they kept to the kitchen or the rec room when they were together at our house, so I wasn't too worried about them getting overly comfortable and into trouble.

I followed Chad and the others out, rolling the big cooler out to the sand where everyone had chosen to set up.

Marie followed along, bringing her own variety of beach essentials—mostly things that would build the greatest sand castle known to mankind.

"Gracie!" Marie squealed when she saw her little niece shoveling sand into a plastic pail. Marie dropped all her gear, swept the toddler into a hug, and immediately set to helping her build a castle. Grace threw more sand onto the blankets than she added to the castle, but they both had a good time being together. Marie considered Grace her live baby doll.

Mandy fumed for pretty much the whole dinner, but between setting everything up, making sure everyone got fed, and taking it all down, I didn't have time to cater to her tantrum. She spent most of the time sitting at a distance from the rest of us and glaring at the ocean.

Oh well. Better than her glaring at me.

"So Kohl's party . . . Have you talked to Dad? Has he agreed to come?" Jessica asked.

"He's a little sticky right now," I said, my eyes on my plate so they wouldn't have to meet hers.

"I don't know why it matters so much to you, Jess," Mike, her husband, said. "If it doesn't matter to him, then it doesn't need to matter to you." He tugged on her braid and kissed her behind the ear—a gesture meant to soothe his words so the truth of them didn't sting.

"I shouldn't do the party. It'll just cause more trouble in the family, and that's the last thing I want," she said with a sigh that bordered on a sob.

"Sure you should," Mike said, looking to me for help in convincing her. "This isn't about your father. This is about your brother. And he needs you. Even if the party is just us and him, it's worth it because then he knows someone cares."

"Mike's right," I said. "You're doing a good thing, Jess. Kohl needs to leave home knowing home is a place worth coming back to. Whether your dad shows up or not isn't the point. It's that you'll be there with his niece and nephew. I'll be there with his other brothers and sisters. Maybe his mom will show up." *Fat chance on that.* His mom was as flaky as his dad was stubborn.

"You're right," she conceded. Then she looked at me, really looked at me. "You said things with Dad were *sticky.* I hope you didn't get into any trouble over this."

I laughed, but even to me the sound came out forced, more like the long, sorrowful bray of an animal than a happy noise of a human. "Of course not."

Why mention the cruise and the one moment in years where Nick looked at me like I worth gazing upon? The moment was forever irretrievable, and no matter how much I wished to call it back, dwelling on it would only make the hurt run deeper.

So I turned my attention to the children—all of them. I took pictures, rolled up my pants, and splashed in the waves with the kids. I let them bury me in the sand and then rose up out of my sandy grave to chase them like a zombie. Chad and Selena stayed to themselves—walking on the beach hand in hand and stealing kisses when they didn't think I'd notice.

I was mom.

I always noticed.

I also noticed that Mandy never warmed up to the event. She barely said two words to Jessica.

Jessica was now a mom herself.

She noticed too.

* * *

A shattering noise came from upstairs not long after we'd been home and unloaded the car. I turned off the water in the sink, where I was doing dishes, and followed the noise to Mandy's room.

I edged the door open to find Mandy cursing and cleaning on the other side of the room.

"What's going on?"

She whirled around then realized it was only me. Her dad had stayed downstairs in his office. "Nothing. I just dropped one of my Goofy statues." She'd collected Goofy stuff since she'd been a toddler.

She had a few ceramic pieces in her hand, and I could see several more in the garbage can that she had already cleaned up.

I wandered farther into the room and inspected the wall where a good-sized hole now happened to be. I smirked at her. "Looks like you dropped it against the wall. Looks like you dropped it real *hard* against the wall."

"It's not funny, Mom." She dumped the contents in her palm into the trash and leaned over to get some more.

"So does this have something to do with the fact that you were pretty miserable company this evening? What was that all about?" I asked.

"All what?" She leveled her very best *I'm-only-listening-to-you-because-you-pay-for-my-room-and-board* look at me.

"Acting like you were some royalty stuck with the peasants for the night. You were really kinda . . . not pleasant." I kept my tone light and as nonaccusatory as possible. Mandy was likely to pitch several other things against walls if confronted with outright accusation over her behavior.

She made that *psh* noise that ground my nerves into dust and said, "Not pleasant? You make it sound like we're going on some fun family activity, and then you invite *them*. How could you just invite them without telling us?"

I sat on the edge of her bed. "Jess and Mike and the kids are family too. Why wouldn't I invite them? Why would that make such a difference in how you act?"

"They aren't *your* family!" she said it quietly. Her dad was still downstairs. She didn't want him to overhear.

I looked at her ceiling. "What is wrong with the people in this house? It's like you all have some sort of anti-relation-disease." I counted to five and then allowed myself to look back at Mandy. "She's your sister, Manda-bear. Those little kids? They are your niece and nephew. They are *your* family. And you are *my* family. And that makes us all family together."

She scrambled to her feet and crossed her arms over her chest as she glared at my every word. I reached out and loosened one of her hands and pulled her down on the bed to sit next to me. "You've never had a problem with Jessica before. What is this really about, Mandy?"

"Dad asked you to go on a cruise with him, and you said no. *No*, Mom. He finally offers us a chance to be normal and happy together, and you said NO!" She shouted the last word then took a deep breath as if remembering her need to be quiet. "You had a chance to fix this so he comes home at night and eats dinner with us and so he actually shows up on your anniversary, so we can be happy as a family together. But instead you said no because you chose his other kids over us. How does that make sense?"

She tried to pull her hand out of mine, but I refused to let go. Instead, I used it to pull her into me so I could hold her and rock her.

She'd started crying.

"Ssshh," I whispered. "You're okay, love. I am so sorry you've been holding this in. You should've talked to me sooner. I wouldn't choose anyone over you." I kissed the top of her head.

"Yes, you would. You did." She sniffed, and for all her anger, she held me back, needing something to hold even if it was the object of her pain and anger.

"I did what I did *because* of you guys. I was thinking of Chad and Tyler maybe someday going into the military and getting a deployment to some faraway country where they wouldn't have family around them and where they would need some sort of internal strength to get them through the hard times. What if, years from now, you decide to throw a party to say good-bye to Chad? Or if Marie decides to throw one for Tyler? Or if Tyler decides to throw one for you? Would you want to send your brothers and sister away without them knowing they were loved?"

"Mo-om! This isn't like that at all. This isn't about us. It's about them."

I tightened my hold on her and shed a few tears of my own. "That isn't true. They are us. We are them. We're a family. The end. And family is sticky sometimes, but if we make sticky work to our advantage and stick together . . . well then . . . we'd be something magnificent. The point is that your brother, Kohl, feels alone. He needs your dad as much as you need your dad. And for reasons I don't understand, he's been cast off like leftovers that have been in the fridge too long. I didn't choose him over you. I chose him *because* of you. If there comes a day that one of you needs me to be there for something important, you can know I'll always be there."

"But Dad—"

"I know. I don't know what to tell you about him. Hopefully, he'll come around. But for now, Mandy, I gave my word I would be somewhere. I may not be so great, but at least people know my word means something."

"I just wish everyone got along," she whispered into my arm.

"You could help that, you know . . . by getting along with everyone?"

Any fight she had left in her deflated with that remark. She pulled away and wiped her eyes. "You're right. I hate it when you're right."

"What is it Ghandi said?" I asked, tilting her chin so she had to look me in the eye.

She moaned and tried to move her chin, but I didn't let go until she rolled her eyes at me and answered, "'Be the change you want to see in the world.' Honestly, Mom. You are beyond cheesy."

I didn't argue with her because she was right, but I did give her another squeeze and a kiss on the forehead. I left her room feeling better about things. Even if things weren't fixed exactly . . . at least Mandy and I were still talking and friends enough that she could call me cheesy. *Cheesy* was not on Mandy's angry-word list. *Stupid*, *moronic*, *lame*, *lame*, *lame . . . those* were her angry words. A bunch of cuss words she'd learned from her father fell on that list too, but she never used those with me.

I went to the downstairs bathroom to get ready for bed since most of my stuff was already there from the morning. The phone rang, and I hurried to answer it before Nick could be annoyed by the late hour.

"Hello?" I kept my voice low.

"Hi . . . Livvy?"

"Yes, this is Livvy."

The voice was familiar but not enough in my distracted state of mind to actually place it until she said, "It's Ruby, you know, from book group."

It had to be about Athena. Ruby wouldn't be calling so late for any other reason. At least I didn't think she would. And her voice sounded tense with worry. "Oh, Ruby," I said. "Hello! Have you heard anything from Athena?"

"Yes, actually, I have. I called to tell her about the new book, and I found out why she couldn't be there last time."

"What happened?" I sat at the island.

"Her mother was in a car accident Halloween night." Ruby sounded so sad to have to break this news to me. "She died in the hospital afterward."

I slumped in my chair, resting my head on the cool counter. It made no sense, but it felt like finding my own mother in her garden all over again. Tears slid down my cheeks and onto the countertop. "Oh, how awful. Poor Athena!"

"I know. It just about killed me to hear such news. That poor girl. Such a horrible blow to lose someone so unexpectedly."

I nodded and sniffed. It always was a horrible blow—expected or not. I'd expected it with my dad. He'd been sick for so long. I hadn't expected it with my mom at all. Both moments felt like I'd fallen down a well with no bottom. I plummeted and plummeted, my stomach in a constant state of dropping. But I was never given the relief of hitting the ground and being done with it all.

Years later, I was still trapped in the eternal freefall of loss.

Ruby sniffed along with me. "I found her mother's obituary in the newspaper. Athena's mother was beautiful—just like Athena. It said the funeral is on Wednesday at Saint Paul's Greek Orthodox Church in Irvine. What do you think about us maybe attending the funeral—to be a support to Athena so she knows people care?"

It seemed a theme for the day—the things we did so people knew we cared. It further proved to me that I'd been right to refuse the cruise. People were important, and they needed to be cared for.

But Nick isn't being cared for . . .

I shoved that thought aside. I'd given him the chance to simply reschedule. He could have had it both ways—the cruise *and* his son. He just didn't want anything unless it was strictly his way.

"Yes, of course we should go," I agreed.

"I knew you'd say that. I've already called Daisy, and she promised to call Paige. The services start at eleven, and I already called the priest, and he assured me it was open to anyone connected to the family. You don't have to be Greek Orthodox to attend. That poor Athena is taking care of all the arrangements herself due to her father's failing health. Can you imagine that? She's so young to lose her mother!"

So was I . . .

Ruby sniffed again. "To have a sick father and no mother . . . I just feel awful."

I felt awful too. I imagined Athena with her dark hair and dark eyes trying to hold everything together and losing the right to mourn because so much needed to be done that there wasn't time. Would Athena know how important it was for her to make time? Would she know that if she didn't allow herself to grieve now and allow people in to comfort her, she'd crack wide open later and it would be worse?

"I'll be there. You can count on me. Thanks for letting me know, Ruby."

"I'm just glad we have each other." She sniffed again, said good-bye, and hung up.

As I pushed OFF on my phone and set it in its cradle, I agreed with her. Women I'd met once or twice, and yet I was so grateful to have them.

* * *

I wore black to the funeral.

We met at Ruby's. Paige and I rode with Ruby. I felt so incapable of focusing that my driving would have surely resulted in a mangle of metal and shattered windshields on the 405. We met up with Daisy just outside the domed building so we could enter and sit together. Everyone wore black except Paige and Daisy.

I'd never been in the St. Paul's church before. It was lovely, with lots of art and stained glass. We sang verses from Psalms, and then the priest offered a eulogy. I straightened as he said, "I ask you to ponder how brief our life is."

My breath hitched in my throat as I saw my mother's casket in my mind. It had been draped with flowers of every variety. She had loved flowers—loved things that grew. Life . . . so brief. A tear slid down my cheek, and I hurried to brush it away so none of the others saw how deeply the priest's words affected me.

When I brought my hand down again, Daisy placed a tissue in my hand and offered the briefest smile of sympathy.

I looked down at the white tissue and remembered something important. I wasn't alone. Not there in the church and not in my life.

I made it through the rest of the service without any more tears, though I held that tissue like a lifeline. For all the frailty of life, there were strong things mingled with it. In God's infinite wisdom and love, He gave us each other.

There was nothing fragile in that.

When the service was complete, Athena stood to follow the casket, along with several other people who had to be her family. It was then that she noticed us. Surprise crossed her features at first, but that surprise was short and quickly replaced with a look of gratitude.

You're not alone! was the message I hoped my smile gave her. I glanced at the unused tissue in my hand—a gift from Daisy.

None of us are.

We followed the rest of the mourners out of the church, where several people headed for their cars. The limo pulled into traffic behind the hearse. I watched it pull away. "Athena's mom sounds like a really neat woman," I said, still watching as the limo and hearse disappeared into traffic.

A few murmurs of agreement followed, and then, out of the blue, Daisy said, "You look really nice today. That outfit really brings out your eyes. I hadn't noticed how blue they are."

I turned to her in surprise, the flush of embarrassment crawling up my neck. How long had it been since anyone had complimented me on anything that wasn't edible? "Thank you." I couldn't keep the wonder out of my voice. Daisy was always put together so well. A compliment from such a woman felt like being crowned queen for a day. "Thank you," I murmured again.

"What do you gals say to lunch?" Ruby asked, shaking me out of my internal thoughts of equal parts gratitude, embarrassment, and warmth from someone saying I looked nice.

"I'm starving," I said, not wanting to go home just yet. Not wanting to face the emptiness of the house. If I planned it right, I could get home at the same time the kids did from school.

"If we don't go someplace that takes too long, I could go," Paige agreed slowly.

Daisy checked her watch and shook her head. "I really have to get back to work, but you guys go ahead and have fun."

I nodded that we would, so she waved, smiled, and headed off toward her car in the parking lot.

I grinned at Ruby. "There's a Ruby's diner just down the street."

She laughed. "Maybe let's go somewhere that doesn't put me on the spot."

I joined in the laugh. "Oh fine. How about we commemorate Athena and eat Greek today? There's Daphne's Greek Café just off the parkway here."

Paige blinked at me. "How would you know where all these restaurants are?" she asked, mystified.

I shrugged. "I really like food." I'd gone to Irvine University. I knew the area well, even with all the changes. It was a place I kept tabs on—

knowing which restaurants were going in and which were going out. Sometimes I felt like I'd left a part of myself in Irvine, and it was good to drive around and visit the area, just to check on it and make sure it was still there and doing well.

They agreed with me, and we went in Ruby's car to the café.

I ordered a traditional Greek salad once we were seated. Ruby ordered a salad as well. Paige ordered a grilled chicken pesto pita melt, which sounded wonderful.

I changed my order when the waitress came back with the drinks to the same as Paige's. Sounded simply delicious. The waitress left again, and we sat in silence for a moment.

But the silence didn't last long.

We didn't dawdle over lunch because Paige wanted to get back to her boys and I wanted to be home when the kids got home, but in that short hour, I learned that Paige had met a lawyer, and though she said it wasn't anything much, her cheeks flushed a lovely shade of pink when she talked about him. I also learned she'd graduated college in Utah and found out she used the name *Carol* as a swear word, which made me laugh until I choked. She was pretty frantic between parenting two small boys on her own and working a full-time job, and I was amazed that she wasn't pulling out her hair and rocking in a corner. She handled this new situation with a grace I couldn't define. Sure, the fine lines of worry crossed her features every now and again, but she was quick to laugh.

"You're amazing," I said after awhile of just watching her.

"Oh yeah. I'm a bundle of amazement." She rolled her eyes and started laughing again.

"I'm serious. Look at how you're handling your life. You're making your own decisions. You're still breathing in and out. And I know from just one visit to your house and watching you with those boys that you are an amazing mom. I just want you to know I'm impressed, and I wish I knew your secret."

"Endure all things . . ." she whispered—the laughter all but gone. Her tone almost sounded as if she were giving herself a lecture.

"What was that?" Ruby asked.

She smiled and shook her head. "It's silly, I guess . . . It's just . . . one of our Articles of Faith—in the Mormon Church—a part of it states that we've endured many things, and we hope to be able to endure all things. Endurance is something I hope to be able to pull off."

"Articles of Faith?" I asked.

"Yeah, they're kind of like a list of what we believe."

Ruby leaned in, hurried to swallow her bite of salad, and asked, "If endurance is part of it, what's the whole thing?"

Paige looked surprised. "You really want to know?"

We both nodded. I knew a little about Mormons because there were some in my neighborhood. They were nice, polite, kept their yards in good order, but I really didn't know anything beyond that. Paige kind of half chuckled, like she couldn't believe we were asking. "Well . . . the Thirteenth Article of Faith states: 'We believe in being honest, true, chaste, benevolent, virtuous, and in doing good to all men; indeed, we may say that we follow the admonition of Paul—We believe all things, we hope all things, we have endured many things, and hope to be able to endure all things. If there is anything virtuous, lovely, or of good report or praiseworthy, we seek after these things.'" She paused and waited to check our reactions. "It's a bit of a mouthful."

"No. I like it," Ruby said, looking sincere. "Kind of what I hope for us as a book club—to seek after things that are lovely and of good report. It's a fine way to live."

I nodded my agreement, committing to memory the phrase *we hope to be able to endure all things.* I think I remembered something like that from my Bible reading. She'd said it came from the admonition of Paul . . . I'd have to look it up.

Definitely a fine way to live.

We laughed and talked all the way through our meal. I laughed so much, stomach muscles I'd forgotten existed started to hurt with the exertion. We drove back to Ruby's to get our own cars and get back to our own lives.

I hated leaving them. Hated to face my life at my house.

Once I was behind the wheel and headed home, I allowed myself to really dwell on the afternoon's events.

It had been hard to hold it together during the actual funeral when it felt like every step of attending this event for Athena's mother was like revisiting my own mother's funeral. There had been no one to help me with the arrangements except Nick. With so much that needed doing, there'd been no time to process, no time to feel the loss that cut a canyon through my soul.

Feeling that canyon had come later. I went to bed one night and couldn't pull myself out again the next morning. I took refuge under the covers and didn't reemerge for nearly a month. The household came to a standstill. Dishes weren't cleaned. Meals weren't prepared.

Nick had stepped in, ordered a lot of takeout, issued commands and chores on the kids, and jump-started the grinding halt of my absence. He'd allowed me to stay in bed—didn't complain about the lack of anything getting done—and held me as I cried into my pillow about needing my mommy.

He'd held me in spite of the unwashed odors coming from me, in spite of the fact that I'd failed the family during that time period, in spite of the fact that I'd offered nothing in return.

Nick had been there for me. And as I turned onto my street, it occurred to me that he'd been the Giving Tree that time and I'd been the little boy doing nothing but taking.

Nick.

How had I forgotten that? How could I have failed to recall that moment when I'd existed only because of his strength?

"I'm sorry, Nick," I said aloud, and when the garage door went up and his car was in its place in the garage, I didn't feel the twinge of panic that I'd have to tiptoe around him.

I found I wanted to see him, actually looked forward to it. I wanted to thank him for being there during that horrible time in my life. Other moments came to my recollection—moments when Nick had smiled encouragingly when I decided to learn to sew, when he'd offered to take midnight feedings for babies so I could get a little rest, when he'd just held me just for the sake of holding me.

I wanted to do that now, just hold him. Whatever was going on with us, we could work it out. We could because we were worth working out and working on.

I scrambled out of my car and bounded into the house.

"Nick!" I called as soon as I got the door to the mudroom opened. "Nick?" I hurried through the kitchen and into his office. He wasn't there.

I took the stairs two at a time to get to our bedroom faster but stopped short at the door.

Nick stood by the bed. Two small suitcases and one big one sat on the floor at his feet.

I stared at the suitcases. All I could think about was the cruise. Was he planning on both of us going early? Did he decide he really could have it both ways? "What's going on?" I said. My voice shook as if my vocal cords knew something was wrong—something that had nothing to do with cruise itineraries.

His shoulders hunched as though he were caving in on himself, and dark circles ringed his eyes. He opened his mouth and took a step forward, away from the suitcases. He closed his mouth and scrubbed his hand through his hair. "I'm moving out."

His words came out in a gusted breath.

My knees gave out from under me.

Chapter 11

I SLUMPED AGAINST THE DOOR frame, incapable of holding up my own weight. "What?"

It had to be a mistake. I hadn't heard him properly over the roaring in my ears. Surely he hadn't said what I thought I'd heard. I rubbed my hand over my forehead, feeling the ridges of my furrowed brow. "What?" I repeated, only this time it came out as a hoarse whisper, like wind blowing over the top of a dusty bottle in the desert.

"I'm leaving." The corners of his mouth drooped low. And his eyes shone with the admission that this gave him no pleasure.

"You . . . Please don't. Please stay. We can fix . . ."

But he was already shaking his head before I could get out any kind of coherent sentence. Why would my brain not function? Why would my lips not form the apology, the hope I'd felt just a moment before?

"It's just not working, Livvy. We walk around each other, talk around each other. I can't do this anymore." He bent to sling one of the smaller bag straps over his shoulder and then to pick up the other two.

"Where will you go?" Why? Why was *this* the only sentence I formed? One that allowed him some sort of permission to leave?

"I rented an apartment close to the office."

He couldn't leave! We had four children. Didn't that mean anything to him?

Anger spread through my limbs, offering strength that the cold shock of his words had sapped from me. We would become like The Ex and her children. We were just another family for him to abandon.

"So what? You leave and to what end?" I asked.

"To think. To give us some time away so we can figure out what we want." He started toward the door with his bags.

"That doesn't tell me what this is!" I stood in his way so he couldn't leave our room. I wanted to punch him in the head. And yet cradle his head and beg him to stay . . . to stay and be again what we once were. "What is this, Nicholas Robbins? Use small words. Define it for me so I can understand."

"Olivia!" He grunted and moved around me. "It's a separation. I need some time to figure things out, to work things out!" He shoved through the door and down the hallway.

I followed after him. "Oh, that's rich. Why not just call it what it is? Everyone knows you can't *work things out* when you aren't even living under the same roof." We were on the stairs now.

"Well, it'll be better than living in—"

"What, Nick? Better than living in *what*?" But he didn't answer. He'd stopped on the stairs and was looking down at the front foyer.

Down to where Mandy and Chad stood.

* * *

Nick did all the talking. He explained that Mom and Dad just needed time apart for a little while. I hated that he'd brought me into this, that my children looked at me with accusation in their eyes. This wasn't my choice, wasn't my fault. He'd dragged me here to this new place—this new jungle. This place where my lips only spit venom when they parted. I finally clamped them closed and hugged my arms around me to ward off the shuddering cold that couldn't be suppressed because it came from the inside.

Chad and Mandy stayed silent and wide-eyed. When Marie and Tyler showed up a few minutes later, the vocal protests began—the protests to the floor of their lives, identities, and belief systems dropping out from under them.

I did nothing to save them from the fall.

My teeth chattered, and my arms stayed around my midsection, my fingers balled up so tightly my fingernails hurt my palms.

The children followed him to the car, crying and begging him to change his mind. I followed them, pulled by the gravity of their ache.

He shoved his suitcases into his car, whirled on me and whispered harshly, "This would have been easier, Olivia, if you'd just have let me leave before they came home."

I stared at him, processing his words.

He'd meant me to tell them on my own?

Hider!

"I'm sorry, Nick. I'm sorry you think leaving your family is something I should make easy on you."

He growled something I didn't understand and got into his car, slamming the door closed. Marie's little hands slapped on the passenger side door, which was locked so she couldn't get in, or she would have—I had no doubt. "Daddy! Stay!"

I had to unwrap myself, to force my limbs to move so I could pull her away from his car so she didn't get dragged under the wheels when he drove away. I pulled her, Tyler, and Chad into me to wrap them up and shield them from the sight of his car getting smaller in the distance before he turned off our street altogether.

Mandy had stayed out of my reach. My fingertips had grazed her hoodie, but she'd managed to evade me.

The other children had their heads ducked down, accepting the shelter I offered. But I looked up to watch Mandy, alone, as she watched her father leave.

* * *

I didn't remember going back to the house, had no recollection of what did or didn't happen the rest of that day. Did we eat dinner? I didn't know. Did we cry? Did we scream? Did we throw things? Did we even talk to each other? Or did we go to our beds and burrow into the nothingness of sleep?

I just didn't know.

But alarms went off the next morning, and I got kids out of bed and ready for school. I considered letting them stay home, but none of them asked for that, and I didn't offer. No one said much to each other aside from a few mumbles and grunts. Mandy's eyes were so puffed and red that she looked like she was having an allergic reaction to something. I grabbed her arm and pulled her into me for a tight, quick hug.

I don't know if it was to give her energy or to steal some of hers for myself, but she gave a half smile that never reached her eyes and went out the door without another word.

And I was alone again . . . in this house meant for a family.

A few days passed with the children and me wandering around the house as if looking for its owner and never being able to find him.

I planned another picnic for the beach. I didn't invite Jessica. Chad didn't invite Selena.

But it didn't matter because on Sunday morning before I could even get them ready for church, the doorbell rang.

I nearly stumbled seeing Nick there. I would have been less surprised to find a ghost lingering on my front step.

How strange for him to ring the bell of the home he paid for.

Mandy peered over my shoulder and squealed in delight to see him. "Daddy!" A name she hardly used. He held his arms out wide as an offering for a hug. She leaped to those waiting arms, something I couldn't do, though part of me wanted to.

The other part of me wanted to pound him until my knuckles bled.

"Hey, Manda-bear."

I bristled at him calling her by the nickname I'd given her when she was just a baby.

He entered the house, carried on the tide of Mandy's excitement.

"I thought we'd all go to the beach," he informed the other kids as they gathered around him, as if he were brilliant to come up with such an idea. "Get your suits and boards, and let's get going!"

They scrambled to do his bidding. And then it was him and me, alone in the kitchen.

"I was planning to take them to the beach this evening," I said quietly.

"Sorry. I should've called, but I haven't seen them all week, and—"

I put up my hand, not wanting to hear any more. He hadn't seen them all week by *his* choice. And all week? He'd only been gone since Wednesday.

"It's fine." My tight voice betrayed the fact that it wasn't fine, but the kids wanted to see him. If I said no and insisted they go with me instead?

They'd never forgive me.

I wanted—hoped for—him to suggest that I come along, that it might be a good start toward us working things out together, but those words remained unspoken.

In moments, everyone was gone, and it was me and the house again.

I wandered, touching things I hadn't really seen in the last couple years—noticing paintings on my wall, inspecting their textures and colors and wondering why I'd bought them.

I ended up in my own room, where I noticed all the things Nick had left behind. Those three bags he'd taken held so few of his belongings.

I traced my fingers along the bookshelves in my room until I spotted the month's book selection. *My Name is Asher Lev*. I'd picked it out because I'd read it once before and it had struck a chord with me. But it had been a long time. And a refresher read was all I had left to do.

I sat on the couch and read, even when the words on the page blurred from the tears in my eyes.

It bothered me a great deal to read about Rivkeh, to read of her checking out of her family's life when her brother died. I'd done that. Had it affected my children the way it had affected Rivkeh's child?

The fact that I had checked out that same way . . . did that make me a bad mother? While reading the book, it felt that Rivkeh was a bad mother. Could she not see how much her child needed her? Could she not see how her inability to cope affected everyone around her? Her husband was a saint to stay with her.

What did that make Nick?

Nick, who had whispered gentle *shhh*'s at my children when they'd walked past my bedroom or when they'd tried to enter. Nick, who had figured out laundry for the first time in our married life. Nick, who had driven to schools and recitals and practices. Nick, who had fielded all the phone calls I'd refused to accept.

What did that make him when he was also Nick, who moved out instead of staying and fixing? Nick, who took my children away when I'd already made plans? Nick, who shoved relationships into a closet where he could shut the door and not be forced to look at them?

I put the book down and stared out the window.

I didn't know what that made Nick.

Or what it made me.

The kids came home happy . . . normal. Their laughter filled the house in a way it hadn't seemed to have ever been filled before. They tracked sand through the mudroom and kitchen in their rush to tell me their dad had fallen into the water fully clothed and how he couldn't get his feet back under him and how funny, funny, funny it all was.

I gritted my teeth and smiled and listened and couldn't help but wonder if they would have come back with this much excitement if they'd gone to the beach with just me.

* * *

Nick picked the kids up every few days and took them on some exciting new adventure. He spoke little to me, a few words of pleasantry exchanged while he waited in the foyer for the kids to gather stuff.

He never moved beyond the foyer of the house he still paid for. Each time he rang the doorbell, a shiver of surrealism passed through my bones. *This isn't happening.*

Yet it was.

We were separated to *work things out*, but we never communicated beyond the stilted chitchat in the foyer. How did we work things out when we were separated by chasms of the unsaid?

And then we were faced with something I'd forgotten about until Marie produced a piece of crumpled paper from her backpack when she arrived home from school on Monday. I smoothed the bright orange paper with autumn leaves bordering the edges and glanced at the school calendar. Marie had Thursday and Friday off school. I almost turned to her to question why when I realized what it meant.

Thanksgiving.

I'd forgotten Thanksgiving.

It was the first time in my married life that I had no idea where the holiday dinner would be and who I would be eating it with.

That particular problem couldn't be ignored. That particular question could not go unasked because I needed to be prepared for whatever answers lay in front of me.

Nick came over that evening with plans to take the kids to a Lakers game. He hovered in the foyer, shifting his weight and looking at everything that wasn't me.

"We haven't really talked . . ." I started. Wasn't the point of separating to give us a chance to work things out?

"Oh? About what?"

"I don't know," I said. "About us? The kids? Our plans?" I took a breath. "Thanksgiving?"

His head turned from where he'd been inspecting the painting above the foyer table to me. "Thanksgiving?"

"Yes. I was wondering what your plans are for Thanksgiving. I thought it might be nice if—"

"I'm going to my mother's for dinner." He interrupted me before I could add the words, *if you came over and we had dinner as a family.*

I nodded. "Oh, well . . . I hope you have a good time." My very bones quivered with relief. He was going to his mother's house. That meant the kids were mine for the day. I wouldn't be alone.

"What are your plans?" he asked, whether to be polite or because he really cared . . . I didn't know.

"The kids and I will just do dinner, and then maybe we'll go to a movie."

He blinked. Then blinked again. Then he cleared his throat and shook his head. "I meant that I'd be taking the kids to my mother's for Thanksgiving. She's already planning on them—bought the food and everything."

I staggered back as if he'd punched me full on in the face. "You're *taking* them? Without asking? Without discussing it in any way—you're just taking them?"

The flush rising in my chest and into my neck wasn't from embarrassment but from sheer fury.

"Well, yeah. It's the holiday. I see so little of them. I don't want them to think I don't care enough to spend the holidays with them. Honestly, Olivia. Keep your voice down. You'll scare Marie if she hears you."

I stepped forward again, grabbing his tie and pulling him in so we were nose to nose. I lowered my voice as directed even while I said, "Don't! Don't you *dare* make this out to be a problem *I'm* creating. You don't see them very much because *you* moved out. But even then you see them more now than you ever did when you actually lived here, so don't try the poor-me card. I am not putting up with that anymore, do you hear me *Nicholas*?" I used his full name the way he'd used mine, only I infused acid into that one word, making it an obscenity. "When were you planning on telling me? Or were you just going to swoop in on Thursday afternoon without any warning while the rolls were baking so I could eat an entire meal for a family all by myself?"

He tried to pull away, but I had a tight grip on his tie. The only way he could escape would be to hang himself with it, which I felt entirely willing to help him with if that's what he wanted to do.

No fair jury would have convicted me.

His eyebrows lifted, and his mouth quirked to the side in a half smile. "I think this is the first time you've ever gotten violent with me."

"This isn't cute. This isn't funny. And this is most definitely not a game to me. Answer my questions, Nick. When did you plan on sharing this information? And what makes you think you have the right to take them on a holiday?"

"Mom?"

It startled me to hear Mandy's voice, and I released Nick. He straightened his tie. He smiled up at Mandy, who was on the stairs with Marie right behind her. "Hey, Manda-bear."

"What's going on?" Mandy asked, her tone and squinted eyes filled with suspicion.

"Nothing," Nick said. "Your mom and I were just discussing plans for Thanksgiving."

"Oh." She slowly descended the stairs with Marie trailing after her—peeking out now and again from behind Mandy's legs to see if we were still there. Marie chewed the sleeve of her shirt, something I hadn't seen in a couple of years. I'd broken her of the habit before her fifth birthday. We'd celebrated when she'd come home from her first day of school with an unchewed sleeve. On such a nerve-wracking day, surely she'd wanted to chew it to shreds, but she didn't. Not then.

But now?

She chewed her sleeve furiously now.

Because she'd seen me grab her father in a way that wasn't playful; she'd seen the anger in my face, likely heard the anger in my words.

I closed my eyes and sent up a prayer. *Dear God . . . what are You doing? What am I doing?*

I forced my lips into the shape of a smile and nodded in agreement to their father's words. *Yes, children. We're just discussing plans for Thanksgiving.*

And I knew what I had to do to make the widened eyes of Marie shrink to their natural size, to make the sleeve leave her mouth, to make the cautious fear leave Mandy's step.

"Dad decided you'd all be going to your nan's house for Thanksgiving; won't that be fun? You haven't had Thanksgiving there for a few years, so this should be a treat."

Blink away the burn in your eyes. Swallow the scream searing up your throat. They need your smile. They need your assurances that they are okay.

My rapid breath left me dizzy.

The boys raced down the steps after their sisters, unaware of the fight, unaware of anything.

"Bye, Mom! Wish us luck!" Tyler planted a kiss on my cheek as he sped past and out the door. He was a huge Lakers fan. The luck he wanted was for his team to win.

"Good luck . . ." I said, keeping the corners of my mouth curved up.

Nick watched me and stepped forward with his hands outstretched as if in plea for understanding. "I'm sorry, Livvy. I didn't mean to—"

"Just go," I whispered.

His hands dropped as he inhaled sharply with my request. He gave a single nod, turned on one foot, and left—the door closing silently behind him.

I counted to three and heard the clicking of car doors opening in the driveway.

To eight, the doors were closed again.

To thirteen, the engine started.

To sixteen, the car backed out of the driveway.

And the scream that had been lodged in my throat for longer than a month clawed its way free and filled the walls of my now empty house.

Chapter 12

I WENT TO THE MOVIE theater alone on Thanksgiving Day. I bought the extra large bucket of popcorn and extra large soda so I could get a free refill of both and watched every single film they had playing, wandering from one darkened theater to the next—the films blurring into one smear of comedy, suspense, and drama. I made it home at nearly midnight.

I ate no turkey. No pie. No yams.

And felt thankful for absolutely nothing.

When I reminded myself how disappointed my mother would be at finding her Pollyanna with nothing to be glad over, I told myself to shut up.

Since Nick had the kids for a couple days, I did the Black Friday sales but ended up going home with nothing that had actually been on sale, all of which I put on Nick's credit card. The claustrophobic crowds nearly drowned me. I almost called Jessica a dozen times. I bought a tree, pulled down the green tubs from the space in the garage, and decorated the tree by myself—all while listening to Christmas music and swiping at my eyes and nose, which hadn't stopped running since the kids left with Nick the day before.

Nick never came in with the kids when he dropped them off, so I knew I wouldn't have to face him, but for whatever reason, I couldn't bear to face *them* either. I didn't want to see the joy in their eyes from the holiday they'd had without me. I went into my room, locked the door, and turned out the light.

Hiding.

That's what I was doing.

Hiding from the pain of life under 1500 thread count Egyptian cotton sheets. I hoped Nick only had 200 thread count cheap sheets in his new apartment. I hoped they were scratchy and miserable to sleep in.

I heard the front door open and the kids call out a merry, "We're home!"

No answer could come from lips pressed tightly together.

And I once again thought of the book *Asher Lev* and the mother hiding in her bed—hiding inside the dark, cool refuge of her own mind.

What are you doing, Livvy? Your children need you.

But my body refused to pull itself from the covers.

"Mom?" The thump of feet on the stairs.

"She decorated the house by herself," Chad observed.

"Without us?" Mandy sounded indignant.

How dare I decorate the house without them when they ate turkey and yams without me?

Get up, Livvy. Show them a smile. Show them their world is still right.

My legs trembled to do as commanded, but the emotional pain shooting through my nervous system won out, and my legs stopped trying.

A knock at the door. "Mom?" Mandy.

A rattle of the locked handle. "Mom?" Chad.

"Mom? You're scaring us!" Mandy.

"Where's Mom?" Marie.

Was she chewing her sleeve?

"Is Mom even home?" Tyler. "Maybe she's not home." He didn't sound like he believed it, but that it was the sliver of hope he chose to cling to over the reality of the locked door.

They had faced the locked door before.

More knocking. More calls for me to come out.

"I told you we shouldn't have gone with Dad. She doesn't have anywhere to go. We left her alone!" Mandy. "She's probably OD'd in there."

"Don't be stupid! Mom wouldn't do that to us!" Chad.

Mandy had told them to stay with me?

It was a shaft of light dispelling the darkness.

Chad had faith I wouldn't leave them. Mandy had *wanted* to stay with me.

My legs trembled and finally pushed out from under the covers.

My feet whispered over the plush fibers of carpet.

The door lock clicked. The door swung open to reveal their wide, frightened eyes. "Sorry, guys! I must've fallen asleep and didn't hear you come in." I yawned the lie. I hadn't slept for two days. "Have you been home very long? And did you bring me any pie?"

Mandy smiled her relief and nodded. "Dad stopped by the bakery because he said Nan didn't know how to make a pie like you did. It's on the kitchen counter right now."

So we went downstairs and ate Nick's peace offering that didn't remotely fill the hunger in my heart. Mandy and Chad watched me carefully. Marie held my hand or my arm or my leg or whatever part of me she could manage. Tyler laughed and cut the pie and served it for everyone. He cleaned up the dishes without being asked, and he hugged me extra tight before going to his room when it came time to sleep.

I'd gotten out of bed.

Without Nick to tug on my hand and make me get up.

And I realized something I'd never known about myself before.

Strength existed inside of me—strength that wasn't Nick's but that belonged to me and me alone.

Good to know.

* * *

Everything seemed a little easier after that. Nick called the kids every night and asked permission from me before he took them out the two times he'd wanted them. I asked him to take them while I went to book club.

I'd dressed for book club in a hurry, having packed Nick and the kids a dinner for their outing. If he could offer a pie, I could offer a whole meal.

It wasn't competition, exactly.

That's what I told myself while I baked and packaged to the very best of my abilities.

It was just me showing my family I cared.

And Nick was still my family, even if he did take off his shoes on the other side of town. I'd spent so much time preparing the food for them that preparing myself wasn't an option. I'd have to look disheveled. I hoped the ladies wouldn't judge what they saw.

I pulled up into Ruby's driveway, and my jaw dropped at the elaborate Christmas lights. Did she hire those out? She must have. A woman her age shouldn't be up on ladders stringing lights across gabled rooflines. Even at my age, no one would ever catch me climbing ladders for Christmas lights. That was one of the major perks of having a teenage son.

Some part of me wanted to back my car up and drive away. How could I go in and talk to anyone when my insides felt flayed open?

I shoved the stick into reverse and then growled and shoved it back into park. I'd chosen the book. And I'd shoved off the responsibility of treat preparation to Ilana. Not showing up would be tacky and rude.

Besides, not showing up to the book club would mean turning around and heading back to the empty house.

I turned the car off and pulled the key from the ignition. *Let it all go, Livvy. Give yourself permission to not think about it for just a couple hours. Life'll still be there when this evening's over.*

I walked up the path of lit candy canes and smiled at the wreath that spanned a good portion of the door—both horizontally and vertically. My mother would have loved such an ostensive display of the holidays.

Ruby answered the door, and the scent of spicy apples rolled over me. Wassail. At least I hoped so. Ruby hugged me tightly, and when she moved to let me go, I clung to her a little longer—using her as a fill-in for the mother I desperately needed. Having my husband living under a different roof validated that need.

"Your sweater is so soft!" I remarked as she closed the door behind me, as if a soft sweater excused me hugging her like a crazy lady.

"Thank you!" she said. "I love this season because it gives me an excuse to wear it."

The season? I blinked until I realized her red sweater matched the red in her earrings and the red in all the bows she had in her front entryway. Of course. Everyone would likely be dressed in Christmas finery. And here I was wearing my laundry day clothes—the ones I only wore when everything else was still sitting in a hamper I hadn't had time to get to. The pants were tight and uncomfortable, and the top was pink.

Not Christmassy. Not even cute. I felt the warm flush of embarrassment but smiled in spite of it. Nothing to be done for it now. I had the choice between preparing a fun picnic and dressing to impress. I didn't regret my choice. They might be eating the dinner I prepared now . . . would Nick notice that it was all his favorites?

Don't think about them. Just get through two hours.

At least that's what I told myself when I entered the living room to find Daisy and Ilana dressed as festively as Ruby. Well, maybe not *as* festively, but at least they didn't look like they'd been dressed by a blind person.

I fixed the smile on my face and stepped farther into the room to talk to Daisy and Ilana. "Hi, guys. How are you doing?"

They both assured me they were fine.

"How was your Thanksgiving?" Daisy asked.

I stopped breathing for a moment. "Thanksgiving?" The word was a rush of air forced over my windpipes. "Fine." I nodded. "Just fine. Yours?"

She smirked. "It was what it was. Not the best day ever but not the worst either."

I allowed a real smile to replace my false one. "Yeah. I understand it not being the best day ever." I gave myself a shake before I went into a long and horridly detailed list of events that had made my personal holiday a nightmare of mythic proportions and turned to Ilana. "How about you? Please tell me one of us had a spectacular holiday."

And then I blinked, wishing I could bite back my words. I had many Jewish friends, but it had never occurred to me to ask if any of them celebrated Thanksgiving. I hoped I hadn't offended Ilana.

She smiled. "It was a good day. Maybe not spectacular . . . That's a tough order to fill, but it wasn't wretched." She didn't appear bothered by my question and hadn't corrected my assumption that she celebrated Thanksgiving.

Shannon showed up, and Ilana moved away from where Daisy and I were talking to greet her.

I shifted and wondered why I hadn't headed back to the movie theater after all. I was in no condition to be in the company of other people. It was one thing to find the strength to pull myself from my bed for my children, but this? This was an entirely new level of insanity.

"I love your polish," Daisy said.

It took me a brief second to recognize that Daisy meant my toenail polish. I'd worn sandals with my jeans, which drew even more attention to the fact that I was completely out of place. Daisy's compliment nearly brought me to tears. I needed so much for *someone* to say *something* kind. I almost pulled her into a hug. "Oh, thanks." I looked down at my pink toes and smiled. "I didn't realize until after I chose my color that I should have chosen something a little more Christmassy."

"Ah," she waved her hand as if her statement hadn't been the lifeline I now clung to. "There's room for pink in every holiday."

Do you have any idea how you've saved me in this moment? I wanted to ask. Instead I blinked back the shine that surely filled my eyes and smiled my gratitude.

Paige showed up not too long after; then the doorbell rang again, and Ruby ushered Athena in. I flashed a warm smile at Athena. Poor girl—losing her mother. I knew what that loss was. I waved to her, but Paige was the one who crossed the room to intercept Athena. "How are you?" Paige's youthful face pinched up in concern. I stopped midsentence in whatever I was saying to Daisy so I could hear Athena's response.

"Doing better," she said. "Thanks again for coming to my mom's funeral." She paused a moment. "It really meant a lot to see you all there."

She looked at each of us in turn who'd been to the funeral. And even though she looked better than she had on the day of the funeral, there were dark circles under her eyes. She'd applied her make-up fairly thickly. Athena didn't strike me as a caked-on make-up kind of girl. So why now? What was with the thick coat of base—especially around her eyes?

Was she trying to hide the dark indicators of no sleep circling her eyes?

Ilana murmured some sort of condolences, but I wasn't listening well enough to hear it. I watched Athena—watched and worried.

It felt good to worry about someone else. To take a moment off from self-pity so I could spread some sympathy to another.

The doorbell rang once more, which surprised me because we were all already there—even Shannon was there. Ruby bustled off to the door and brought back a newcomer to the book club.

"Ladies, I'd like you to meet Victoria Winters." Ruby kept her arm around Victoria. Victoria surveyed us from a set of beautiful brown eyes. She had on a green headscarf that held her hair back away from her face, highlighting regal, high-set cheekbones under her milk-chocolate-colored skin.

Victoria was stunning, as in take-a-second-look, breath-caught-in-your-throat stunning.

Her green blouse matched her head scarf. Even the new girl knew to wear Christmas colors.

"Victoria has assured me she's a great reader and ready to dive into whatever we're in the middle of," Ruby said.

Victoria laughed—laughed like it was always the first reaction she had to anything. "I was really excited when Ruby invited me to the club. I hope I can contribute a little and not bore you all to death."

We joined in her laughter. It was easy to do. Ruby playfully swatted Victoria's arm. "She's far from boring. She works in the film industry and has some amazing—and horrific—stories."

"That's true." Victoria settled herself on a chair. "But before telling you any of them, I'll need you all to sign a nondisclosure form."

Everyone laughed—immediately put at ease by this newcomer. The film industry. Now *that* was something interesting.

"Well!" Ruby clapped her hands. "Let's get started." She glanced at us all with absolute delight. "Anyone have anything new to share?"

My heart dropped into my intestines somewhere. She wanted us to share news? I genuinely liked these women, but to tell them about my husband moving out? I hadn't told anyone—not that I had anyone to really share the news with. I let out a slight laugh that came out as a nervous bray. "Not much going on here . . ." I said.

"Yep. Same as usual," Paige agreed. She said it too fast, like me. My reason for nervous fast speaking was that I'd outright lied. My world had been knocked off its axis. Did Paige have the same problem? Had something happened in her life that she needed help with?

I hoped not. I genuinely liked Paige.

Daisy appeared as unrevealing as Paige and I had been. Victoria shrugged and said with a wry grin, "Since it's my first time here, everything about me is new. Trust me; you don't really want all the details at once."

Victoria had a way about her. She calmed me. She was a walking lullaby. She put people at ease. Even Ilana and Shannon gravitated toward Victoria, although Ilana and Shannon also refused to tell anything newsworthy about their lives, whether they'd been put at ease or not. Ilana smiled politely but did little more than bob her head.

Athena, on the other hand, had come with the intention to talk. "Last time I was here, I made an announcement about my pitiful dating life." She smiled wider, her eyes widening at the same time as her mouth, as if even she were surprised by what she was about to say. "The fact is, things have turned around. I'm dating a man named Grey Ronning."

"From the bookstore?" Ruby said, clapping her hands together. Dang, I loved that she did that!

"Yes."

"That's simply wonderful," Ruby exclaimed.

I couldn't have agreed more. A new relationship in light of what Athena had lost would definitely do her some good—even if nothing serious came out of it. Having someone there beside you made all the difference. I thought about Nick again. Losing my mother would have been so much worse if he hadn't been there to pick up all my shattered pieces.

Everyone was quick to offer congratulations and sly little comments about Santa bringing a man for Christmas. When we'd finally quieted down, Ruby brought us back to order. "Keep us updated, Athena. This is no small news." She turned to me. "Now, let's start with Livvy, who chose the book. What are your thoughts on *My Name is Asher Lev*?"

I opened my copy, where I'd made a few notes. I knew I'd be leading the discussion because I'd chosen the book and so came prepared, as much as preparation was possible in my current state of insanity.

I cleared my throat. "This book seems to revolve around the suffering caused from conflicting traditions. The story really deals with the decisions these three people made in their lives that ended up affecting not only their traditions but the people they loved the most. And yet . . . none of them could have chosen differently or they would have been betraying themselves." I took a breath.

Athena opened the book she had on her lap. "After a few pages, I actually started underlining some of the sentences." She scowled slightly and bit her lip. "The relationship between Asher and his father really affected me." She looked up. "You see, my mother was always pushing me to get married—to a Greek man. Time after time, I dated men who didn't have marriage potential for me. Maybe it was a rebellious act to show my mom I could make my own decisions."

"Is the bookstore guy Greek?" Daisy asked.

"No," Athena answered slowly. Daisy nodded at the answer, but Athena went on. "When Asher goes against his parents' wishes to not only become a painter but to paint the crucifixion, I guess I was reminded of myself. Listen to what he says." She hesitated while scanning the page. "'I turned my back to the paintings and closed my eyes, for I could no longer endure seeing the works of my own hands and knowing the pain those works would soon inflict upon people I loved.'"

Silence filled the room.

"I guess it really hit me hard," Athena continued when no one else said anything. "I was doing the same thing. Living a life or, more accurately, rejecting a life those who loved me wanted me to have." She blinked back the shine. "I don't want to turn my back anymore. Although I don't know if marriage or children are in my future, I'm willing to open my heart at least and consider the option."

I understood what she meant and leaned over to pat her hand and offer encouragement.

"I found some letters my dad wrote to my mom," Athena said. No amount of blinking could stop the obvious tears at that point, and I noticed Daisy's eyes were getting a little wet too. "Their marriage wasn't what I thought it was. They had their challenges but loved each other dearly." Athena swiped at her wet cheeks. "What I saw as a child was only a glimpse. I misunderstood greatly."

"Isn't that true of many things in life?" Paige asked in a quiet voice. "We go around assuming we know or understand another person. When we find out the truth, our whole perception changes, for better—or for worse."

I knew about worse too. Nick had shown me worse. But hadn't he also shown me better?

"This book is filled with layers of family dynamics," I added, thinking about all the layers of my own family. "Each character has intense flaws, yet you can't help but relate and understand their motivations for doing what they do, even when it tears down another family member."

"Families are sticky," Victoria said.

Her words made me think of the conversation I'd had with Mandy. *Families are sticky sometimes, but if we make sticky work to our advantage and stick together . . . well then . . . we'd be something magnificent,* I'd told her. But I'd since discovered that *sticky* and *sticking* weren't the same thing.

Ilana weighed, having been raised in a Jewish home. She seemed very analytical about the whole thing, as if she had merely observed the goings on of her childhood rather than experienced them for herself.

Victoria hadn't brought a copy of the book but jumped into the conversation. "You know when Asher got into trouble with the Mashpia, which I took to mean as his school principal—I didn't take the time to look it up . . ." She glanced at Ilana who nodded as if to say, *close enough*.

Victoria continued. "So this Mashpia is talking to Asher when he's in trouble for drawing a rabbi on his scriptures . . ." Victoria frowned and leaned over to Paige. "Can I borrow your book for a second?"

Paige relinquished her book, and Victoria flipped pages until she found what she was looking for. "Here it is. So this Mashpia says, 'Many people feel they are in possession of a great gift. But one does not always give in to a gift. One does with a life not only what is precious to one's self but to one's own people. That is the way our people live.' Don't you think that's sad?" She handed Paige her book back. "To have a gift and not use it because you might feel selfish doing something that makes you happy? I'm around artists all day: writers, directors, actors, set designers, costume designers. They use their gifts because it makes them happy. The side benefit is that their art makes other people happy too. I guess I just don't understand Mashpia's attitude."

Ruby beamed brighter than the decorations on her house. "You read the book!"

Victoria shrugged. "Told you I'd jump in wherever you were all at."

After that, everyone talked about art and what art meant to them until Ruby, sensing we were winding down, said, "Paige has the next book selection; would you like to tell us a little about it?"

"Sure." Paige nodded. "I chose a classic that some of you might have read in high school or college. *Silas Marner* by George Eliot."

"Oh, I love that one," Ruby said. "It's definitely worth reading more than once."

I'd never heard of the book, let alone read it. I felt a little dumb for them to talk about it being a classic when I hadn't even heard of it.

Ruby and Paige entered a lively conversation about how the author was really a woman when Daisy, tugging at her shirt, caught my eye. She acted as if she felt uncomfortable with her choice of wardrobe, which was crazy since she looked great. And after all . . . she hadn't worn *her* laundry-day outfit. I thought about how nice she was to make me feel comfortable at the first of the meeting and wanted to return the favor. "I think those kinds of shirts are so cute, Daisy. But I can't wear them; any time I try, I totally look pregnant."

Daisy didn't look pregnant. She looked adorable, which is what I *meant* to say but not how it came out at all. With a jolt, I realized my words sounded wrong entirely.

"I wonder if you are," Ruby said, practically bouncing with the idea of a baby. "How exciting!"

Daisy smiled but didn't look very happy. I wanted to crawl into a hole for bringing it up. "I'm *not* pregnant; trust me," Daisy said in a tone that left no room for argument. "I got that taken care of permanently fifteen years ago, remember? I can't get pregnant."

Ruby went on as if she hadn't heard Daisy's tone, or words, at all. "I had a friend back in '87 who had a tubal ligation, and then ten years later, poof! There she was, expecting a surprise little caboose! He's a teenager now."

"That's pretty rare," Daisy said with a faint chuckle. "I'll just make a point of not wearing this shirt again."

Then I really felt bad. I'd meant to compliment Daisy, not insult her—which I'd obviously done.

"Well, let's serve up the dessert." Ruby moved to her feet. "Or rather, the refreshments, since potato latkes aren't sweet. Ilana brought them for Livvy. Wasn't that nice of her?"

It was nice of her. I wished I'd known how to make latkes so I could have brought them, but it would've been foolish not to take advantage of Ilana's firsthand knowledge. I had just bitten into a forkful of latke when Paige turned to Athena and asked about her father. I didn't exactly mean to eavesdrop but leaned in closer to hear the answer.

"It's getting harder," she whispered. "He doesn't sleep well and usually thinks I'm my aunt Fran, his younger sister. I don't know how my mother did it by herself for so long. Since I've stepped in, it feels like it's all been downhill. I can't work as much as I need to, so I'm always behind, and I can't seem to get a routine figured out to save my life."

That explained the extra make-up and the blue-ish rings around her eyes. She wasn't sleeping at all, poor girl. To add that burden to losing her mother?

Athena tried to smile, but it didn't look like a smile so much as it did a grimace. "My sister thinks we should put him in a care center now. But it's so expensive, and this is a bad time of the year to put my parents' house on the market."

"Had your mother ever talked about a care center?" I asked.

"Not that she told us." She shoved her food around her plate with her fork.

"Have you checked into any of them?" Daisy asked.

"It might be worth looking into," Paige added.

I almost felt bad that we were all sort of ganging up on her, but caring for someone with late stages of Alzheimer's wasn't easy—or even safe, especially for a single woman to handle on her own. I'd heard stories that made my hair stand on end.

Athena took a shuddering breath. "I looked up a couple of locations, but I feel so . . ." She tilted her head up and stared at the ceiling. "Guilty. I'm his daughter; he raised me and took care of me my whole life. I'm the only one who can really take care of him—my sister has three kids. It's not his fault my mother is gone; I have to take her place as best I can. I just can't bring myself to put him away."

"You're not putting him away," Paige said quickly.

"Nursing homes are awful," Ruby declared.

"Not all nursing homes are the same," Paige contradicted, which heightened tensions enough to make me duck my head and not meet either Paige's eye or Ruby's. "Back in Utah we had a care center that my church provided worship services for. It was beautiful, and the residents were happy there. The thing is, your mom was his caretaker, and she did what she thought was best. You're his caretaker now, and it's not wrong to make a choice in both of your best interests."

Athena nodded, which meant she was considering the option.

We finished our dessert in relative silence, aside from a few murmurs of compliment on the latkes. Ruby tried to get Athena to eat more, saying Athena was too skinny. No one urged me to take seconds, but

I took more anyway. Why not? It wasn't like I had anyone at home to impress with my body.

I left book club feeling lighter. The kids were staying at their dad's for the night, which they all loved since they had to crash in sleeping bags in the living room, which felt like camping to them. But even knowing they wouldn't be there when I arrived home didn't fill me with the hollow ache that usually nibbled away at me when they weren't there. Attending book club had been a good choice as it seemed it would sustain me through an entire night.

Chapter 13

Every day leading to Christmas seemed like I was waiting for the proverbial shoe to drop. And I wasn't even all that sure what that phrase meant. What did dropping a shoe have to do with anything? I'd found some strength on my own, but was it enough to keep me moving through Christmas without my kids?

If Nick took them for Christmas, I wasn't sure what would happen to me.

I didn't bring it up to him when we saw each other in passing. I couldn't bear the idea of him taking them, and yet, what would I say if he wanted them?

DeeAnn called once to ask how the kids were, but it felt like she was really calling to see if I'd be a wreck after having Nick gone for this long. I was polite and even pleasant with her. *I will not give that woman the satisfaction of seeing me come apart,* I thought as I laughed and talked about how great Chad's play had been. He'd been a wonderful Professor Higgins. I made sure to bring it up since DeeAnn hadn't bothered to come to the play of her own grandson despite the fact she had nothing going on and lived a short drive away. It was petty, sure, but I would talk to my minister about my sins later.

I hadn't started reading the book club book yet—hadn't even bought it—and had decided I'd get to it today once the chores were done and the kids were home. I'd make it an outing. We could all get a book and maybe read them together by the fire. The image made me smile and feel warmth from a fire that didn't even exist yet.

I'd just finished the dishes when my phone rang. I wiped my fingertips on the towel that hung from the oven handle and compulsively checked the caller ID, hoping it would be Nick's name on the screen so he could tell me he loved me and was moving back and that he would go to Kohl's party after all. But it wasn't Nick. And even if it had been, his saying all those things was as likely as my sprouting an eye in the middle of my forehead.

It was Paige.

"Hi, Paige," I said once I'd hit the talk button and wedged the phone between my shoulder and ear so I could pour the cleaner into the tray and close the dishwasher. "What's up?"

She wasn't bothered by the fact that I knew it was her before answering the phone. The beauty of the young. They took for granted things like knowing who was calling before picking up a phone. At my age, that was still something to get used to.

"I really need some help." She sounded near panic.

I shut the door of the dishwasher with a click and gave my full attention to the phone call. "What's going on?"

"It's Daisy. She's . . . well, she's pregnant."

I blinked. Hadn't seen that one coming—not after all the protesting she'd done when I'd insulted her shirt. I still felt sick about that.

She explained that Daisy was at work and was in a dark place due to some pretty awful happenings in her office with her coworker and needed someone desperately. "She shouldn't be alone at a time like this. Can you help?"

"I'm free all afternoon." I grabbed my car keys from the dish and my purse from the counter. "Well, except for grocery shopping and sorting laundry, but all that can totally wait. As long as I'm home by four, I'm good."

"I'll call later to see how she's doing and what she might still need," Paige said.

"Great. I'm heading over now." I sighed deeply. Was no one's life sparkly clean and happy? "Poor Daisy."

"No kidding. Thanks for stepping in, Livvy. You're the best."

"Any time." It felt good to be needed, to be trusted with something huge like Daisy's situation. With my life falling apart and Christmas looming in the next week, I desperately needed to know that I was necessary—that I wasn't a background character in my own life. And this? Daisy pregnant? She had been so adamant that she would never have children. She was planning out her retirement and life with just her husband again. This news had to be devastating to someone who was looking forward to being on her own.

I found the office building where Daisy worked, rushed onto the elevator, and tapped my foot impatiently as it slowly ascended to her floor.

I found Daisy in her office after a quick chat with her boss and after a secretary pointed me in the right direction. Her head was on her desk, and the contents of her purse looked like they'd been emptied by a junkie looking for cash to buy more drugs. "Oh, honey . . ." I said upon seeing her. I rounded her desk and put my hand on her back briefly before stuffing the contents on the desk back into her large purse. I wasn't sure if everything I'd picked up actually belonged in the purse, but Daisy didn't stop me, so I went with anything that looked logical. "You're going home," I said.

She shook her head. "I can't until—"

"I already told your boss. Can you walk?" I didn't wait for an answer but instead tugged her gently to her feet. I put my arm around her and led her out of her office. She didn't protest, just followed along with me. People stared as I led her back to the front desk and the elevators, but I smiled and nodded at them as we passed.

"Are you okay to drive?" I asked once we'd reached the parking garage. She nodded, and with little other choice, I folded her into the driver's seat of her car and shut her up inside before crossing over to my own.

Daisy had barely said anything. She looked blank, as if shock had taken over and her ability to process had fled altogether. I really worried about her driving but watched closely as I followed to make sure she didn't have any troubles. I parked behind her in her driveway.

"You haven't eaten lunch, have you?" I asked once we were in her house. It was still early enough in the day that it seemed unlikely she'd taken care of feeding herself. She glanced at the clock and then shook her head.

That was good news indeed because it saved me from having to just idly stare at her while twiddling my thumbs. Meal preparation was something I could handle.

"Why don't you lie down? I'll have something ready in a jiffy."

She nodded but kept the motion small, as if she were nursing the worst headache ever, and shuffled to her feet. She made her way down the hall into what I assumed was her bedroom.

I could hear her cry—it sounded like the quiet mewling of a new kitten taken from its mother, sort of sad and pathetic. I closed my eyes and said a quick prayer for her. *Please, God, Daisy needs You so much right now.*

The quick prayer of strength for Daisy actually made me feel a little better myself. And I turned to the cupboards to scavenge for ingredients that would make a nutritious meal for a woman and her baby.

I smiled when I found the can of tuna. *God is looking out for you, Daisy. I have the tuna can to prove it.*

I hurried to mix the fishy chunks with salad dressing, adding a shot of red wine vinegar and a small dollop of relish. I wasn't a huge fan of tuna and found it necessary to hide the fishy flavor in other things.

In the fridge, I found some not exactly fresh but still edible spinach leaves and smiled again. Daisy would definitely need some iron about now. I put the sandwich together. I added a few baby carrots on the plate for good measure. I wasn't hungry and *really* didn't want tuna, but it seemed weird to consider watching her eat alone. It would probably put her more at ease if we were eating together like a little luncheon.

I swallowed hard and forced myself to make another sandwich—adding an extra dollop of relish. I hadn't eaten tuna since I was pregnant with Marie. I didn't miss it at all.

Voilà! Lunch.

And it had taken fewer than ten minutes. I wandered back to where I'd seen Daisy disappear. I knocked lightly on the doorframe. "Hey there . . . sorry you didn't get longer to rest, but lunch is ready."

Daisy pulled herself up with a visible reluctance, half dragging herself to the table, where I'd placed one of the two sandwiches, and slumping into a chair.

"Tuna with spinach leaves." I lifted the top piece of bread from one of the sandwiches to show Daisy and to give it a stare down before I forced myself to eat it. "I have anemia issues, especially when I'm pregnant, and this is what my OB called a lunch of champions. I ate it every day. It's packed with protein and iron." I didn't mention to her that I had to gag it down every day. No pregnant woman needed to hear the word *gag* unless someone was trying to make her sick.

Daisy offered a smile that, though tired, also looked genuine. "Thanks," she said.

"So," I began after we'd each made our way through the first half of the sandwich. I'd already started the mental pep talk I'd had to give myself through every one of my pregnancies. *The sandwich won't win over your will. You're halfway there, Livvy. You can finish this!* "Do you know what you're having?" I cringed. Hadn't she just barely discovered she was pregnant? *Dumb question, Livvy.*

"No," she said. "I haven't been to a doctor." She hesitated. "Well, actually, I went to a doctor this morning, but it didn't work out."

I put my sandwich down, promising myself the sandwich hadn't won, and looked at her. I'd never heard of a doctor's appointment not working out. "What didn't work out?"

"The doctor." She nibbled another bite, chewed, swallowed, and said, "If it hadn't happened to me, I would be sure it was a poorly written soap opera episode."

"Really?" That sounded bad. I didn't want to pry, but I did want to help. Turned out I didn't even have to ask any questions or coax her into doing the talking that I knew in my heart would do her some good. She began the story on her own. She must have known that talking would do her some good too.

"There's a girl at my work, Amy. She and her husband have been trying to have kids for like . . . forever. I told her I was pregnant, and what kills me? What really kills me is that I worried about telling her. I worried myself sick over hurting her because I know how bad she wants this!" She put her hands on her stomach and shook her head.

"But she took it great. She acted perfectly fine. She had me so impressed with how grown-up and kind she was to me. She even referred me to her OB because she said he 'handled special cases' like mine." She tapped her toe wildly on the tiled floor. "So I made an appointment with her OB and then told her how Paul wouldn't even talk to me about the baby, so she offered to come with me to my appointment so I wouldn't have to go alone." Tears welled up in Daisy's eyes.

It killed me to hear that Paul wouldn't go to the doctor's appointment for his own child. For all Nick's faults, there hadn't been one appointment he'd missed. He'd been there with me every step of the way.

She shook her head sadly. "I so didn't want to be alone. Again."

I wanted to prompt her to continue, to reach out and hug her, but instead let her go at her own pace. She almost acted like she'd forgotten I was there to hear the story she relayed.

She sniffed. "So anyway . . . Turns out she tricked me. She set me up with her doctor so the two of them could talk me into—into adoption."

I was pretty sure I gasped. I covered my mouth with my hand, shocked and horrified by the tale. "That's so awful," I said, though *awful* didn't begin to describe that kind of betrayal from someone you thought was your friend. "You poor thing."

She gave a short nod of admittance to the awfulness of it and took another bite of her sandwich.

My mind swam through all the details. The girl's desperation to have a child almost made me feel some degree of sympathy for her. Desperate people did desperate things. But the doctor? The doctor was in serious breach of professionalism. "I bet you could turn him into the medical board for that," I said finally. "That's a horrible thing for him to have done."

"I suppose I could," she said with a deep breath, "but I'm not sure I have the energy."

"And you still need to go to a doctor," I informed her in my best bossy mommy voice. "Paige said you were about fifteen weeks?"

"Closer to seventeen, I think, but I'm so big." She framed her belly with her hands. "Maybe I'm further along than that." She stared at her belly as though she expected an alien to pop out and tap dance on the table.

I'd missed these stages of pregnancy with Jessica—things were so awkward after Nick walked out of her wedding. I could've been there for her—been a good *mom* to her. But I'd failed her and in so doing failed myself. I'd missed bonding with a beautiful young woman as she entered motherhood. My own mother would have wept to know how I'd failed.

Daisy finally looked up from her belly. I gave her a half smile.

"You make a cute pregnant woman," I said, grateful even more to be there for another beautiful woman entering a new phase of motherhood.

"I don't know about that," she said, obviously embarrassed by a compliment. She pulled at the purple top, which reminded me of when I'd told her I looked pregnant in baby-doll shirts and made her uncomfortable. Now I was the one blushing, still feeling awful that I'd made her feel bad.

"Paul's never liked me in purple," she said softly. "He once called it a color for old ladies and little girls." She laughed, as if there were something funny about her wearing the color her husband didn't like on a day she'd needed him and he hadn't been there. He hadn't been there. So what difference did it make that she wore something he didn't like?

"It's always been one of my favorite colors though, so he's learned to deal with it."

I thought about my hair. I hated my hair but kept this ghastly fake blonde because Nick liked it. But what difference did it make to him when he never saw it? I was the one still looking in the mirror every day, dealing with a head of hideous hair. Maybe it was time to change that.

"How many children do you have, Livvy?" Daisy asked, pulling me from my silent revelations.

"Four—of my own, at least. Nick has two kids from his first marriage, but they're grown. His oldest has two kids of her own." *Two grandkids I barely see, and when I do see them, I cause friction in my own family. I've had to abandon them for the sake of marriage preservation, and the marriage crumbled anyway.*

"Oh wow, you're a grandma." She sounded genuinely surprised. I tried to smile to hide my internal thoughts. "You're not old enough; do you love it?" she asked.

"I think I *would* love it." The smile left me. "I don't get to see them much. Nick has been a little . . . hard on his kids." I shifted uncomfortably and stared at the half sandwich still left on my plate.

"Oh." She looked worried about me, which was just silly. Daisy had enough to deal with on her own. What she did not need was for me to have a breakdown over my husband leaving me.

"I'd have loved to have more." I changed the subject to something that wasn't Nick and tore the crust off the remaining half of my sandwich, determined to finish it no matter what. "Just wasn't in the cards for me though."

Daisy frowned, looked down at her plate, and took another bite. I wondered if she hated tuna too and was just too nice to say anything. But it had been in her cupboard, and even if she did hate it, the nutrients were as good for her as they had been for me. Pregnancies were no picnic, no matter who you were. A woman who can't have babies complains she's barren, and another complains because she has to eat crummy tuna or she has morning sickness or toddlers trashing her living room.

"It's funny how that works, isn't it?" I said, partially voicing my thoughts.

She hurried to swallow. "What?"

"Pregnancy and babies. I can't think of a single woman I know who has exactly what she wants in regard to that. It seems everyone wants more or fewer than they have."

She surveyed me as if looking at me anew. "You enjoy being a mom, don't you, Livvy?"

I almost laughed at that. She totally called it. "I do—well, most of the time. The whole teenager thing is taking its toll on me, but I really do enjoy being their mom, even when they hate me."

"I can't imagine your kids hating you." She shook her head like the idea was insane.

But she didn't know what had happened with Mandy. She didn't know how my relationship with Mandy was still strained even though we had talked about it. Mandy had always held Nick accountable for his own behavior until Nick had walked out. Then, suddenly, his behavior was all my fault. How had that happened?

"Oh." I laughed. "Trust me, they do. Just like I hated my mother, and my mother hated hers—at least for a while. Part of growing up, I suppose. Don't you have a teenage daughter?"

"Yes, and an older one," she said. She told me about her two daughters, December and Stormy. December had recently had a new little boy of her own whom she'd named Tennyson, which I thought was just the most adorable name I'd ever heard. I'd always been a sucker for poetry.

"So you're a grandma too." I grinned at her. "We're definitely too young to be running around with people calling us Grandma. I could've sworn I needed to be collecting social security before I got that title."

Daisy laughed—a sound I was growing to love.

I talked about my own kids then, telling her about everything they did that made me laugh and even a few things they did that made me crazy.

"You love your kids a whole lot," she observed.

"I do." I nodded my agreement. "They're my world."

I would still be hiding in that bed if they hadn't pounded on that stupid door.

"I wish I were more like that," she said with a tone that sounded frighteningly like envy. "I'm not sure I ever really enjoyed my own kids the way I could have."

"Then it must be exciting to have another chance." I nodded at her stomach and smiled. "I sometimes think about what a better mother I would be now, as opposed to when I was in my twenties with so much growing up left to do." I wished I'd been a better mother to Nick's kids. My conscience pricked at me every day over that—especially now that

I realized how letting it get out of hand the way I had led us all to this place of separation.

"That's a good point," she said.

"So is your husband getting used to the idea?" I felt awful that he hadn't gone to the appointment when she so needed someone with her. And then to have it turn out to be the ultimate friend betrayal . . .

Daisy looked at her plate again. I felt bad that I kept asking questions that kept her from looking me in the eye. She shook her head. "I'm not sure he's going to stick it out." Her eyes widened as if she were stunned to have said such a thing.

I was also shocked. Shocked because that same fear continually ran through my whole soul with my own husband. What would I do if he didn't stick it out? I loved Nick. I really, genuinely loved him. For all his faults, all the silence, and all my working to please when he seemed incapable of pleasing, I loved him. And yet, we never communicated. He said we were going to work on things, but we didn't work on anything. I blinked rapidly, trying to keep myself from throwing a pity party while Daisy sat here needing someone to worry about her. She looked up and caught me blinking back tears. I tried to smile, but I wasn't good at false smiles. "I'm sorry," I whispered. She was alone with a new baby coming. Her alone was worse than mine. "No wonder this is so hard for you."

She nodded. And with that motion, her head swayed as though she were simply too tired to hold it up anymore.

I slid my chair back. The tuna sandwich won this round; I would've rather swallowed my own tongue than consume another bite. I took Daisy's hand and helped her to her feet. "Let's get you back to bed. It's been a long day, and you need rest."

She didn't argue, which must have meant she was more tired than I'd thought. I led her to her room and waited until she'd slid under her covers before clicking the door shut.

I stayed until three o'clock, catching up Daisy's laundry and mopping her kitchen floor while she napped. I had to leave to be there for my kids when they came home from school. I hated to disturb her but didn't want her to wake up, find me gone, and feel any sense of abandonment. So before I left, I stopped at her door, knocked lightly, and said, "Hey, Daisy, I've got to get going now. Can I get anything for you before I take off?

Daisy got up and gave me a hug, peeking out into the hallway where the basket of folded laundry sat. "No. You've been great. I can't believe you cleaned and everything. Honestly, Livvy, I don't know how you did all this."

"It's what I do." I shrugged, feeling a little lame over the compliment. "I love it; it makes me feel connected to the people I care about." I hoped she would understand that she made the list of people I cared about.

"My mom's like that," she said. "Always doing stuff for people."

"Sounds like my kind of woman." And even as I said it, I thought of my own mom and her Heaven Reminders. *My mom was like that too*, I wanted to say. I'd learned from the very best and fell so far short of all she'd accomplished that it shamed me.

"Thank you," she said, her eyes filled with genuine gratitude. "I know it couldn't have been easy for you to give up your entire afternoon, but I feel so much better. I was in a very dark place."

"I know all about dark places." My mom's death had been a dark place. Nick's leaving was a dark place. I really hated dark places. "And it's often someone else who needs to help you get out of it. I'm glad I could be that hand for you to grab on to. You call if you need anything at all, okay?"

"I will."

"Promise?" I gave her the look that meant I expected a promise that would be kept.

She laughed and got the eye shine. "I promise."

As I made my way home, I pondered over the entire day's events. I'd told her that someone else needed to help get you out of dark places. Nick had been there when my mom had died, but with Nick gone, who would get me out of this? I would have leaned on Daisy a bit for support, except she needed it more than I did.

Maybe Athena?

But she'd just lost her own mother. Considering that fact made the hairs on the back of my neck prick up. *I should visit her*, I thought. She very likely needed someone who understood what losing a mom was all about. I couldn't go to her with my own burdens, but I could help her with hers.

Call Paige.

I snorted at that thought. Paige was a young mother with as much trouble as any of us. No, I couldn't call Paige.

The thought came to me several more times, but I shoved it aside. I would not call Paige. Instead, I sent an e-mail with an update on Daisy and no updates about myself.

Chapter 14

Jessica called at about the same time I arrived home to tell me she'd mailed the invitations to Kohl's party. "I mailed Dad's invite to his office so he would have to see it directly and couldn't just assume you'd be taking care of it," she said.

I let out a noise that might have been mistaken for a laugh over the phone. I hoped so anyway. "Good idea." I hadn't told her that he didn't live with us anymore. She would feel guilty, like it was her fault—which it most certainly was not.

"What are your plans for Christmas?" I asked, trying not to think about the holiday and yet knowing the holiday subject had to be addressed with Nick at some point. I had four days until Christmas Eve. Four days to confront him. I was putting my foot down this time. He'd had Thanksgiving. He couldn't leave me without them for Christmas. He had his mother and his father and his other kids. I really had no one else. And I couldn't spend another day at the movie theater alone.

"We're going to spend the day with Mike's parents. Mom and her husband are going on a cruise to Catalina Island, so I invited Kohl over with me. I don't want him to be alone."

Jessica referred to her stepfather as "her husband" in the same way I referred to her mom as "The Ex." I hoped she didn't have vague nicknames for me.

"What are you guys doing?" she asked.

"I don't know yet," I said, feeling hollowed with that teensy bit of confession.

"Well, call me when Dad talks to you about the invitation. I want to know how he reacts so I'm prepared for when I call him."

I nodded then spoke up because she couldn't see the nod. "I'll let you know. He has to come. He and Kohl need to make things right before Kohl goes away. They can't keep on like they are. It'll end up hurting both of them."

She agreed, and we said our good-byes. I set the phone on the counter and turned to see Mandy standing in the doorway. Her narrow eyes and tight lips meant she found no joy in whatever she'd overheard.

"Are you serious? You're still pushing him into that stupid party?" Her face darkened with her every word.

"They need to make up. You know why it's important."

"I thought you were done with all that!" she yelled.

"And I thought you finally understood." I didn't yell.

"Just let it go, Mom. Let it go before Dad decides not to come back!" She stormed off before I could answer her. And by the time I'd made it to the bottom of the stairs, her bedroom door had slammed closed.

It slammed closed hard enough that several pictures fell off the wall in the hallway that passed her room. I closed my eyes, said a quick prayer for patience so I didn't sell her to the circus for throwing a tantrum, and followed the wake of her anger.

I had to sidestep glass and found I should've said a longer prayer because patience was the last thing on my mind as I bellowed, "Amanda Robbins!" I went to open her door but realized she'd slammed it so hard, she'd cracked through the wood molding, and her door now swung out a bit into the hallway.

"You have got to be kidding me. Amanda!" I shoved at her door, making it go back inside her room where it belonged.

"Get out!" Mandy shouted. "Get out and leave me alone!"

I about yanked my hair in frustration and confusion. What I'd said on the phone was not enough to merit this sort of psychotic episode. "What is your deal? You're acting like a lunatic. And the door? How am I supposed to fix that?"

"You're ruining everything!"

"How am I ruining *any*thing? How is any of this my fault?"

She hesitated before jutting out her chin and actually answering the question. "Nan said."

"Your *grandmother* told you I was ruining everything?" I wanted to scream. That horrible old woman with her pretend Southern gentility had been the bane of my existence since she'd called my wedding day a disaster.

"Nan didn't say it to me. She told it to Dad. I just overheard her. She told him if you couldn't learn to be a team player, then he should file for—"

She didn't finish the sentence. She didn't have to.

DeeAnn had told her son to divorce his wife.

I couldn't say why that surprised me. I couldn't say why it cut into me in a way that made me feel like my insides were spilling out. I'm not sure what my face looked like that Mandy's eyes suddenly went wide, that her mouth fell open, and she started shaking her head. "I didn't . . . Mom, I'm sorry, I . . ."

I didn't stay to hear her apologies.

I marched through the door that swung out into the hallway, down the stairs, to the kitchen where my purse and keys were, and out into the garage. I didn't even tell Mandy to watch Marie and Tyler. Would she think to take that responsibility on her own?

I almost prayed again for patience as my temper flared hotter.

What did it matter to pray for patience? God had obviously abandoned me.

I peeled out of the driveway with no idea where I was running to.

Just knowing I was running.

Running from the words no one could take back.

Nick had been told to leave me.

Maybe I'd paint *evil* or *dragon lady* on the side of DeeAnn's house.

I drove around until I realized I needed to fix Mandy's door before the hinges were pulled out entirely by the abnormal swing. I could focus my energy on that because I didn't know where else to focus.

I finally stopped the car at the hardware store.

It was while glaring at the many options for wood moldings that I heard my name.

"Livvy? Livvy Allred?"

The use of my maiden name startled me. It had been a long time since I'd heard anyone call me that. I turned and saw someone I hadn't seen in nearly two decades: Alison Howell. She'd married Tony Fredericks, a guy I'd actually dated in college before he turned his affections to Alison. It wasn't a big deal when he'd started seeing her because Tony and I had already discovered we made better friends than anything else.

"It's Robbins now," I said and then swallowed hard. "Well at least it used to be. I think he wants a divorce." The flush of red heat raced up my neck all the way to my ear tips. *What possessed me to say all that?*

"Are you okay?" Her eyes were furrowed in concern. Her hand was on my shoulder, and she'd leaned down to peer into my face. "Seriously, Livvy. Are you all right?"

I shook my head, aware that suddenly my cheeks were wet. Was I crying? When had that started up? "I have to fix a door. My daughter broke the door frame molding thing. I have to fix it, and I don't even know *how* to fix it." My words came in broken sobs and shudders.

"Livvy . . . c'mon, let's find you somewhere to sit down. You should *not* be here. Hardware stores are terrible places for the brokenhearted. They just remind you of all the stuff that needs fixing."

She led me to a bench at the front of the store and made me sit down.

"What happened?" she demanded while digging around in her purse and finally pulling out a package of tissues. She gave me the package and waited while I wiped the mascara trails off my face.

I didn't go into details but instead made it all out to be a simple disagreement with my headstrong and passionately driven teenager. I tried to play it off like it was even a little funny. After all . . . Alison and I hadn't spoken since we were practically kids.

"I just need to fix the door," I kept insisting. "And it's a little overwhelming since I don't have any idea where to begin." I left out any further information about my marriage. She didn't pry, though she had to know there was more information to be had since I'd started with the divorce bombshell.

Her phone chirped, and she answered it. "I'm at the front of the store . . ." she said, then she cast a long, sad, sideways look at me. "And I'm with an old friend. Why don't you meet us up here?" She hung up and offered me a smile and a pat on my leg.

Tony Fredericks showed up a few moments later—at least a slightly balder, heavier version of the Tony Fredericks I'd known in college.

His face broke into a smile. "Is that Livvy Allred?"

"Robbins now," I said automatically and then clamped my teeth together so nothing else came out the way it had when I'd corrected Alison.

"That's right," Tony said. "I remember. What was his name again? Mark?"

"Nick."

"That's right. Nick. We went to the wedding. How you guys doing? Do you have kids?"

Tony either didn't notice my red eyes and sniffly nose or he purposely chose not to mention them. I gave one word answers. "Good" and "Four." Tony inquired after my reason for being in the hardware store, and Alison explained the situation, saving me from losing control and having another breakdown.

"I can help you with doors. C'mon. Let me show you what you need." He helped me up, and he and Alison led me back to the department with the wood moldings. He picked out a bunch of stuff and put them on a flatbed cart he'd acquired.

Tony and Alison stepped aside for a brief moment to have a quick, quiet talk, and when they turned back, they were all smiles. "I got a great idea," Tony said. "Why don't I come over to your place tomorrow and fix all this stuff for you? I'm a contractor. I totally know what I'm doing and promise not to mess anything up."

"He's really good," Alison said, nodding and smiling.

"I can't let you go to all that trouble. I can figure it out. You've been more than helpful in explaining the materials to me."

"Nope, sorry. I insist. It's my Christmas present to you."

Arguing with Tony and Alison proved impossible. They took the materials with them since Tony said he didn't trust me not to just fix it myself before he could show up.

"This isn't necessary. I promise not to touch any of it until you show up," I insisted as he loaded his truck with my purchases.

Tony laughed. "Should we believe her, Ali?"

Alison shook her head violently. "Not a chance. The Livvy I know never accepts help because she's too busy helping everyone else."

They both laughed, and my face warmed with the fact that I'd apparently been like this even back in college.

"See you tomorrow," Tony said and hopped in his truck. He and Alison drove away with my hardware, leaving me feeling grateful for their help and uncertain of what to do next. I'd managed to pause the breakdown in front of Alison, but how long could I keep that up? Going home was out of the question since the desire to hide in my bed again felt overwhelming.

I didn't know where I was headed until my car ended up parked in front of Paige's apartment building.

Go in. Talk to her. She can help.

These were the words a little voice in the back of my head whispered to me.

"She's already divorced. She's half my age, which means she has only half my experience. She has her own troubles."

These were the words I whispered back to that relentlessly calm voice.

My feet opted to listen to the voice instead of to me as they moved out of the car, up the steps, and down the hall to Paige's apartment. My hand had also gone rogue as it knocked on the door my feet had led them to.

What am I doing here?

Before I could answer that question, Paige opened her door. Her widened eyes indicated her surprise at seeing me.

I burst into tears—giving into the breakdown completely.

Chapter 15

I'm not sure how I got from the doorway to the kitchen table. Paige sat next to me, her body facing me entirely because she sat sideways on her chair. She had a hand patting me gently on the back and her voice cooing gentle noises, as if she'd found a squalling infant in need of comfort on her doorstep instead of a full-grown woman.

I spilled the story, leaving out no details, no matter how trivial or embarrassing—and all this before Paige had even asked what was wrong.

"He's leaving me." I ended with those three horrible words, and I felt hollow and stretched at the same time—a balloon completely emptied of air.

"You don't know he's leaving," she said, though she said the words through tight lips. Did my coming here force her to relive ugliness from her own divorce? "That was your mother-in-law talking. And though I don't have in-laws like that, I've heard enough stories. You can't let her be a part of this. This is between you and your husband, not you and some disgruntled mother-in-law."

"But he has to be considering it, or Mandy wouldn't have looked so terrified. She broke her door!" I blew my nose into the paper towel she'd given me at some point, though I didn't remember receiving it or thanking her for the courtesy.

"Is there . . ." She took a deep breath and looked like she'd rather eat barbed wire than ask the question hovering on her lips. "Is there another woman?"

"No." There was that at least. I wasn't competing with a yoga-attending, salad-eating, size-six female.

Paige scowled. "Are you sure? How do you know for a fact?"

I understood her disbelief. She'd just come from a situation where some other woman had flirted her marriage away.

"There aren't any indicators—not anywhere. This isn't about an affair. This is about his children from his marriage with The Ex. Something's wrong there—something happened—and he won't open up to me about it. He almost acts like those first two kids don't exist in his life. It's weird, and it's wrong. And I've tried to fix it, but instead I've made him mad, and he's closed up even more. I just don't understand. I've done everything I can think to do."

"Could you talk to his kids about it?" she asked.

I shook my head. "They're as confused as I am." I took a shuddering breath. "It's just not fair. Why is this happening?"

"Sometimes you just have to have faith that there's a reason for everything—even when you don't understand it."

I stared at her. Faith felt like pretty shaky ground to me, and I told her so. "I'm not a terrible person," I continued, my voice shrill. "Why would God do this to me? How could any loving God allow crap like this to happen? Look at you, Paige. You're a nice, good person. What is the point of all this stupidity? How can you have faith with all the horrible things that happen in life?"

Paige smiled and looked away as if afraid to meet my eye. She dropped her hand from my back and stood. "Do you want some hot chocolate?" she asked in an obvious attempt to veer me away from the topic of God.

I nodded. It wasn't exactly cold enough outside to worry about hot chocolate, despite the fact that it was December. But it was cold inside my bones. I could almost feel them rattle together as I shivered in my own uncertainty.

"You know . . ." she said as she ripped the top off a foil packet and dumped it into a mug. "You really are a good person, Livvy. You're the kind of person who should have good things happen to you, so I understand why you feel like it isn't fair that bad things come instead. But . . ." She had two mugs ready now and placed them into the microwave and set the timer.

She turned to me, leaning back on the counter. She appeared to be thinking—to be making certain she said exactly what she really meant. "But when I was a little girl, I went to Primary. It's like Sunday School for little kids."

I nodded my understanding.

"Anyway . . . we sang a song there. It was about the wise man who built his house upon the rock and the foolish man who built his house upon the sand. In the song the rains come, and the house on the sand washes away, but the house on the rock is fine."

The microwave dinged. She pulled out the mugs, dumped in some big marshmallows, and grabbed a couple spoons before returning to sit by me at the table, pushing one of the warm mugs my direction. "Later, when I was an adult, I heard a talk by one of our Church leaders. He talked about that song, and he said something that's kind of stuck with me—especially when times get hard. He said that nowhere in the song does it promise that the rains won't come just because you built your house on the right spot. It only promises that if you build in the right place, you'll be able to withstand the rains, no matter how bad they get." Her voice softened as she spoke until she was almost whispering.

Her eyes had the shine, and tears dripped down my own cheeks in steady streams.

Just then, Nathan, the smaller of her two boys came out from a room I assumed to be their bedroom. He was followed by his older brother, Shawn. It hadn't even registered to me that they hadn't been present until that moment.

"I like that song," Nathan said.

"Will you sing it to me?" I asked at the same time his older brother showed up.

"Uh-huh." He scratched at his ear but didn't sing. "Can I have a cocoa too?" he asked, eyeing my mug.

"Sure, buddy." Paige got up and readied two more mugs.

"She asked you to sing her a song," Shawn reminded his little brother.

"Oh. Wight." And he began singing in a cute little boy voice. His pudgy little hands did little actions along with the words, and when he washed the house away, he did it with a dramatic sweep of his arms.

I listened to the words.

Paige was right.

Nowhere in the song did it promise rain wouldn't come for the wise man. And if a wise man couldn't earn such a promise, who was I to think I should get better?

"Thank you, Paige," I said once I'd stayed long enough that the boys felt like they'd had an adequate visit. Paige had followed me to the door.

"Are you sure you'll be okay?" she asked.

"I'm much better now. I don't know why I came here, but I'm sure glad I did." I gave her a tight hug, hoping to convey my gratitude.

"Call me if you need anything. Anything at all," she said.

I agreed and went down the hall. "Merry Christmas!" Paige shouted after me as if the holiday just occurred to her.

It had been easy to forget Christmas, but now I thought I needed to feel the Christmas spirit more than ever—no matter what Nick did or didn't do. My faith couldn't waver based on his whims. I believed in God and in that baby in a manger. I knew where my house was built.

Bring on the rain.

* * *

Paige's reminder of the holiday gave me the courage to buy myself a Christmas present. Nick wanted a divorce? Fine. I wanted a lot of things too.

I found a hairdresser who kept her shop open late, went in a blonde, and walked out a brunette. I also had a cute new haircut—completely different from what I'd always worn. It was short and sassy. Maybe not as cute on me as it was on Athena, but I still loved it and felt lighter because of it.

Mandy met me in the garage and was at my car door as soon as I'd pulled the key out of the ignition. She opened the door, and her apologies spilled in.

"Mom, I am so sorry. I didn't mean to say that. I really didn't. It's just, I overheard Nan saying stuff, and it's been really freaking me out. But I know it isn't your fault. I just—"

She stopped midrant in her apology when I stepped out of the car.

"What?" I asked.

"Your hair." She pointed slowly to my head.

I smiled. "Do you like it?"

"I do. I really do, but . . . why?"

I took her hand and pulled her into a hug. "Because I need to feel like me again. And your apology is accepted. Someone will be by to fix your door, though I'm thinking about leaving it as a swinging door to teach you a lesson."

"I'm really sorry," she said again, her voice muffled against my shoulder. "I just want Dad to come home."

"Me too," I said and meant it. "In fact, I think I'll invite him over for Christmas dinner. I can't think of one good reason why we shouldn't spend it all together." I gave her a tight squeeze. "So are we okay?"

She nodded. "Are you really going to invite him?" she asked. "Do you think he'll come?"

My heart tightened at the fact that two of Nick's daughters had asked me a question I had no ability to answer. "I hope so. I love you, Manda-bear. Your dad loves you too, even if he decides not to come, even if this all ends differently than I'd like. I know this isn't easy on any of you. It isn't easy on me either. But we need to stick together. No falling apart, okay?"

She nodded again. I released her and went into the house to make the phone call but yelled over my shoulder, "You still owe me dishes for the rest of this week to help pay for the door repairs."

She didn't argue—further proof of her penitent attitude. I didn't know how long it would last before she was mad at me again but took heart that, for the moment, we were okay.

Stupid Nick. Stupid Nick and his stupid mother.

No, Livvy. Be glad. Your hair looks great, and your daughter doesn't hate you at this exact moment. You know where your house is built.

I stared at the phone.

Make the call to Nick.

I glanced at my reflection in the chrome on the microwave. My blue eyes looked so vibrant alongside the dark frame of hair. I smiled, feeling beautiful for the first time in years.

I picked up the phone and dialed Nick's cell number.

Of course, I almost chickened out when his voice, rich and low, answered with a warm, "Hello?"

"Hello . . . Hi." I closed my eyes. *Just ask.*

"Is everything okay? The kids?" he asked.

"Yes. Everything's fine. We were all just hoping you would join us for dinner on Christmas Day. And the kids would really like it if you could be there in the morning when they wake up to open their presents."

That's it. Just assume he's planning on the kids being with me.

The pause felt painfully long—long enough to serve as evidence that he *had* planned on taking them. My heart dropped with the unspoken confession. How could he really have planned on leaving me utterly alone for Christmas? Thanksgiving had been horrible enough but Christmas?

"Dinner would be wonderful, Liv." He said the words slowly as if they made him uncomfortable, but he also used the shortened version of my name, which had always been his casual term of affection for me.

Such a contrast—the discomfort and the affection. "Thanks for inviting me."

"We wouldn't want you anywhere else." How I meant those words. I wanted things fixed, to be the way they were in the beginning of our marriage. Perhaps if I worked hard enough at Christmas, he would see what he was missing by not being home and decide not to listen to his mother's advice.

We said awkward good-byes and hung up. I measured the conversation from all sides, trying to find meaning in every tone and word. Was that the voice of a man on the verge of serving me divorce papers?

Was that the tone of a man who still loved me?

Or was it the tone of the man who had planned on stealing my children from me on Christmas?

That man deserved a Christmas dinner of ashes to match the coal in his stocking.

But the voice belonged to all three, which left my mind battered in the wake of Nick's multiple personality disorder.

Who are you, Nick Robbins?

I took a deep breath. There wasn't time to focus on any of that because Chad stood in the doorway to the kitchen, gaping at me.

He had keys dangling from his hand as he took in the scene before him. I looked around me as well to try and figure out why he looked so aghast. And then I remembered.

Dinner.

Chad was looking at the kitchen as if it were enemy territory because it was quiet and clean and lacking in the smells that should have come from me cooking something.

He'd invited Selena over for dinner since it was the last night she'd be home until after the holidays. Her family apparently always went to Catalina Island to celebrate Christmas and New Year's.

I hadn't made dinner because I'd been crying in my car, crying at the hardware store, and crying at Paige's house. Then I still hadn't made it because I'd stopped in to get my hair done.

Chad didn't even notice my hair in his panic over the lack of meal preparation. He was likely leaving to go pick her up at that exact moment.

"I think you should take her out to eat—just the two of you. That's why I haven't made anything yet." I turned to the counter to hide the flush in my face that came from my horror in forgetting and to fetch my purse so I could get him some money.

"Mom. No. It's okay. I should have known that with everything going on there wasn't time to get dinner done. But I'd like Selena to spend time with my family. So if it's okay, we could just order pizza and have it delivered."

The relief I felt in such a gesture. He wanted to spend time home. He wanted his girlfriend to really get to know his family. The enormity of his request did not escape me, so I grabbed hold of him, kissed the dickens out of his cheek, and squeezed him tight until he wriggled out of my arms. "Mo-om!"

"What? You're too big to kiss?"

"No. I'm too big to smother. And what's Selena going to think if I show up at her place with my mom's lipstick on my cheek?" He swiped at his cheeks while scowling at me.

I grinned—entirely unapologetic. If he only knew how much I needed the little lifeline he'd thrown me.

He shot me a half smile with a shake of his head as he bustled out the door to pick up his girlfriend.

Maybe he did know.

Dinner went well, and I was glad I'd taken the precaution to get a garden pizza because Selena turned out to be vegetarian. She'd eaten at our house on several occasions, but I'd always had meals that allowed her to eat around the meat factor. Chad gave me a thumbs-up for the vegetables, though he was lucky the stars aligned well enough for me to make such an order, and it would have been better if the darn kid would've mentioned her dietary habits sooner.

Chad drove Selena home at the end of the night, and when he returned, he sat on my bed, stretching his long legs out and putting his shoes on my bedspread. He must've been to the beach recently because grains of sand sifted from the cracks in his sneakers onto my bed. "Mandy told me what she said to you—told me what she'd overheard Nan talking about with Dad. What will you do if Dad asks for a divorce?"

I thought he'd come in to talk about his love life and found myself completely unprepared for a discussion on mine. I couldn't respond. What should a mother say in such a situation?

"I don't know what his problem is," Chad continued as if I hadn't just ignored a significant question. "He's been different lately . . . have you noticed?"

I nodded. Not noticing Nick's differences would be like not noticing when someone punches you in the side of your head.

"Dad won't talk to me. Mandy thinks I should mind my own business, and Nan is impossible. I didn't want to make things harder for you, but I needed to know what was going on. So I called Kohl."

I gasped and covered my mouth with both hands. "Oh no, Chad. You didn't! Did you tell him what was going on? You didn't indicate any of this was his fault, did you? Oh, he must feel so horrible right now."

Chad grunted and shifted his shoes on my bedspread. "I'm not stupid, Mom. Of course I didn't tell him what was going on. I asked him for advice on my relationship with Selena."

I gave him a look that must have exhibited every shred of confusion I felt because he smiled and ducked his head into his shoulder.

"Well, I had to ask somebody. And he's been through a few relationships—even one where he almost asked the girl to marry him. He *is* my big brother, so it's not like this is anything weird—"

"No." I sat next to him, shoving his feet back off the bed. "I don't think it's weird at all. I think it's marvelous. I'm glad you're good enough friends with your brother to call him. So how did you end up going from love advice for you and Selena to getting information about what's going on with your dad?"

"He mentioned Jessica and the party you guys were planning. He asked if I'd heard anything. I think he wanted to know if Dad would be showing up."

"That *is* the question of the day. Will your dad show up?" I groaned. "So what happened?"

"I didn't really know much. He seemed to be waiting for me to tell him something huge. He seemed to think I had information—like some huge family secret information. I didn't have any. When I asked him to tell me what he was even talking about, he said to ask you guys. So that's what I want to know. What's going on? What's the secret? Time to let the skeletons go free."

Skeletons? Family secret? Our family wasn't interesting enough for secrets, let alone anything that would qualify as important enough to be a skeleton in the closet. I blinked at my son for several moments, but before I could form a response, Chad grunted.

"You don't know anything either, do you?"

I shook my head slowly.

"I didn't think you did." He looked genuinely sad to discover my ignorance. "You need to talk to Dad."

"I've been trying to—"

"No. I don't mean talk to him like you always do where he shuts you down. I mean you need to demand he tell you whatever it is he's been hiding." Chad stood and moved toward the door. "Kohl knows, but he isn't talking. And we can't fix what we won't talk about."

When did my oldest child become so wise? "What do you think he's hiding?" I asked.

Chad shrugged. "Maybe he's CIA. Or maybe he has a terminal disease." He grinned. "Or maybe he's really a used car salesman and he sold a piece of junk to a drug lord seeking revenge, so he's distancing himself from his family to protect us."

Such were the imaginings of a teenage boy.

Chad never mentioned the possibility of a secret girlfriend or maybe Nick being a criminal needing to hide from the police. Chad imagined his father a hero, even when nothing in our lives indicated heroism.

"What about you?" I asked before Chad could leave me to my darker thoughts of what Nick could be hiding.

"What about me?"

"You called your brother for advice on a girl. This makes me wonder how you're doing." I smiled at the way he blushed. This was definitely a better topic for discussion than pondering what could be wrong with Nick.

Chad came back to sit on the bed, his feet back on my bedspread. His grin could only be described as goofy.

He stayed in my room a long time, telling me all about Selena, how he thought she could be *the one,* how she made him feel like he could accomplish anything, how he'd decided he was in love.

I envied him his excitement, his eyes shining with hope. He was barely seventeen, with all the romantic notions youth associated with love. I didn't tell him love wasn't always roses and candlelight and walking on the beach with your nerve endings gone electric because you're holding that other person's hand. I didn't tell him all the other things that were love—the things that didn't put a grin of stupidity on your face, the things that weren't nice, the things that were downright infuriating but that you dealt with because love demanded it of you.

Let him have his youth.

The reminder of sweetness in love was good for me. Love wasn't always the hard things. Love was a balance of both the good and the bad.

Balance.

Definitely good to remember.

Chapter 16

Paige and I had been exchanging e-mails—sharing jokes and inspiring quotes. Her e-mails had become a nice way to start the day.

As I was laughing at a comic strip she'd forwarded to me that morning, the phone rang. I answered with a distracted, "Hello?"

"You sound better today."

It took me several confused moments to know who the voice belonged to. It was Tony, telling me he was sorry he couldn't come that day to fix Mandy's door, promising me he hadn't stolen the hardware I'd purchased and also promising he'd be there the day after Christmas. I'd almost forgotten the door needed repairing and assured him that the day after Christmas was fine. He was doing me a favor, and I'd wait for it to be convenient for him.

I readied the kids for Christmas as much as I could, keeping my fingers crossed that everything would be perfect for the day, praying that Nick would actually show up because that was the only thing that could prevent perfection. I wondered if he would come with his own presents for the kids and wondered if it would be weird for me to get him a gift.

Christmas Eve was quiet. Chad seemed to be mourning the loss of Selena. We popped popcorn and watched Christmas movies. After the presents were tucked under the tree and before I went to bed, I pulled out my Bible and read the accounts of the very first Christmas story.

I didn't know if Nick would show up or not, but I knew where my house was built.

I almost called Paige to thank her for that little song. But it was late and Christmas Eve. I doubted she wanted a phone call in the middle of the night.

I kept thinking I ought to call her. But I didn't. And I didn't know why I felt bad about *not* making that call.

My alarm went off earlier than normal. Marie and Tyler were still small enough that they'd likely already be up. I didn't want to miss a moment. I raked a brush over my hair, delighted by the fact that the new haircut really didn't demand much more than a brushing, and went downstairs to see who else might be up.

Tyler and Marie *were* up. So was Mandy. Chad still slept. The rule was that no one could open presents until everyone was up and all together. *Should I wait for Nick? Does the rule still apply here?*

I didn't know and was glad to put off the decision since Chad still hadn't made an entrance.

The worry resolved itself when the rumble from the garage door sounded over the quiet Christmas music Mandy had turned on when she first came downstairs.

Marie squealed, and Tyler grinned as they both rushed out to the mudroom, knowing what that noise meant.

Dad was home.

And that meant everything.

Nick bustled in with kids hanging off him, dragging them over to where I stood by the tree. He stared at me once the hugs were all done and the squeals of delight finally quieted—more specifically, he stared at my hair. I dropped my gaze and tried to discreetly smooth the tangles of my hair, thinking it must look especially awful for him to be staring at me like that when I remembered it had been cut and dyed.

I blinked, my heart rate speeding up as I forced myself to meet his gaze—to see what he thought of this change in me.

His eyes were locked on me, filled with heat—not the heat of quiet anger that I'd grown used to but the heat that had led to his marriage proposal and to us ending up with four children. It was the heat of attraction. For a moment, it seemed there were only the two of us by the Christmas tree.

"You look . . . amazing, Liv."

My breath caught at the compliment, and my toes tingled in the warmth of his gaze.

Did I dare stoop to the silliness of a school girl and stand under the single sprig of mistletoe by the front door?

No.

But oh, how I wanted him to close the distance, sweep me up in his arms, and kiss me completely.

He didn't.

But he had shown up. I was sure that was all the kids had wanted from Santa this year. Any other presents were a side note compared to getting a day with their family all together. Chad had loved coming down and finding his dad by the tree.

I caught Nick watching me every now and again, but he hurried to glance away whenever he realized he'd been caught. I moved carefully under the weight of knowing he watched me, hoping I didn't look stupid in my clothes, hoping my hair looked right, hoping he thought good things about me.

He helped me set the table and put dinner out. He helped the kids clean dinner up. He stayed and played the new game Tyler got for Christmas.

He stayed until Marie yawned and asked to be taken to bed.

She really was too big to carry anymore, but Nick obliged her by picking her up and carrying her to her room. Her head rested against his shoulder, and my heart swelled with the sight.

"I'm sorry," Nick finally said as I walked him to his car in the garage.

I didn't ask him to expound on what exactly he felt sorry for. Did it matter? An apology from him was as rare as a solar eclipse at midnight. He had made the day good. I could have kissed him for that—and *would* have kissed him if he'd given any indication he wanted that kind of affection from me.

"Thank you for coming today. It meant everything to them to have their father there."

"I doubt it meant everything . . ." he said with a slight shake of his head.

I touched his arm. "No. It did. I heard Marie tell one of her friends that she didn't want anything for Christmas except her dad. Coming from a seven-year-old . . . that sounds like everything to me. They love you. *We* love you."

For a flickering moment, the heat in his eyes returned, and I thought he *might* kiss me. But he backed up a step, pulling his arm from my hand.

"Thanks for letting me come, Liv. It was good to be here."

"Don't thank me. It's your *home,* you know. You can come home anytime you want, and we'll be glad to have you." *Secrets and all.* I wanted to ask about the secrets Kohl had told Chad about. But to ruin another perfect day would be like spitting on heaven's gates. I would ask. But not today. Maybe not even tomorrow.

He nodded while shuffling back another step. The night air sweeping through the garage was cool, not cold like it was on all the Christmas movies but cool enough I had to hug myself to try to keep warm. I didn't know where Nick and I stood together. His mother had told him to leave me. Did he plan on doing that? Was that the reason for the apology? Was this Christmas one last final good-bye?

A good-bye with no kiss?

Stop it, Livvy. Don't panic when the day ends so well. But I felt like panicking, watching him toss me over a sad sort of smile as he pulled his car door shut.

"I love you," I said as his engine started up. His eyes met mine again. I don't know that he heard me over the car, but I hoped he did.

It had been hard for him to come today. But he'd done it. He'd shown up. I loved him for that. It was a step—one that took us all in the right direction.

I really should have invested in a houseful of mistletoe.

* * *

Tony showed up bright and early the next morning with all the hardware I'd purchased from the store. "Hey, Livvy," he said as soon as I'd opened the door to find him on my front step. I was still in my nightgown. The flush flamed up my neck and cheeks. At least I'd put on a bathrobe before answering the door.

I raked my fingers through my hair and ran my hand under my eyes to wipe away the sleep.

"Wow," I said. "You're early."

I was an early riser too, but this? This was insane.

He shrugged. "Yeah . . . I wanted to get this done before I went to the day job. I'd have waited until after work, except Alison and I are taking the kids to my mom's tonight." He bounced a little on the balls of his feet and looked past me into the house.

Flushing hotter, I swung the door open wider to allow him to come inside. "Oh! Right. Come in. Sorry. I don't know where my manners are."

He grinned. "Probably still in bed. Sorry about waking you up. I really would've come at a different time if I'd had any choice."

I felt bad for making him notice my discomfort in him being there so early. He was doing me a favor. It was only right I accommodate his schedule.

He crossed the threshold and eyed the house. "So where's the offending door?"

"Upstairs." I pointed. "Second door on the right. But let me get my kids up before the hammering starts."

"Sure thing. I have to get a few tools anyway." He set the hardware down in the entry hall and went back outside to his truck.

I ran upstairs and woke the kids up, letting them know they should meet me in the kitchen so we could have what we called a scientist breakfast. None of them would grumble being forced out of bed for that.

The scientist breakfast had started when Mandy and Chad were little and we'd had Jessica and Kohl for the weekend. We didn't have enough ingredients to make more than a few of anything—a few pancakes, a few slices of toast, a few eggs to either scramble, hard boil, or make into an omelet, and a few strips of bacon. Trying to keep four kids from whining over not getting the exact same breakfast and the exact same amount of breakfast, I'd devised the mad scientist concept.

They'd all drawn strips of paper from a hat that told them what their ingredient was, then they'd had to come up with something wacky but edible to make with that ingredient. We'd divided the concoctions into teensy portions so everyone got to try everything.

We'd laughed a lot that day.

We'd laughed a lot every time we'd done it ever since.

The kids were stumbling down the stairs when Tony showed himself in with a bunch of tools. Tyler stopped short on the stairs and pointed. "Mom, there's a strange man in the house."

"He's not strange." I rolled my eyes at the intended sarcasm of my youngest son. It was completely obvious from the tool belt at his waist what Tony was doing in the house.

Tony grinned. "You don't know I'm not strange."

I rolled my eyes again. "This is Tony. He's a friend of mine from college, so be nice to him. He's here to help fix Mandy's door."

Mandy had the good sense to drop her gaze and look sheepish.

That's right, daughter. This one is your responsibility.

I settled the kids into what they were planning on making then went to check on Tony to see if he needed anything. He assured me he was fine, so I went back to the kids. Every once in a while, the whir of the miter saw filtered down to where we were cooking. That would be followed with the thumping of a hammer. Mandy looked guilty with each new noise, but I finally put my arms around her and told her it was okay. We all had mad moments where we did crazy things.

"Maybe that's why they call crazy people *mad*," Tyler said as he eavesdropped on Mandy's further apologies. "Maybe they aren't really crazy; they're just really mad."

I had to admit, the kid had a thought. I'd done plenty of crazy things when I was mad that felt pretty stupid once I'd stopped being mad.

The kitchen was starting to fill with wonderful smells. The kids were all pretty good at the scientist breakfast, perfecting their dishes as the years went by. Mandy made this amazing oats and applesauce batter to use as a dip for her French toast. Chad had omelets perfected into something that could only be called art. Marie cut up green and red apples as well as a bunch of other various fruits and arranged them on plates so they formed pictures, and Tyler made a drink that consisted of warm milk, caramel, vanilla extract, cinnamon, and whipped cream.

We were all talking and so intent on the food that we didn't hear the garage door open. I almost dropped the stack of plates I was taking to the table when Nick said, "Wow. I picked the right time to come. I love scientist breakfast."

"Dad!" Everyone squealed—delighted to have him there in their kitchen with them, where he belonged, two days in a row. He hugged Marie, who was closest to him. "Christmas trees! They look beautiful, sweetheart."

Marie beamed from where she'd arranged the fruit to look like a forest of Christmas trees.

"Nick . . ." I couldn't keep the wonder from my voice. Why hadn't I showered and dressed before now? I looked messy in my nightgown and bathrobe. I hadn't combed my hair or brushed my teeth or anything. "What's up? Is everything okay?"

He looked tired, as if he hadn't slept at all since going home the night before. But his eyes stayed on me in a way that made me blush under the intensity of his inspection.

"I wanted to talk to you, Liv . . ." he started.

"Let's eat in the rec room," Mandy suggested, nudging Chad, who immediately took the hint and helped her gather the younger kids and their plates of food so they could leave their parents alone.

We stayed still while they moved around us, scurrying to vacate the kitchen. I *couldn't* move. I felt seared into place by the heat of his gaze.

Once the kids were gone, he edged closer to me. He lifted his hand and sifted his fingers through my hair. "So, here you are."

I wasn't sure what he meant. Where else would I be? And yet the words and whatever they meant weren't nearly as important as his fingers in my hair and the back of the fingers on his other hand tracing over my jawline carefully, as if I might break like a bubble on a breeze.

I tried to keep my breathing from stuttering as he tilted his head down and pressed his lips lightly over mine. My eyes closed of their own accord. My hands wrapped around him and pressed him in tighter to me.

Nicholas Robbins. I love you. Love you, love you, love you.

I didn't say the words out loud, but they felt like an eternal echo in my head as I kissed him and he kissed me, until we were caught up in a tangle of kisses that had no beginning and no end. Who needed mistletoe?

"Livvy?"

The voice.

It was a man's voice, but it wasn't Nick's, and it wasn't Chad's.

Why was there a man's voice calling my name, pulling me down from this new heaven I'd found?

Nick pulled away, his eyes dazed, confused as he shook his head and his mouth formed a question he didn't voice.

"Livvy?"

That's right. Tony. Tony was here fixing Mandy's door.

"In here," I called back.

Tony pushed through the swing door and stopped short upon seeing me there with Nick. After my outburst with Alison, who had very likely filled him in on everything later, Tony had to be surprised to find my husband home—and not just home but kissing me—when just a few short days ago, I'd cried about a divorce.

Nick's eyes went from Tony to me. He trailed them down my robe and nightgown and then he let out a breath. "Oh." Nick raked his hands through his hair, raking it back into place where I'd ruffled it up.

Tony looked to me for some clue as to how to respond to Nick, but with my head still full of kisses and hope, I was as confused as everyone else. Finally, Tony took the initiative and extended his hand to Nick. "Hi, I'm Tony. I'm an old friend of Livvy's. We've actually met before. I was at your wedding. It was a great day, if I remember correctly."

Nick slowly took the offered hand. His eyes showed his bewilderment as they swung back and forth between Tony and me.

Tony pumped Nick's hand for a second and said brightly, "Well, I'm off. Just wanted to let you know I was leaving now. If you need anything . . . you should call me. You have my number. Nice to see you again, Nick. Bye, Livvy. Merry Christmas to you both, or is it Happy New Year now that Christmas is over?"

Tony didn't wait for an answer and was gone through the door when I realized I hadn't thanked him for all of his help. I glanced at Nick, who looked pale and swayed as if he were going to fall over. "I'll be back in just a second. I just have to thank him and show him out."

Nick mumbled something and nodded, his movements slow.

I hurried out of the kitchen to find Tony had already exited the house. I caught him just as he was getting into his truck. "Thank you!" I called. "For all your help! Tell Alison thank you as well. You just don't know how much a few kind words can mean to someone having a bad day. And tell her how much I appreciate her loaning you to me today."

Tony smiled as I finally made it to his truck door. "Well, I can see you didn't actually need me. Because *that*, that wasn't a man leaving. That was a man coming home. You're going to be okay, Livvy. Looks like a happy New Year to me." He gave me a quick hug, winked and closed his truck door.

The words he'd just said, *a man coming home*. Those kisses had *felt* like a man coming home.

I grinned at the thought and swung my arms out as a giggle escaped me. I spun and hurried back to the kitchen where Nick waited for me.

But the kitchen was empty. I heard the slam of a door and followed the noise through the mudroom and to the garage. Nick was in his car and reversing already. I tried to run out and stop him from leaving, but he'd already made the turn to the street. His eyes met mine briefly before he turned them back to the road and drove away.

Those eyes weren't the eyes of a man coming home; they were the eyes of a man who'd been broken.

Chad and Mandy had followed me out. "What's going on?" they both asked.

"I think your father got the wrong idea," I said with a growl, looking to the empty place on the street where his car had been.

"About what?" Mandy asked.

"He saw Tony here. And I'm still in my nightgown, and it isn't even eight in the morning yet. I think he thinks I . . ." The words were too horrible to utter.

Chad laughed. Mandy punched him. "This isn't funny, bonehead. This is serious."

"Yeah right! *Mom* having an affair. Dad is *not* dumb enough to think Mom could even—"

"Shut up, Chad!" Mandy demanded as she wiped her hand down her face—the same way I did when things went beyond my control. "Mom, go call his cell phone right now. You need to explain before this gets insane."

"You mean any more than it has?" Chad asked.

"Seriously, Chad?" Mandy said.

I nodded. Mandy was right. I had to call him and explain before he went off the deep end. I hurried back into the house and dialed his number. He didn't pick up.

Chad and Mandy both tried, using their cell phones, but by that point, it went straight to voice mail. He must have turned his phone off.

"He's such a baby sometimes," Mandy declared after trying his office phone and getting no answer there either.

Well . . . another potentially good day crumbled to dust.

Because he refused to answer my phone calls for the next day, I sent him a long and detailed e-mail explaining everything. He didn't respond, but I knew he had to have received it. I invited him over for New Year's Eve, practically pleading for his presence, but it was out of my hands. I explained myself, in spite of the fact that I hadn't done anything wrong. I told him I loved him and hadn't wanted to hurt him, and anything else was up to him.

Chapter 17

I PASSED INTO THE NEXT day with still no word from Nick. He had to have received my e-mail by now, which meant he either felt stupid for jumping to such lame conclusions or he just really didn't want to talk to me.

I'd pulled myself out of bed, missing my mother more than ever. Her laugh, her soft voice telling me everything would be okay, her way of seeing the world that made my world look better.

And missing my mom made me think of Athena. I'd had four years to *heal*, yet I still needed my mommy. Athena had barely had any time at all, and with Christmas having come and gone . . . was she making it?

When my mom died, I'd gone to bed, completely incapable of facing my own husband and children. But I'd had a husband and children to help me through it. Athena had an ailing father who couldn't be any kind of support.

Call her.

I pushed the thought away as Chad came into the mudroom where I was opening the lid to the washing machine. "Selena's perfect," he declared, leaning against the dryer so I couldn't switch the laundry out.

Instead of shoving him aside, I said, "Will you take the clothes out of the dryer for me?"

He shrugged and did as asked while continuing to tell me why Selena was all things angelic and heavenly. "You know . . . this is gonna sound weird, but she kinda reminds me of Grandma sometimes."

I raised my eyebrows at that and tried unsuccessfully to stifle a laugh. "You know a boy has totally lost it when he starts comparing his girlfriend to his grandma."

"Not Nan. But Grandma—your mom. And not in any creepy way either. It's just that every once in a while, she *knows* when people need things . . . like

Grandma did. You know, when Grandma said she'd had a Heaven Reminder and then rushed off to go save a baby from a burning building."

"Grandma never saved any baby from any burning buildings," I informed him.

He smiled and pulled the last of the warm clothes out of the dryer and into the basket. "You know what I mean. It's just cool that she's like that—Selena, I mean. She's just so . . . perfect."

I smiled and shook my head while pointing to the washer. He took the hint and moved the wet clothes from there to the newly emptied dryer. I started folding the warm clothes but stopped with a warm fuzzy towel in my hand. *Heaven Reminders.*

Call Athena.

Was I ignoring something important?

Chad left, and I used the kitchen phone and dialed the number to Athena's phone.

"Hello?" she sounded a little dejected.

"Hey, Athena. I was just calling to check on you, to see if you needed anything."

"No. I don't . . . need anything," she answered.

"Oh." I felt a little stupid for calling. She was fine, and my call was likely an annoyance, as it took time out of her day. "I've just been thinking about you lately," I continued. "My own mom died just four years ago. I couldn't have made it without other people to help me. I just thought maybe you could use a friend. I know this is hard."

A soft snort came through the line. "Yeah. Really hard. I had to put my dad in a nursing home yesterday. The house feels empty. Honestly, Livvy . . . I just want to crawl into bed and not get up again."

My breath hitched in my throat as tears swelled in my eyes. It was absurd how much I cried lately. "Oh, sweetie, I know exactly how you feel," I whispered. "But don't do that. Blankets are shallow comfort, and they can't do anything to warm up the places where you really feel cold."

"I just have so much still to say to them. And she can't hear me, and he doesn't even know who I am," she said softly. "Why wasn't I a better daughter, Livvy?"

I made sympathetic noises when I realized she was crying and sincerely wished I'd done more than just call. I wished I'd gone over to check on her in person so I could hug her and rock her. "You've taken on the burden of caring for your father pretty much by yourself because you thought that's what your mom wanted. How is *that* being a bad daughter?"

"She wanted me to get married and to give her grandchildren." Athena's voice sounded smaller, as if she were caving in on herself.

"And you think you're a bad daughter because that hasn't happened yet for you?" I sighed. "Something I read once a long time ago in a book I can't even remember the title to is that the best way to honor the dead is to keep living yourself. You're still breathing, Athena. You can still get married someday and have kids someday. You can still fulfill all your mother's wishes. But you can't give up. You can't go to bed because it's so hard to get out of bed again. Trust me on this one. You need to keep breathing. Live your life, Athena. That's the best way to prove you love your parents."

I thought of my own children and how they would continue even after I was gone. They would remember me, and they would remember things like scientist breakfasts and Halloween costumes. And they would tell their children and maybe even carry the traditions on in their own families.

Immortality at its finest.

Athena and I talked a while longer. Well, mostly Athena talked, and I listened while she recounted memories of her mother. She talked about a digital scrapbook she was putting together. She talked about some clock that had the loudest tick in the world when the house was empty like it was.

She talked.

I listened.

And by the time we were done, I felt better for having listened. I still missed my mom but not in that painful way. It was more that way that made me smile and feel closer to her.

Her and her Heaven Reminders.

Four days more passed with still no word from Nick. Mandy went out with friends for the new year. Chad was out with Selena, and DeeAnn asked for the little kids. She even came and picked them up. I suspected she was getting them for Nick so he didn't have to talk to me and almost told her to tell him that if he wanted them, he could man up and get them himself—but I was too tired to fight over it. I went to the beach again and then to the movie theater.

I received an e-mail from Paige, telling me that Daisy was in worse shape than ever. She was bleeding, and her pregnancy was at risk, which meant she was on bed rest despite needing to move out of her house because Daisy's husband had decided he didn't really want to take responsibility for his own baby. I'd heard of unmarried fathers doing that when they found out their girlfriends were pregnant, but I'd never actually heard of a married man turning his back on his pregnant wife.

That was completely incomprehensible to me.

I wrote Paige back and told her I'd do anything to help. She promised to call for the details, so I waited for the phone to ring.

Daisy was moving out. It broke my heart to think of her dealing with the trial of becoming a mom again all on her own. How could he not want to be a part of his own child's life?

And then I felt guilty for thinking horrible thoughts about the guy. What made him more monstrous than my own husband? Nick didn't want to be a part of his kids' lives either. But that wasn't exactly true. Nick didn't want to be a part of the lives he'd created with The Ex. He still wanted the kids he'd made with me.

What was the difference between those two sets of kids? I'd sent e-mails, texted, and called Nick at all hours of the day for several days running. He wasn't going to talk to me even though he knew he'd been wrong to jump to conclusions about me. Shame did that to him. He hated to be wrong about things, hated to feel like he'd been made a fool of or that he'd acted the part of a fool. Apologies were hard for him. Which meant he would not be apologizing to me anytime soon or coming anywhere near me where he'd have to face his shame up close. If he couldn't talk to me about something as simple as a misunderstanding, how could I ever get him to talk to me about Kohl?

Because something *had* happened with Kohl; Chad had said so. And Kohl knew something the rest of us didn't know. Somehow, he had to feel ashamed of himself for something. That was the only reason possible for this excessive and continual neglect of his oldest son.

* * *

On Friday morning, Nick was waiting for me in the kitchen. I'd thought the house was empty. The kids were already in school, and I'd gone up to shower. I'd thought I was alone, so I squealed like a little girl in a haunted house when I saw him.

"You nearly gave me a heart attack!" I said, panting, huffing, and wanting to throw the laundry basket I'd just dropped at his head.

He had the decency to look abashed for scaring the wits out of me, and though he stepped up to help pick up the dirty clothes that now lay scattered all over the floor, he didn't get closer to me than necessary.

He picked up the basket for me and hefted it to the mudroom and then turned to face me.

He didn't need to say the words out loud. I could see them on his face.

"You're not coming back," I said. Why dance around the reality of it?

He dropped his gaze to the floor and nodded. "I just think it would be better if we just . . . if we . . ."

I steeled myself for the words he seemed loath to say.

But it didn't hurt any less when he actually pushed them out past his lips. "Get a divorce."

I gripped the cold tile counter to keep myself on my feet. "Is that your mother talking? Or is this really what you want?"

"My mother never—"

"You have children, Nick. They have ears, and they hear what people say around them. Don't defend her. It's insulting."

"I just think this would be better . . . for both of us. I've got a lot going on that you just don't understand and—"

I spun on him. "Don't. This is not a question of *my* competence. This is a question of *your* communication. I cannot understand what is never explained. I'm assuming this isn't about Tony from the other day. I'm assuming you read my e-mails and heard my voice mails, so you know that he was there only fixing the door, right?"

He nodded, his fingers toying with the ring he still wore on his hand. "I got the messages."

"Then what is this about? Don't tell me this is better for both of us. It's not better for me. It's only better for you. So what is it? Another woman?" I knew the answer but had to ask.

"Of course not." He finally met my eyes, anger at the accusation burning in his own.

"Okay, no other woman for you, no other man for me . . . That means you're running. But you're running away because of what?"

"It's complicated."

I crossed my arms over my chest. "So is molecular biology, but I still passed the class. Don't undermine my intelligence with such a stupid word."

His eyes shot up in surprise at the fact that I stood my ground, even if it did feel like that ground quaked and gave way beneath me. There was more than surprise in his face. He loved me. You don't tell a woman you want a divorce and then look at her like she's water in a desert.

I stepped closer to him so I could stare directly into his eyes. "Why are you doing this to us?"

"I just don't know how to make things right." He turned and walked away, but he didn't look back. I followed him.

He was out the garage door and in his car.

I yanked his door open again. "Then ask for some help, you stupid man!"

"Livvy, please . . ."

"Please what? Please let you self-destruct without ever telling me why? No. You can forget it."

His fingers tightened on the steering wheel. "It's not open for debate. I plan on telling the kids on Sunday. I was hoping we could do it together to make it easier for them."

This isn't happening! I slammed the car door closed and turned away from him. I retreated to the house and slammed that door too. I sank to the floor and wrapped my arms around me.

His car didn't move for a long time. I barely breathed, waiting to hear the door open again, to hear his footsteps come back to me, but eventually the engine fired up and his tires rolled away.

I called DeeAnn and asked her to pick the kids up from school and to keep them overnight. She didn't ask why, which made me wonder if she'd known he'd come to me about this today.

It was Friday. He wanted to tell the kids on Sunday.

And then I screamed until it hurt too much to utter any noise at all.

I didn't dare go to my room. The bed was my enemy, and the best way to defeat it would be to avoid it.

I fell asleep on the couch.

I woke up feeling sluggish and wounded. I could have been on a cruise, sipping at drinks with umbrellas and getting vitamin D from lounging on the deck soaking up sunshine. I should have been dancing out of rhythm to the rumba.

I lay on the couch, knowing a shower was necessary, knowing I couldn't stay there forever. *At least it's not my bed.*

My cell phone vibrated, and I vaguely remembered it had done that all night.

I picked it up—nineteen new text messages. Most of them were from Chad and Mandy. They wanted to know why they were stuck at

Nan's. Chad wanted to know if he could go to Selena's house instead for the day, even offering to take the other kids with him as long as he didn't have to stay at Nan's watching *The Sound of Music*.

Mandy simply wanted to know what was wrong. Eight of those messages carried those three little words along with a paragraph of question marks.

And one was from Paige, reminding me that book club was at Daisy's house tonight because she was on bed rest, reminding me that Daisy needed us in her life. Right. Book club. I hadn't even thought about book club. I'd bought the book, *Silas Marner*, last month and now didn't even know where I'd put it. I hadn't read it—not even the back cover.

Daisy was on bed rest and in a precarious place as far as her marriage was concerned. Paige had lived through a divorce and still breathed every day. Ruby had lost her husband. Athena had lost her mother. They still smiled. They still read books.

And what's more . . . they were my friends. I needed them.

I also had to talk to Kohl. I had to know what had happened, which meant I had to get up and get dressed.

Nick would be furious if he found out I'd gone to Kohl, but really, it was his own fault. He'd left me with no alternatives. And could I be in worse trouble than I already was? What more could he do beyond asking for a divorce?

But Kohl was so much like Nick. The thought of talking to him scared me just a little.

You can do this . . .

I needed answers, which meant I got up, stuffed my feet into shoes, and drove to get them.

Chapter 18

THE PEELING PAINT ON THE door and the smudgy black smears around the handle testified that the apartment belonged to poor starving *male* college students. Even in poverty, girls would have found cheap paint somewhere and found a way to make the entrance to their home look inviting.

A lanky, long-haired kid in cutoff jeans and no shirt answered the door. "Yeah?" His fingers drummed the side of his leg, and he didn't appear thrilled to have some older lady standing on his front porch.

"Is Kohl Robbins here?"

The kid opened the door wider in response as he called out, "Cold! It's for you!"

Cold. I remembered how some of his friends used to call the house asking for *Cold.* It morphed every once in a while, depending on the friend. Some called him *Ice Box* and other variations on the cold theme.

I stepped into the dimly lit apartment and blinked to adjust my eyes. Boys. The whole place vibrated with the presence of boys without moms. Clothing hung from the sides of chairs and the shabby couch as if tossed there like confetti at a party. Several long wires stretched from the only light source—the television—to the couch, where a couple of guys were playing a game that split the TV screen into four parts. They were shooting at characters within the divided screens. Kohl sat on the floor with his controller and a triumphant grin, which meant he must be beating the other guys. He looked up at me, and his smile melted into surprise.

"Livvy?" He jumped to his feet and wiped at his jeans as if making sure he didn't have dust on him, though to look at the floor, dusty jeans were the least of his worries. Unlike his roommate, Kohl wore a clean, pressed, button-up shirt. "What's up?"

I smiled brightly and pulled the kid into a hug. He hugged me back tightly. "Just wanted to see you. How are things going?"

"Things are good." He glanced back at his friends, who were still playing the game. "Hey, guys, I'll be back in a bit." He smiled at me. "Maybe we should go outside. My roommates aren't the tidiest people ever."

I grinned in agreement and followed Kohl out the back door to a smallish sort of patio that overlooked a common grassy area shared by all the apartments. He sat on the table, leaving the one lawn chair for me. I sat even though I felt more like pacing than sitting.

"I can take a guess as to why you're here." He started the conversation I had no idea how to begin. Score points for Kohl.

While I fumbled to say the right thing, he continued. "Nick finally told you, didn't he?"

It startled me to hear Kohl refer to his dad by his first name rather than as *Dad* like the other kids did. Things were worse than I'd thought. "Your father's got a little sickness right now. He's got a bad case of pride that apparently rendered him incapable of having discussions with me. He hasn't told me anything." I couldn't bring myself to mention the *D*-word. I couldn't tell him my marriage, my entire life, was on the line. "And . . . I can't solve a problem I don't understand. I need your help, Kohl. I need to know what happened between the two of you. You're a great kid; you've accomplished so much and deserve to have a strong family backing you up. I just want to help make things better for everyone."

Kohl listened, his eyes focused on the grassy common area. He didn't say anything for several moments, and then he finally groaned and gave a self-deprecating chuckle. "No one can solve this problem . . . and I don't think it's my place to talk to you about it. You need to ask Nick."

"Kohl—"

He hopped off the table and finally turned his eyes to me. I cut off my pleadings, unable to give voice to anything under the gaze of those tortured blue eyes.

"Seriously, Livvy. You can't fix my broken family life. I love that you want to try though. You've always been good to me, and I appreciate that. Some of my best memories from my childhood were at your house with your picnic lunches in the living room under the blanket tents and your scientist breakfasts. You were good to me without any reason to be. But I can't help you with this. Thanks though, for everything." He moved to go back into the apartment. I followed him.

"I had every reason to be good to you," I said to his retreating back. "You were always a good, loving little boy. So don't you go talking like that. Just tell me what I can do to make things better for you *now*."

"I'd help if I could, Livvy." He wove his way to the front door, apparently through with the conversation.

"You *can* help!" I insisted. "You're just being stubborn. You're just like your father."

His face darkened. "I hope not. Go talk to Nick, Livvy. It'll all make sense then."

"You mean go talk to your *dad*." I followed after him. It grated on my nerves to hear a child speak so disrespectfully about a parent—no matter what had gone on between them.

Kohl laughed, the sound entirely vacant of humor. He held the front door open as I stepped through it. Kohl reached out and gave me another hug. He held on tightly, as if he was certain this would be his last chance to hug me. "He isn't my dad."

The whispered words seared through me. "Kohl, don't talk like that . . . please. Families are worth fighting for. If we just stick together . . ."

Kohl shook his head; his eyes had the shine. "He isn't my dad. There isn't anything anyone can do about it. Bye, Livvy . . . Thanks for coming over. It means a lot." He shut the door, closing off any hope I had to reason with him.

* * *

It was as I slammed my car door shut in frustration that the words took root in my mind.

He isn't my dad.

My mouth fell open as the meaning struck me. But no! Kohl couldn't have meant that . . . "Oh, Nick!" I said out loud. That had to be it. What else would have made Nick turn his back on those kids?

I rested my head on my steering wheel and breathed deeply.

What if he'd found out that Kohl wasn't really his son? The Ex had cheated—that was the whole reason for the divorce, but how long had she been cheating? I covered my face and shook my head.

"You're being melodramatic, Livvy," I told myself. "You've watched too much daytime television." The scenario I pictured about Nick and his children didn't happen to regular people. It didn't happen to my family.

"It isn't true," I said out loud. But somewhere deep inside my soul, something else confirmed it was.

I turned on the car, gave one last long look at Kohl's apartment, and drove away.

I considered going to Nick's apartment. He might be there. It was Saturday, after all. But what would I say? *Hey, I know you said you want a divorce and everything, but about that kid of yours . . . He really doesn't have your eyes after all, does he?*

No.

I had nothing to say to Nick at the moment. Too many emotions fought for ownership of my heart, and I didn't know which one would win out. I needed to calm down and get control of myself.

I considered not going to book club at all, but that seemed wrong too. If ever I needed support, it was now—now when everything I'd known had unraveled into something else.

I needed to just see them—the women who reminded me that I was an individual with value. That I wasn't just The Wife to my husband or The Mother to my kids but a person with her own thoughts, her own value. Whatever happened with Nick, I needed to reconfirm my own identity in order to handle it. I needed *them* before I faced *him*.

Book club provided the much-needed escape from the questions beating each other up for space inside my skull.

I ended up being late, which was proof of how *off* I felt. I was never late for anything. I tumbled through the entryway of Daisy's house, hoping to outrun the phantoms of my troubles, though it felt as though all my troubles shoved their way inside with me—refusing to allow me to escape. Daisy was set up on the couch so she was comfortable in her new state of bed rest. I tried to smile. "I'm so sorry I'm late. I just couldn't get away from home, and then the traffic . . ." I shook my head, not able to finish the lie. Traffic had been fine. I'd just seen a lot of it because I'd been driving. I called it windshield time. The car was a good place for me to think. "Crazy," I finished.

Daisy tilted her head and raised a finger at me. "Your hair."

I reached up, worried that it was as disheveled as my insides, when I remembered the haircut. I wondered when I'd finally get used to it and stop being startled every time I passed a mirror or surprised when people commented on it. Daisy's eyebrows went up, and she nodded with a smile of approval. "It looks awesome."

Thank you, thank you, thank you. At least something about me isn't falling apart. Something about me isn't dying.

"You like it?" I asked.

"I love it. It's perfect for your face," Paige said.

I smiled at everyone's assurances that the haircut and coloring were perfect for me. I didn't know what tomorrow would bring, but at least

I'd stand tomorrow as myself. I ran a hand through my hair. "I was ready for a change."

"Well, it was a good one," Paige affirmed.

Yes. It had been a good choice to come here and be among friends. I glanced around, aware of the heat crawling up my face with their compliments and attention. I sat between Paige and Athena and smiled. *I have friends, Nicholas Robbins, even though you said grown women have a hard time finding real friendship. I am not alone.* Knowing that helped me sit straighter and taller.

"So," Ruby said, singling Daisy out, "you need to give us a bit of an update, young lady. An awful lot has happened since we met in December."

Daisy isn't the only one who's had changes.

As I glanced around the room, I realized we'd all done our share of stretching and character building over the last few months. Athena with her mom and dad and her relationship. Paige with her learning to stand on her own. Me.

Me.

I'd changed too.

Daisy gave Ruby a half smile. "Well, my daughter December had a serious case of toxemia last month, so I flew out to Ohio to be with her. She delivered the sweetest little boy ever—a little early but healthy. They named him Tennyson. Then about a week ago, I started bleeding, and the doctor put me on bed rest for the baby. Livvy and Paige have helped me out quite a bit, since I can't do much of anything."

Daisy left a lot out, not ready to share everything yet. I understood that. How much of my troubles did these women know? And despite their not knowing, they had helped me through everything just by being *them*.

Ruby smiled wide. "Do you have pictures of the baby?"

"I do." Daisy grabbed her phone from the end table beside her recliner, clicked around a minute, then passed it around the circle. The baby was a sweetheart. You could tell from the pictures that his parents were glad to have him in their lives. Didn't every baby deserve that chance? To be loved and wanted where they found themselves growing up?

Daisy set the phone down once we'd all had a chance to see several pictures. "So anyway," she said, "I'll see what the doctor says next week. Until then, I am your token bump on a log, but I sure appreciate you guys coming all the way up here tonight. I'd have hated to miss it."

Ruby waved the concern away. "Of course, of course. Athena was gracious enough to pick me up on her way. It was a wonderful visit." Ruby turned to Athena. "Athena's had a big month too."

Everyone turned to Athena. She smiled, uncomfortable in our waiting for her to spill whatever Ruby intended for her to spill. Athena shifted and looked like she might bolt out the door if we stared at her for much longer. I was trying to think of a way to change the subject so she could relax, but with my brain jumbled with thoughts of my own problems, it was really hard to come up with anything.

Paige finally came to the rescue by starting book club officially. "So. *Silas Marner.*"

Everyone got out their copies. Everyone but me. I still had no idea where my copy had gone. Athena smiled gratefully at Paige, who offered a smile in return and said, "As I said last month, I chose this one because it was short—always nice for the holidays—and because it had kind of a Christmas message. I read this the first time in high school, and I liked it then, but I found that reading it as an adult was even more powerful. Now that I have kids of my own . . . like Silas, I've felt mistreated by some people I trusted." What could that have meant? Had something new happened that I wasn't aware of? Paige and I had become pretty close and exchanged e-mails almost daily as well as several phone calls per week. I hoped she was okay.

"Both of those things stood out to me in regard to Silas's story, and I felt like I was reading it on a different level than I had before," Paige said. She smiled at the group. "What did you guys think?"

I looked around, waiting for someone else to speak. I certainly had nothing to say about a book I'd not even read. Ruby spoke up first. "I've always loved the classics, as you all know, but I hadn't read this one for years and years." She patted her copy lovingly. "Reading it this time reminded me what it was about classic literature that first made me love it so much. Brought me back to thinking on my years at graduate school when I finished up my master's in English literature."

I blinked. Had I heard that right? Ruby had a master's degree? And in English literature. No wonder she wanted to start a book group. This was something she loved enough to study it in depth. People were full of surprises. Ruby continued explaining her feelings regarding *Silas Marner*. She loved its simplicity, its way of teaching without being overly didactic, and the beautiful symbolism. Her description made me sorry

I hadn't read it—no matter how good my excuse of being a complete emotional wreck had been.

She turned to Daisy, expecting her to continue. Daisy smoothed her hand over the bent and crumpled cover of her book. She must have been reading in the bathtub and dropped it to get it to look like that. "Oh, I really liked it."

"Well, not at first," Paige said and tried to hide a smirk.

Daisy sketched a glance to Paige and smiled slightly. Looked like I missed an inside joke somewhere. Daisy cleared her throat before saying, "But once I really gave it a chance, I was struck by the fact that some of the most horrible things that happened to Silas were actually building blocks that prepared him to be the man he was by the end of the book. That was refreshing to me."

"I noticed that too," Athena said, leaning toward Daisy. "Up until he found Eppie, it was like he wasn't really there. I mean, it was as though he didn't even remember his life or relationships before he came to Raveloe—like they were a dream. It was like he was asleep, so absorbed by his gold, caring and seeing nothing else. And then Eppie came into his life and became everything to him—she brought all of his life lessons to a head and solidified his life. Does that make sense?"

Ruby nodded, seeming excited to agree. "That's a great way to put it—solidified. Became whole."

The conversation on the book moved around me with everyone but me adding their thoughts.

"The people we love have so much power," Athena said, but her shaky low voice betrayed that she was thinking about more than just the book. "I told you about my mom's life. She was an amazing person. She loved the people in her life—she gave them everything she had. I miss that . . ." She looked up and smiled at all of us. "I mean, I miss her."

I turned to Athena, grateful to have something to say—even if it didn't have anything to do with the book. "How's your dad?"

Athena straightened. "I finally did it—he went into the care center right after Christmas." I'd known that already, but apparently few others did as they assured her she'd done the right thing.

"Thank you," Athena said. She seemed hesitant, which made me wonder if she still didn't feel confident in her choice.

I patted her leg. "I'm sure he's being very well taken care of."

She nodded then choked out, "He is." Her face crumpled, and all I wanted was to hug her. "He's all alone in there. I feel like I should have done more, especially with my mother gone."

"Dear Athena," Ruby interrupted. "Your mother would have done the same thing."

But she shook her head. "You don't know my mother."

"How is he when you visit?" Paige asked.

"He's in his own world." Athena tried to dry the tears off her eyelashes. "I don't remember the last time he called me by name."

"It's a terrible disease," Paige said. "But you did the right thing."

Athena looked right at Paige then around at the rest of us. Everyone from the book club currently present were the ones who'd gone to her mother's funeral. We all loved Athena—genuinely cared for her and for each other. I was sort of glad that this month's meeting was small, with the members who knew one another best. I doubted Athena could have opened up with Shannon, Ilana, or Victoria there.

I needed comfort company the way I usually needed comfort food. These women, the ones surrounding me here, were exactly what I'd hoped they'd be for me tonight. Apparently Athena had needed some of the same.

"We can trade off and visit your father with you," Ruby offered. That was an excellent idea. Many hands make light work, my mother used to say.

"Thanks, everyone," Athena whispered, still trying to mop tears away from her eyelashes with her fingers. I thought of Daisy handing me the tissue at Athena's mom's funeral and rummaged through my purse until I found a rumpled but clean and unused tissue for Athena. She took it gratefully and pressed it against her lashes then said, "And while I'm spilling my heart, Grey and I broke up."

Oh, that was terrible news. Couldn't any of us have a happy ending where men were concerned?

Before I could offer any sort of words of comfort, Athena held up a hand. "Don't worry, I'm fine. It turns out he wasn't so perfect after all."

"Are they ever?" Daisy said.

That was for darn sure. I laughed along with everyone else. At least, I laughed until Ruby eyed me and then said, "Livvy, we haven't heard your thoughts on the book."

Oh great. Caught. I ran a hand through my hair again as I tried to think of *something* to say. "Oh, um, I liked it." I smiled, feeling my insides wince at the lie. "You guys have pretty much summed up my thoughts. It was a touching story."

A touching story? I shook my head and tucked my hair behind my ears. The book was short. Any idiot could have read a book that size in a couple hours. I'd had a whole month. What had I been doing that I couldn't read a simple book?

Oh yeah. Holding my family together, I answered myself. Now I was sorry I'd missed it. From all the things the women had said about the story during their discussion, it sounded as though the book had centered around a man who loved a child that was not his own. Who knew I might end up dealing with such a scenario in my reality?

"It was, wasn't it?" Ruby mused. "I'm very glad you chose it, Paige."

Daisy tried sitting up a bit in her chair. "Me too."

"Good," Paige said. "I'm glad we all enjoyed it. Daisy, it's your month to choose one now."

"Oh, really?" She sat back and held her breath, putting her hand on her belly—which visibly moved as the baby did. I smiled at that. Motherhood was incredible on so many levels. "Um, well, Paige brought me some books. One of them, *The Help*, was really good. I know there was a movie, but I never saw it." She pointed toward the TV, where a stack of books were piled. *The Help* was on top.

Paige leaned over, picked up the book, and said, "I really liked this book and the movie. I only know about the Civil Rights movement from the History Channel and movies, but I felt like this got to the heart of the situation. I had no idea what it was really like for both sides."

"I like her writing a lot," Daisy said then talked about how the book was about several very different women. "Which seems like the perfect fit for us."

Yes. Very different women . . . but not so different. We loved and lost and cried and carried on. We fought for our children, wanted to be loved, and needed and leaned on each other. I felt better, stronger just for having shown up, even if I hadn't read the book. I knew that whatever came my way, I could call these women, and they would be there for me. I wasn't alone.

We all agreed on the new book option, and we set the date—but not the location—for the next meeting. With Daisy on bed rest, she might be somewhere else next month. And though no one knew it, I might be somewhere else next month too.

Paige passed out the plates of gelatin cheesecake, all the while apologizing for her scheduling disaster and promising that if we ever gave her another chance, she'd bring something better. Daisy took a bite and said, "Wow. This is pretty good."

I tasted it. It really was good. Athena took a bite. "Mmm." She closed her eyes as if relishing the flavor. Good food and good friends made everything better.

We chatted some more, and everyone finished their lime cheesecake. When I was sure Paige had the cleanup under control, I made my exit. Daisy needed rest, and as much as I wanted to dump my frustration and troubles, dumping them on a confined, pregnant woman seemed like a horrible idea.

And even though I hadn't read the book, I'd gleaned something from their conversation. Loving a child had nothing to do with blood. The little girl in the story had the chance to go with her biological father, who was apparently wealthy, but she'd chosen to stay with the man who had cared for her and about her.

Nick had once been that sort of man to Kohl.

I saw in my mind how it all must have been. Nick hated to be made out as a fool. Discovering the paternity of a son he'd thought was his own had to cause him a horrible amount of shame. I wondered if he'd discussed parentage with The Ex, wondered if she was aware that he knew. I hadn't even noticed—not really. Nick said they were his and paid child support without a bit of hesitation. Who was I to question?

Finding out the truth must have felt like one gigantic joke. It must have seemed that everyone was in on it, laughing at his stupidity and naiveté for believing something other than the truth. How that would torture a man like Nicholas Robbins!

And to carry the burden of knowledge alone. What could I have done differently?

I couldn't change anything in the past, but I had some choices about my future.

I drove straight to Nick's new apartment. I hadn't dared go there before. I didn't want to see the life he was living without me. It was almost as if I believed that by not seeing it, it didn't exist.

I rang the doorbell three times and knocked until my knuckles hurt before he finally answered the door. His eyes were red like he wasn't sleeping well. I wasn't either. After eighteen years of marriage, sleeping alone proved nearly impossible.

"When did you know?" I asked before he could say anything to me.

He looked behind me as if he expected to see the kids there. "What are you doing here?"

What if I'm wrong? What if this is just a conclusion I jumped to? He didn't look unhappy to see me. Underneath the surprised widening of his eyes was something similar to relief at having me there close to him.

"I came to rattle some skeletons out of our family closet."

"Liv—"

"You're not going to invite me inside?" This was not a discussion I wanted to have on the doorstep of an apartment complex.

He stepped to the side so I could pass through.

There were a few differences between his apartment and the apartment Kohl lived in. Nick's was nicer, and there weren't smudges of dirt around the doorknob. But Kohl had more furniture and a big-screen TV.

Similarities existed too. Clothing lay like puddles of fabric on the floor. Dirty dishes formed a tower in the sink. And the smell of recently burned food still hung in the air.

He had a couple fold-up chairs in the living room area, and he motioned to one as if he wanted me to sit. I eyed the uncomfortable metal seat and declined the offer. Wasn't I uncomfortable enough?

"So . . ." he started.

"So." I tried not to think of the day after Christmas when he'd sifted his fingers through my hair and kissed me with the urgency of a drowning man trying to find his last breath. I tried not to hear his voice whispering to me in the darkness of my bedroom that I had to get out of bed, that he needed me, that he couldn't live without me. I tried not to remember the glance of his toes on my ankles as he stretched himself out to sleep. Because here was also the man who'd gone silent. Here stood the man who'd asked for a divorce.

But I tried not to remember those things either. I could not love him, and I could not hate him. I was there to uncover truth. And for that, I could have no emotion at all.

"I talked to Kohl today," I said, hoping that would inspire an explanation without me having to dig for one.

His mouth formed an *O*, but no sound came out. He sat on one of the metal chairs instead.

"We had an interesting talk—an enlightening one."

His breath left him in a gust. "I see." He stared at the beige carpet and nodded. He kept nodding for several seconds.

"So. I want to hear your version now. I want to hear things the way you see them."

Silence ticked past us. But we'd suffered through years of silence. What were a few moments longer?

"What do you want to know?" he finally asked.

"I want to know when you realized Kohl wasn't your child." I held my breath. What if I was wrong?

Well, what if I was? What did I have to lose when I'd already lost?

But Nick didn't look surprised by my words. If anything, he looked relieved. He nodded some more and started talking. "When I realized how much he had in common with Andrew. I met Andrew when we were in grade school. Fifth grade."

Andrew was the best friend Nick had caught with The Ex before the divorce. She'd married Andrew after the divorce, and they were still together, though it was anyone's guess as to how they could stand each other. They were both equally flaky . . . equally prone to laziness, equally prone to tantrums worse than mine or Mandy's put together.

"We spent every day after school together. I got to know all his quirks," he continued. "Kohl was eleven when I really noticed the difference. I mean, Kohl was always different with his light blond hair and blue eyes, but then . . . he looked more like his mother. That made sense. It was the mannerisms that finally gave it away, the way he twiddled his spoon and fork at mealtimes, the way he laughed and held his head when he was paying attention to something. I tried to tell myself those things made sense because he lived with Natalie and Andrew, so it would be natural for him to pick up Andrew's habits. But I finally admitted to myself that something was wrong. What kind of dummy does that make me? Eleven years?"

I didn't interrupt. What could I say?

"I had a paternity test done during his physical checkup at the doctor before he went into middle school. It basically told me to gather back the cigars I'd handed out when the kid was born. That was a bad week."

"The week you flew to New York for a convention," I supplied.

He nodded. "I didn't go to the convention. I stayed in my hotel and watched the History Channel."

My turn to nod. It didn't matter whether he'd gone or not all these years later.

"I didn't know what to say or how to tell you. And Jessica . . ." He closed his eyes and scratched at his forehead. "I didn't dare check to see if she was mine. I just didn't want to know."

"Does . . . Natalie know about the test?" I didn't call her The Ex. In my distracted frame of mind, that seemed a miraculous feat.

He grunted. "Does Natalie even know herself? She's so self-centered, it seems highly unlikely she's aware she has two children—let alone who their fathers are. I never talked to her about it. She might know. She might not. I don't really care."

"What about your mom? Does she know?"

He shook his head before I finished the question.

"So you didn't tell anybody?" I asked.

He shook his head again. "To what end would I tell someone?"

He'd paid child support and allowed me to throw birthday parties in his house and never said anything to anyone.

"Why didn't you tell anyone? Why didn't you tell *me*?" I didn't care about him not telling anyone else. It hurt like crazy that he hadn't told me.

His neck muscles tightened as he stretched his neck in agitation. "I felt stupid. All those years later, Natalie still managed to betray me, to lie to me, to cheat me." He got to his feet and paced around, walking right on top of the clothing puddles on the floor. "What should I have said, Livvy? Hey, those kids we're raising . . . they aren't ours? Should I have told you we were basically paying some woman to help raise *her* kids? Are you kidding?"

"So you didn't tell anyone because your pride was hurt and you didn't want to look like a fool?"

He opened his mouth to argue but closed it again.

"And *that's* when Nicholas Robbins went missing," I finished. I moved aside some fast-food wrappers and scooted back so I was sitting on the counter. It was more comfortable than his dumb chairs.

"I didn't go missing. And what difference did it make? You were so busy with the kids all the time, you barely noticed when I was home."

"I noticed," I said softly.

"So what else did Kohl tell you?" he asked, only his tone carried something new, something that went beyond his pride being hurt, something that felt soaked in shame and self-loathing.

"He actually didn't even tell me that much," I confessed. "Not really. I figured it out on my own."

When he looked genuinely surprised, I felt irritated and lost my ability to be neutral. "Wearing an apron and cleaning your toilets doesn't automatically make me stupid."

"I never said anything like that," he insisted.

"No. You're right. You never said *anything* at all."

His gaze dropped back to the floor.

I leaned my head against the wooden cabinet. "Okay. So we now have a truth. That's a good start. You have a child you've paid for who doesn't share your blood but who does share your last name. That kid followed you around like you were some Olympian god. And then one day you find out he wasn't exactly what you thought and you scraped him off emotionally."

Definitely not neutral.

He didn't look up from the carpet, but his teeth were grinding together. I could tell by the way his jaw flexed and the veins in his neck bulged.

"What I want to know," I continued, "is why you don't want to come home. I want to know why you think leaving the rest of us fixes something that we have no ability to change?"

"You keep pushing, that's why! You want some sort of Thanksgiving picture where we're all around a table of food, smiling at each other and feeling good about who we are and what we've done, but not all of us can do that! Not everyone is like you. You don't know what guilt feels like. You love everybody, and everybody loves you. You've never done anything wrong."

I hopped down from the counter in disgust. This fight was better than those words living forever unsaid in my own head. We were shouting, but at least we were saying something. "Yeah . . . those are terrible traits. I can see why you'd want a divorce from someone like that. You don't want me pushing? Why wouldn't I push? I learned how from the best of them. What did that kid ever do to you to deserve to be *pushed* aside like that? So he isn't you biological son? So what? Big deal. What he was, was a little boy who needed a father. And you were a father who could have shown him how to grow up to be a man."

He shot up, and his eyes looked manic. "You think I don't know that?" he shouted. "You think I don't know what I did wrong?" He raked his hand through his hair, and he swallowed hard, looking like he about choked on his own words. "I know what I did! You don't know . . . you don't know the half of what I've done." His face twisted as if he was trying to control tears that came anyway.

I stepped back. Nicholas Robbins didn't cry.

"I told him, Livvy! At Jessica's wedding. He grabbed my arm and told me to stay for Jessica's sake. He was just doing the right thing. I should've stayed. I just felt so betrayed—*again*. She didn't want me to walk her down the aisle. My own daughter. And then it got me to thinking . . . what if she wasn't my daughter? And then I realized I was wasting my time being there. But Kohl was right." Nick nodded.

I didn't move, didn't dare.

"I should've stayed. And when Kohl tried to keep me there, I was more cruel than I've ever been in my life. I told him he wasn't mine. I called him something you shouldn't ever call a kid. I called his mom some pretty awful things too. And I saw him for what he was, a little boy looking for a father and losing his father all in one moment. But instead of doing the right thing, I yanked my arm out of his grasp. He called back to me. He said, 'Dad! Just stay! Let's talk about this!' And I turned to him and told him to be sure he knew who he was talking to when he called someone dad. And I *walked away* from him. Who does that, Liv? Who tells a kid something like that?" The tears were immediately replaced with anger.

"Idiot!" Nick jabbed at unseen demons in front of him, and I was glad I wasn't standing too close.

After a moment of the two of us standing there, Nick glared at me. "What? You have nothing to say? No words of wisdom? No bandages to make it better? Go home, Livvy. Now you know the truth. Just go home." He went back to his metal chair and slumped down onto it, his elbows on his knees and his fists gripping his hair, his entire body heavy with the shame he could no longer stand.

I stood still, not obeying the direct command given by my husband. Rapid heartbeats inside my chest marked the passage of time as he sat in his chair with his eyes closed, and I stood nearby with my eyes open.

Open. And seeing.

I weighed and measured what I saw. He was the man who had kissed my hand good night when we dated, who'd put his mouth to my belly to welcome Chad to the family when I'd told him we were having a baby, who had said a prayer over the cardboard box holding the small dog that had been hit by the neighbor's car while his children wept softly at his side, who had held me and rocked me as I wept over the grave of my mother. He was the man who'd told me I was unlikely to make new friends, who had been charged with and found guilty of emotional neglect of his family, who had asked me to join him in the morning to tell the kids he wouldn't be a part of my family anymore. He was the prankster, dumping cold water over me when I was in the shower; the lover, whispering kisses in the darkness; the friend, laughing in the movie theater with me when no one else was laughing; the dictator, storming around when things weren't perfect; the hider, working long hours to avoid his own shame; the dad, lifting his children high up on his shoulders so they could see the world with a broader perspective. And here he was now, the broken man, lost beneath years of shame and secret keeping.

He was Nicholas Robbins.

And he was my husband.

And I still loved him—because of, and in spite of, all of those things that made him, *him*.

"No," I said.

He turned his head to look at me. Red rimmed his eyes. He had the shine.

I stepped toward him, carefully, as though he were a small injured bird I didn't want to frighten away. I knelt by his side and lightly tugged his hands away from his hair. I gazed up at him. He looked confused.

"I'm leaving now because, honestly, our children are sick to death of your mother, and I won't curse them by making them stay with her another night. Sorry if that was harsh, but it's true. But tomorrow, I will not be standing by your side while you tell our kids you're never moving back home. I will not make a divorce easy on you, Nicholas Robbins, because you aren't trying to leave me; you're trying to leave all of this." I let go of his hand so I could wave mine over him.

I pointed at him. "And *this*? This isn't going away if you leave me. It'll only get worse, and that smell from those dishes on the counter is only going to get worse too."

He actually almost smiled at that.

"If you're coming over to give my children bad news tomorrow, don't bother coming over. I won't let you in."

I lifted his hand to my lips and kissed the hollow of his palm.

He closed his eyes and shook his head some more. "Did you not hear a thing I just told you?" he whispered. "I hurt that kid so much. I can't fix this. I'm not the boy's father."

"Don't be stupid, Nick. He isn't looking for a father. He's looking for a dad." I kissed his hand again and stood up, leaving him alone with his clothing on the floor and his metal chairs.

His defeated voice followed me to where I held the door open. "I don't know what I'd say to him."

"Sometimes dads have to say sorry too," I answered then closed the door behind me.

Chapter 19

He didn't show up on Sunday. I didn't bother communicating with him in any format. I'd done what I could. The rest was up to him. I wasn't sure he wouldn't leave anyway, but I thought a lot about my mom on that first day I'd gone to work at that fast-food restaurant. "You can't quit," she'd said. "You have to make sure you never quit until you know you did everything in your power to give your best."

I'd given my best. There was nothing left to give.

Daisy was still on bed rest but also had an appointment so the doctor could check on her and see if she could start moving around again. She needed someone to go with her, and I volunteered.

She went into the exam room alone, leaving me in the waiting room to read parenting magazines and to stare at the saltwater fish tank in the corner. I didn't mind. I liked fish and liked reading about parents. These were all things to be glad about.

I'd gone to visit Athena's dad and planned on going again soon with Ruby. I'd also gone over and properly introduced myself to my Mormon neighbors in the hopes that they had a son Paige's age who might be date worthy. They didn't, but I planned on keeping a lookout.

I had wanted to tell Daisy about Nick and me, but I still didn't know anything. Nick hadn't communicated, and it was his turn. He knew where I stood, and he knew I wanted him to stand with me. I decided to wait before spilling my guts—wait until I knew something one way or the other. Everything was too much in the air for me to be okay discussing it. So I waited and watched the fish.

Daisy finally returned with a grin. "My sentence has been commuted," she said. "Sort of."

"Sort of is good." I stood. Daisy looked tired but handling it. I admired her for that. I had to make a decision every minute to keep handling my own life mess.

I had a new list of goals. I wanted to be as strong as Daisy, as independent as Athena, as loving as Ruby, and as faithful as Paige. They had been the things saving me during this communication blackout with Nick. I chanted the words, *I am not alone*, to myself all the time.

Daisy fell silent, and I was perfectly content to live in my own thoughts for a moment. I peeked in her direction. She'd certainly changed me. All of the women from book club had. I'd made real friends. And I'd made time for myself again. Nick had been right when he'd called me the Giving Tree. I still swelled a little with self-righteous pride when I thought about it, but something I'd learned from *The Poisonwood Bible* was that I did only have a life that was my own. I would no longer be a secondary character in my own life story. I couldn't blame the things I didn't make time for on anyone else. My life was *mine*, and—for better or worse—I filled it with things of my choosing. I had loved reading in high school and college and felt relief to have found that part of myself again. *My Name Is Asher Lev* had reminded me of Nick's sacrifices when I'd checked out of the world during the time after my mother's death. I had vilified him so much in my own head that I'd forgotten all the reasons I had once believed him to be my hero.

I'd never found my copy of *Silas Marner* and finally checked out a copy at the library. I'd have just bought a new one but was certain that as soon as I did, I'd find the one I'd lost. The book was short and yet so *full*. I was too late for the discussion but not too late to gain from having read the book. When Daisy felt like talking again, we discussed all the details of her life changes as we drove, and we discussed the books as well.

I'd zoned out again—thinking about Nick—when Daisy interrupted my thoughts with an offering. "I've already read *The Help* if you want to borrow Paige's copy."

"Next month's book?" I asked.

She nodded. "Have you read it?"

"No . . ." I paused, hating the confession but knowing it needed to be said. "In fact, I didn't finish *Silas Marner* before the meeting. I meant to, but I . . . lost it. But then after you guys were all so touched by the story, I found a copy at the library. It really had some good messages."

"It did," she said. "Did it ruin the story for us to have discussed it before you finished?"

"Not at all," I insisted. "Just the opposite; I knew what to look for. I've always believed it's the choices we make in our lives that define who we really are at our core, and I felt like the book emphasized that. I can see that I've made a lot of good choices in my life, but I've made some mistakes—actually, I've made the same few mistakes over and over again, and I'm going to do better now." I smiled.

"I think you're a wonderful person, Livvy," Daisy said. "And I misjudged you."

I glanced at her and blinked.

Before I could ask what she meant, she hurried to explain. "The first week we met, I saw you as . . . less than you are. I didn't see past my own fears and stereotyping to get a sense of who you really were. I'm ashamed of myself for having done that because I can't imagine how I would have dealt with all of this if you weren't so . . . you."

"So me?" *So me* from before was someone who was lost in her own branches. I gave a nervous laugh. "That's not always a good thing."

"Well, it's been good for me," she said, leaning back against the seat. "I want to be the kind of mom who loves her family, Livvy, who wants to take care of them and who takes pride in what she's done. I haven't really been that kind of mom; my goals and priorities have been mixed up, but I have another chance." She glanced at her bulging belly and smiled. She was going to be the best mom ever to this child.

"Second chances are priceless," I whispered, wondering if Nick and I would get that chance . . . if he even wanted it.

"Yes, they are," she said.

I was glad to have Daisy in my car so I wasn't left alone with my own thoughts. "I'm feeling like ice cream," I said as we came to a light. I shot Daisy a questioning look. "What does the pregnant lady think? Drive-through on the way home?"

Daisy laughed. "The pregnant lady thinks that's a great idea." She put her hands on her belly. "We both do."

I grinned. Ice cream it would be, then. Ice cream for my friend.

Chapter 20

The night of Kohl's party came. Jessica had called me eleven times to try to cancel it the week prior, but invitations were already out. The only way I'd allow her to cancel was if I was dead and couldn't argue with her anymore. Jessica was there with her husband and their kids. My kids were all in attendance. Chad had invited Selena. The Ex was there only fifteen minutes late—a record. DeeAnn had been fifteen minutes early and looked utterly bored for the half hour it took The Ex to show up. I tried not to grit my teeth as the two of them sat at a table together and giggled like long-lost sisters. Kohl's friends from high school and college were all there, devouring the food and making me glad I'd planned for so much extra. The girl Jessica had hinted to Kohl liking was there also.

Nick was not there.

I swallowed my disappointment. I had so hoped.

Kohl disappeared for a good fifteen, twenty minutes before he returned with the shine in his eyes. My heart sank further. Nick's absence had affected him after all.

Kohl cast sidelong looks my direction for the first hour as I made sure the buffet table remained adequately stocked. He finally separated himself from the girl who Jessica had apparently been right about and stood next to me. "Need some help with anything?"

"Not at all, sweetheart. You just enjoy yourself and talk to your friends."

He lowered his voice. "Just thought you might like to know he's here."

I jerked my head up, scanning the room for the familiar form among all the guests.

Kohl grinned. "He's out back by the duck pond. He's been there awhile, trying to get the guts to come inside. We had a good talk. He told me to tell you thanks for loaning him your *Silas Marner* book—whatever that means. But I thought you might want to see what he gave me." Kohl held out an envelope. He shook it slightly in front of me. "Go on, take it. You know you want to."

My fingers reached for the envelope carefully. I pulled out the handwritten card. The cover said, To MY SON . . .

My hands shook. Was this real?

Inside, the card was filled with words. Every spare inch of white space was taken. It started out with the day Nicholas Robbins brought home a baby Kohl from the hospital and how excited he was to have that red, crying mess of an infant grow big enough to play basketball with him and to go to Lakers games with him. He went on to say how proud he was when Kohl won this spelling bee and that science fair and brought home A's on all those report cards. He detailed memories of watching Kohl play with Chad, teaching Chad to handle the ball so he didn't lose control of it while he dribbled, and Chad letting his baby sisters color in his sketch pad even though all they did was scribble.

A whole letter dedicated to all the ways in which Kohl belonged to Nicholas—of fishing and body surfing and checking out tidal pools. Of ice cream and learning to ride bicycles and teasing Jessica. It ended with the confession that he was too afraid to talk to Kohl, too ashamed to face him man to man. He supposed he still had some growing up of his own to do, and then he quoted me as "a wise woman who once said even dads needed to say sorry sometimes."

I met Kohl's eyes when I'd finished reading.

He smiled and shrugged. "Guess this means I'll need to add a Father's Day card purchase to my budget while I'm gone."

I laughed and pulled that kid into a hug. "I love you, Kohl."

"Love you too, Liv. Now give me back my letter before you get it all wet with that crying." He took his homemade card back and carefully put it into the envelope as if it were a rare document that needed protecting.

And so it was.

* * *

I rushed through the kitchen entrance leading to the duck pond behind the clubhouse. Nick stood there, just like Kohl had said, gazing out over the water, but I could tell by the way his body stilled that he knew I was behind him.

He didn't turn to face me but said, "I was hoping that maybe you'd give me the chance to say I'm sorry for the rest of my life."

"If telling me that being with me is going to make you sorry for the rest of your life, then you're about to be pushed into that pond with the ducks," I said.

"You know what I mean. I *am* sorry. So sorry I didn't trust you enough to tell you everything, sorry I was a complete jerk for the last I don't know how many years. You deserved better—all of you. I'm asking you for the chance to give you better."

I shook my head. "I already told you . . . that's the only thing you'll get from me—chances to do better. There aren't any other options."

He relaxed and took my hand, pulling me into him slowly, as if waiting to gauge my reaction in his movements. When I didn't protest, he smiled softly. "You're beautiful, Liv."

The heat crawled over my cheeks and eartips. "So here you are, Nicholas Robbins."

He smiled, his fingers still in my hair, his face close enough for me to feel the warmth of it. "So here *we* are." He pressed a kiss softly over my lips.

And I discovered a whole list of things to be glad for.

Livvy's White Chocolate Chip and Cranberry Cookies

½ C. butter
¼ C. white sugar
¾ C. packed brown sugar
1 egg
1 tsp. vanilla
1 C. all-purpose flour
½ tsp. baking soda
¼ tsp. salt
½ tsp. cinnamon
1¼ C. quick oats
1 C. cranberries
¾ C. white chocolate chips

Cream butter in a mixing bowl until smooth. Add sugars and mix until combined, scraping down the sides halfway through. Add egg and vanilla, and mix until combined. Add flour, baking soda, salt, and cinnamon. Mix until combined. Add oats, and mix. Add cranberries, and mix. Add white chocolate chips, and stir until combined.

Place rounded tablespoons of cookie dough on an ungreased cookie sheet. Bake at 375° for 10–12 minutes or until edges are just browned. Cool on cookie sheet 2 minutes before removing to cooling rack.

Daisy: Coming June 2012

The Newport Ladies Book Club: Daisy
By Josi S. Kilpack

Chapter 1

"Would it kill you to take a day off, Daisy?" Paul asked over the phone.

"Yes," I said, glad he couldn't see my smile so the game would play out a little longer. "It just might."

Paul laughed, a laugh that was too high-pitched for a man of forty-four. When we first started dating six years ago, I'd found it annoying and knew that I would never be able to marry a man who laughed like a teenage girl. Somewhere between that first date and a marriage proposal—complete with swans, if you can believe it—I came to love that laugh and a hundred other things that made Paul a husband extraordinaire. "You know I can't take time off at the end of the month—too many policy renewals."

Commercial insurance policies tend to renew annually on the first day of the month, meaning my clients bombard me with questions a week before they're supposed to re-up for another year, even though I've been reminding them for the last sixty days.

"The thirtieth is a Saturday," Paul said. "We can leave Friday afternoon after you finish your renewals, and you can take Monday off—it won't set you back too far. Come on," he prodded. "You know you want to."

"You are so bad for me," I said, lowering my voice seductively. Meanwhile, I flipped through my planner almost a month forward to check the dates for this romantic escapade. I had a ten o'clock meeting on Monday, November first, but I didn't think it would be hard to put off. My hopes were rising as I flipped back a page to be sure I'd properly evaluated the weekend.

"Shoot," I said, scowling at October thirty-first. "Sunday is Halloween." It was part of the unspoken code of parenting ethics that you had to be around for any and all holidays—even pointless ones I swore were instituted by the American Dental Association and Mars Candy, Inc., as a means of job security. My next thought, however, was, why did I have to be there? Stormy was in her final year of high school, and with ten years between her and her older sister, December—who was about to make me a grandma at the age of forty-six—I'd been doing the Halloween thing for a very long time. Couldn't I take one off?

"Maybe Stormy could stay with Jared," I said, feeling the building excitement of a weekend away. Stormy didn't spend many weekends with her dad since she had things going on with her friends most of the time, but Jared *was* there. It was perhaps the only perk of having my ex-husband live just a half hour away.

"Your call, Mama," Paul said, causing me to scowl. He knew I hated it when he called me that. It always made me defensive of the many things that I was, mom only being one of them. Paul, on the other hand, claimed to find my maternal aspects very sexy, and I took that at face value. His fifteen-year-old daughter, Mason, lived in San Diego and found it hard to come up on the weekends now that she was in high school. She came for a couple weeks each summer and alternating holidays. Paul missed her.

I bit my lip and stared at the page in my planner. "I'll talk to Stormy about it," I said, hoping it would be an argument I could win. I flipped back to "Today" in my planner and wrote a note to myself.

Stormy Halloween w/ Jared?

Then I leaned my elbow on my desk and rested my head in my hand as I continued the sweet-talk with my sweetie. "So where are you taking me, Romeo?"

"It's a surprise," Romeo said.

"Not even a hint?" I pushed. It was Paul's year to plan our anniversary celebration, and I felt a thrill run through me at the possibilities. Say what you will about second marriages, but so far, mine had been a wonderful ride. Maybe because both of us wanted to make sure this one worked, maybe because we were both grown-ups now and knew how to make better choices in a mate, or maybe because we had a better idea of our future and therefore could plan it out exactly as we wanted it to be. Whatever the reason, Paul was the sugar in my coffee, the tread on my tire, or as he liked to say it, the Shasta to my Daisy.

"I'll give you a clue: bring your bikini."

"Nice one," I said, narrowing my eyes. Bikinis don't come in a fourteen, but I had a very flattering one-piece I'd be happy to bring along, with control panels in all the right places. "I don't know why I put up with you sometimes."

"Because I pay the mortgage," Paul said.

It was an offhand comment, but it pinged in my chest, and I responded without thinking about it. "Careful, sailor, or you're on the next boat out of here."

That fell even flatter, and we both went quiet, having sufficiently stepped on one another's toes rather harshly. We could banter and tease all we wanted, but Paul's wife had left him without warning ten years ago, so jokes about me leaving were never funny. I wondered why I'd said it. My next thought, however, was that him making comments implying that I couldn't take care of myself was equally difficult for me to take in stride. Did I say second marriages were *perfect*?

I cleared my throat. "Well, I'd better go," I said. "But the weekend sounds like fun. I'll talk to Stormy about it tonight and then give Jared a call. I'm sure it's a go though—he totally owes me for Labor Day." He'd had to cancel Stormy spending the weekend with him because he said he had a last-minute business trip, but I suspected he'd taken his newest girlfriend to New York for the opening of a Broadway play he'd told Stormy about the week before. He'd been a theater major in college; it was probably how he'd tricked me into marrying him—he acted out the part of faithful suitor. What a joke.

"Right," Paul said, also trying to recover from the moment. "She's got that Shakespeare thing at school tonight, right?"

I groaned. "That's right," I said, looking at my planner again. I hadn't written it in. Instead, I had a list of errands I was hoping to do on the way home: the hair salon for my favorite shampoo Stormy had left at the pool on Saturday, the library for a new novel, and the grocery store for some more Lean Cuisines. I'd brought my last one to work for lunch today. "Um, is there any way you could go solo so I can run some errands?"

"Isn't Jared going?"

"I think so," I said.

"Daisy," he said, a reprimand in his voice that caused me to let out my breath in a huff. Paul and Jared did okay together, but Paul was always anxious about seeming as though he were overstepping his boundaries as stepdad when dad-dad was around.

"Okay, okay. Don't worry about it," I said, trying not to sound as annoyed as I felt. After working all day, I wanted to run my errands and go home, not sit through a high school drama performance where my daughter probably had three lines. "I'll try to leave a little early and get my stuff done before it starts."

My stuff, I thought after I hung up a minute later and looked at my list again, a familiar frustration rising in my chest. I yearned for *my* stuff, *my* time, *my* schedule. After so many years of putting it after *their* stuff, *their* time, *their* schedules, my patience was wearing thin. Of course, Paul was different. He was a grown man, and he was wonderful about giving me my space. My girls? Not so much. I was their mother; I was supposed to put them first, but that didn't mean I didn't long to just do my own thing. I'd been so young when I became a mother—barely seventeen—and I felt like I'd been trying to catch up with the role ever since. Now the end was in sight. If it made me a bad mom to look forward to being done with this phase of my life, well, so be it. I'd given so much for so long.

I pushed my planner to the side of my desk and opened up my e-mail folder; my break was officially over. I glanced at the clock—it was almost two. If I kept a steady pace, I should be able to leave the office by four-thirty. That would give me time to get the shampoo and the microwave meals—I could move the library to tomorrow. "Nine more months," I said to myself—that's how much longer I had before Stormy graduated from high school. She was already planning to go to California State after living with Jared for the summer—applications were due in November. I could go away on the weekends anytime I wanted once she was up and out. Paul and I planned to buy a trailer and hit the open road. My office was getting closer and closer to telecommuting options all the time, so I could still work part time. We wanted to trace the Oregon Trail then visit the thirteen original colonies. There was so much we wanted to do, and we were so close to having the green light to do it.

For now, however, I was sentenced to high school plays, budget-busting prom dresses that were worn one time, and overseeing homework.

"Nine more months," I said one last time before getting back to work.

About the Author

Julie Wright started her first book when she was fifteen and was surprised to get it published. She's written over a dozen books since then, is a Whitney Awards winner for her novel *Cross My Heart*, and she feels she's finally getting the hang of this writing gig.

She enjoys speaking to writing groups, youth groups, and schools.

She loves reading, eating, writing, hiking, playing on the beach with her kids, and snuggling with her husband to watch movies. Julie's favorite thing to do is watch her husband make dinner. She hates mayonnaise but has a healthy respect for ice cream.

Visit her at her website: www.juliewright.com.